M000197990

PRAISE FOR
THERE'S NO BASKETBALL ON MARS

"There's no question that today's young readers will be tomorrow's first humans to reach the Red Planet. And if they're reading Craig Leener's inventive and heartwarming tale of a teenage astronaut overcoming challenges to get there, this just might be the book that inspires them."

MARC HARTZMAN
Author of *The Big Book of Mars*

"This book is the author's best work yet—and that's saying a lot. Imaginative and engaging, the story shines from page one. Mr. Leener's ambitious choice to tell the tale through the eyes of the autistic Lawrence Tuckerman is a brilliant stroke that colors the story with beautiful insight."

DR. BOB DICKSON
Associate Professor and Communication Department Chair
The Master's University

"Lawrence's characteristics and non-typical behavior patterns relate well to his diagnosis of high-functioning autism. Craig managed to make this person extremely endearing. I found that Lawrence grew on me, and the more I read, the more I rooted for him."

ELLEN McLEOD
Two-time Teacher of the Year, Special Needs
Garden Grove Unified School District

"This futuristic ride to the planet Mars is well-grounded with the actual scientific and technological history of spaceflight, but the author takes it a step further with the addition of his own special insight into the future possibilities of space travel."

BOB CONROY
Engineering Faculty Member Emeritus
California Polytechnic State University, San Luis Obispo

"Much like the various levels of basketball, there is a spectrum of autism. It's important to understand that each person needs to be seen as unique, with wonderful thoughts and perspectives, but who may not be able to articulate them. Lawrence is a great example of following your head and heart."

HOWARD FISHER
Advocate for Autism Speaks
Head Coach, Youth Men's Basketball Team for Team USA

"After reading the author's trilogy, I was surprised to find that this book was in the point of view of Lawrence Tuckerman. It was interesting to see how Lawrence thought about things and faced problems in his own seven-loving way."

SANTOS RODRIGUEZ
Avid reader and youth basketball player
Murrieta, California

"Leener offers a unique first-person perspective of a character on the autism spectrum in a story peppered with interesting factoids and quirky takes that make for a lively and lovely read. As long as Lawrence Tuckerman has his Bazooka Joe and chili mac 'n' beef, he can find himself at peace."

KEVIN WHIPP
Mechanical Engineer
NASA Jet Propulsion Laboratory

"Craig has a vast understanding of those with special needs, especially the attendant numerical and physical mannerisms and behaviors. His references to conditions and his highly descriptive writing style will enable young readers to learn a great deal about those on the autism spectrum."

GORDON "GORDO" DURICH
Artist, Writer, and Special Needs Community Coach

"The unique friendship between Lawrence and Zeke was heartwarming. And even though they were total opposites in many ways, they were totally connected, because after all, this was always about basketball."

HAILEY STAR DOWTHWAITE
Avid reader and high school basketball player
Los Angeles

"Neurodiverse readers will appreciate the quirks Lawrence has, including his affinity for numbers and his preference for communicating through the written word. It's important for readers to see neurodiverse characters being accepted for who they are and for what gifts their unique traits bring to this world."

ALIX GENEROUS
Autism Neurodiversity Activist

"The author takes the impossible and makes it not just real, but strangely familiar and comforting."

CHRIS COPPEL
Author of *Legacy* and *Lingering*

"Basketball serves as the pathway for Lawrence Tuckerman to understand and navigate his increasingly complex world."

DEREK JOHNSON
Host, Rock Chalk Sports Talk
KLWN 101.7 FM and 1320 AM
Lawrence, Kansas

"I wish I'd had this book when I was Lawrence's age."

MIKE HULYK
Artist
Milwaukee, Wisconsin

THERE'S NO BASKETBALL ON MARS

ALSO BY CRAIG LEENER

The Zeke Archer Basketball Trilogy

This Was Never About Basketball

All Roads Lead to Lawrence

This Was Always About Basketball

THERE'S NO BASKETBALL ON MARS

CRAIG LEENER

GREEN BUFFALO
PRESS

Cover design by Tabitha Lahr
Designed by Brent Wilcox

ISBN: 978-0-9905489-8-0 (print)
ISBN: 978-0-9905489-9-7 (e-book)

10 9 8 7 6 5 4 3 2 1

To Elio Laszlo

1

My Brain Wonders Why

It is Saturday.

I pull the envelope from my pocket, and I study the four-digit number written on the outside of it.

And then I look up and analyze the four numbers spray-painted onto the corrugated steel roll-up door in front of me.

It's a perfect match.

SPACE 1046.

I have the right storage unit.

I wonder why Biffmann Self-Storage uses four numbers to identify its individual storage units, instead of seven.

My brain works best when sevens are involved.

But the thing is, Chett Biffmann owns Biffmann Self-Storage, not me, so I have no say in how the spaces are numbered.

I dig my key ring out of my backpack, and I slip a shiny silver key into the padlock.

And I swivel the key precisely one-quarter turn to the right. It causes the shackle to release from the padlock body. I feel the click. I hear it too.

Feeling and hearing things are two ways that I make my way through the world and stay out of trouble.

Seeing too, but never, ever by direct eye contact, which I avoid because it's overwhelming, and it makes my brain twitch—meaning there's a direct correlation between direct eye contact and the sudden convulsive movement it causes inside my skull.

I'm used to people avoiding me because of this aspect of my behavior. I know my fellow students at Ernest T. McDerney Continuation School sometimes feel uncomfortable because I avoid eye contact with them. I know it makes me appear rude or not interested in them. And that makes it a whole lot harder to make friends.

And I also navigate my way through the world by my sense of taste, especially with pepperoni pizza, but only from the best pizzeria in Los Angeles, Mike's Pizza on Broadhurst Parkway, and only when my pizza has been cut into seven slices, instead of the customary eight.

Whenever there's a rookie pizza-slicer guy hired at Mike's, and he slices my pepperoni pizza using the conventional eight-slice pizza-slicing method, I don't eat it.

Ever.

Once I threw a whole pepperoni pizza against our kitchen wall because it was cut into the standard eight slices instead of seven, and my dad told me if I did that again, it would be a long time before we had takeout pepperoni pizza from Mike's.

So I stopped doing it.

When the angle of the sunlight streaming in through our kitchen window is just right, I can still see the shadowy grease stain on the wall, because Mike's pepperoni pizza is as greasy as it is tasty.

And we have pepperoni pizza from Mike's every Tuesday because it's the only day of the week whose name is constructed using precisely seven letters.

And now my brain shifts back to the padlock. The click sound is *lock language*, the padlock's way of saying to me, *Hello, keyholder. I thought you were never coming back.*

It's how I feel whenever I meet someone new, and they're nice to me at first, but then they disappear for a long time—maybe forever. Although technically, it's hard to know how long forever is, especially if the person disappears for longer than I am alive.

I'm familiar with the inner workings of a padlock because I once took apart the one my dad used to secure the garage door at our house, at 26488 Laszlo Lane.

I needed to find out how a padlock works, how all the parts—the springs and pins and counterpins—move together in sequential harmony to protect the forty-nine boxes of my dead mom's stuff that my dad keeps in the garage.

There are so many boxes in there that my dad has to park our 1987 Ford LTD Crown Victoria station wagon with 145,656 miles on it in our driveway.

My dad was unhappy when I was unable to reassemble the padlock, but he didn't say anything about it on the drive to the hardware store to buy a new one, or when he handed the store clerk a crisp twenty-dollar bill, and he only got back three quarters and two pennies in change.

Seventy-seven cents.

I considered mentioning those two sevens to my dad on the way home, but I thought better of it, and I did quadratic equations in my head instead.

And now my brain shifts back to space 1046. I grab hold of the roll-up door's rusty metal handle, and I pull it open. And there it is, a 1965 sea-foam-green Chevrolet Fleetside shortbed pickup truck.

Or at least it once was.

Now it's completely dismantled.

The truck bed, fenders, hood, side panels, bumpers, and sideview mirrors are geometrically stacked in one corner of the storage unit.

The truck chassis is sitting in the other corner. The chassis looks neglected and lonely all by itself. I'm not a car, but I recognize the feeling.

And the truck's cab is resting dead center atop the storage unit's cold concrete floor. It still has its doors, windows, and steering wheel intact, but without all the other parts working in sequential harmony, it's not going anywhere.

I reach inside the envelope, and I pull out its contents: the Chevy's California certificate of title.

My best friend, Ezekiel Archer, was the Chevy's previous owner. Zeke signed over his truck to me exactly sixty-three days ago. And when he did, he referred to that perfectly square piece of paper as the vehicle's "pink slip."

Zeke explained that it is called a pink slip because it is pink.

I like that.

My brain wonders why the rest of the world isn't as uncomplicated.

2

I Don't Like It When
People Ask Me Questions

I recall taking apart the pickup truck, piece by piece, with the help of a guy named Brock Decker, who wears smelly cologne, and who I don't like at all, but for the life of me, I can't remember why Brock Decker and I did that to Zeke's truck.

And whenever I try hard to remember what happened, my brain twitches, and I have to stop. And then I get angry, and I try to remember again, but the twitching only intensifies, and the cycle starts all over again until I give up, which makes me even angrier because I don't like to give up on anything.

Zeke was supposed to drive that pickup truck to the University of Kansas. He had enrolled there after graduating from Jefferson Community College.

But since the truck was in too many pieces to be drivable, Zeke signed it over to me, and he drove his father's pickup truck to Kansas instead.

And Zeke wasn't even mad at me, which was a relief, because

my life up to that point consisted of people who either got mad at me, or ignored me. Zeke never does either of those things.

And neither does my other best friend, Nathan Freeman.

Nathan is angry all the time, but he almost never directs his anger at me. It's mainly aimed at Zeke, like when they worked together over the summer at Chip's Sporting Goods, when Zeke was earning extra money for college. Nathan was the assistant store manager, which gave him ample opportunity to hassle Zeke and boss him around a lot.

And Nathan is also the captain of Jefferson's chess team. During matches, he likes to focus his anger on his chess opponents. Fans of competitive chess might call this a *tactic* or even a *strategy*, but anger is Nathan's natural state of mind.

I met Nathan at the Vernon Shields Community Recreation Center, and since then, we've had a chess match every Thursday after school.

The first time we ever played, Nathan became enraged when I employed the Dutch Defense tactic, checkmating him before he had time to settle into his folding chair and pop the top on his twelve-ounce can of root beer.

When Nathan realized that he lost, he screamed at me, and then I slapped him hard across the face.

Nathan never got mad at me again after that, and we became instant friends, and we drank a lot of root beer together on that day, and we still do, and Nathan has never fallen for the Dutch Defense again.

Zeke and Nathan are my best friends because they understand me despite how anxious I get in social situations and how much I resist variations to my established routine.

And now my brain shifts back to space 1046. This is the

first time I've gone to see all those Chevy truck parts since I became their new owner. And since I'm mainly the person who disassembled the truck—although I can't remember why I did it, and I'm still frustrated about not being able to re-member why—I'm the logical choice to put it back together.

And since I'm planning to get my driver's license in ninety-one days, when I turn sixteen, I need to get started soon.

And now I look at my watch. It's 4:55 p.m. Biffmann Self-Storage closes at 5:00 p.m. The bus back to my house will leave in eight minutes. The walk to the bus stop takes seven minutes. It's time to go.

I snap the padlock shut to secure the roll-up door, and I walk back to the main office.

Chett Biffmann is sitting on a barstool behind the counter. He has short, chubby fingers and a beard that's mostly gray, but it's also brown on the bottom parts from his chewing tobacco drippage.

And Chett Biffmann smells like dirty gym socks that've been soaked in Old Spice and then left out in the Biffmann Self-Storage parking lot to dry under the hot L.A. sun.

"You make any progress putting that ol' heap back to-gether, Larry?"

My brain counts off seven seconds before I respond, not by speaking, but by writing Chett Biffmann a note.

My name isn't Larry.

I hardly talk at all, preferring instead to communicate my thoughts through written messages. And my workflow is simple and consistent: I select one of the seven No. 2 pencils from my pocket protector, and I pull out my writing pad, and then I write a note, and I fold it in half, and I hand it to the person I'm not talking to.

Although in Chett Biffmann's case, I always fling my notes onto the counter and then take a step backward.

I write him a follow-up note to clarify my self-nomenclature.

My name is Sherman, Sherman Tuckerman, but my friends call me Lawrence.

"Suit yourself, padnah."

Chett Biffmann turns his head and sends a wad of chewing tobacco mixed with saliva directly into the center of the brass spittoon he keeps on the carpet next to him.

No doubt Chett Biffmann's spittoon is made of brass because of that metal's resistance to corrosion. My brain recalls that brass is an alloy of copper and zinc, which are listed as 29 and 30, respectively, in the periodic table of the elements.

Lawrencium, a radioactive metal that's the final element on my chart, is number 103. And even though Lawrencium is my favorite atomic element, especially since only fourteen isotopes of it are currently known to exist, and that number is divisible by seven, Lawrencium isn't named after me.

It's named after Ernest O. Lawrence, inventor of a type of particle accelerator called a cyclotron. In 1939, Ernest O. Lawrence was awarded the Nobel Prize in Physics for his invention. I plan to earn that same Nobel Prize some day through my own practical application of mathematics.

I'm into numbers.

Super into them.

I have a particular way of seeing numbers as they relate to other numbers, and I do all my calculations in my head.

Zeke calls it my superpower, meaning he thinks I have some sort of superhuman ability, which I don't, because it's just my natural state of mind.

Nathan has a different word for it. He calls it annoying.

Calculations continuously flood my brain, streams of numbers that are like river water rolling and tumbling over miles and miles of stones that somehow filter out all the water's impurities to isolate: *the answer.*

And what emerges in the downstream sector of my brain is the pure truth, the only conclusion a mathematical formula can reach.

Math equals truth.

That's why I never lie.

Ever.

I have so few friends because the friend-making process requires my brain to identify and separate out the parts of someone that don't serve a friendship, mathematically speaking. I find that few people can withstand this test.

I was diagnosed with autism spectrum disorder at the age of four. My doctor, a pediatric neurologist named Dr. Morton Tidewater, calls me high-functioning. The thing is, I am normal to me.

Dr. Tidewater also diagnosed me with a rare condition known as savant syndrome, which means I have massive memory skills and perfect recall. I also face challenges with social skills and nonverbal communication, and I'm prone to lapse into conspicuous repetitive behavior. I am aware of all these things.

And I don't like loud noises.

And I don't like to be touched.

And I don't like it when people ask me questions.

And I don't like it when someone feels sorry for me.

And sometimes I wonder why other people can't analyze numbers and interpret them the way I can. And sometimes I get upset about it, like the time I smacked Nathan.

My teachers at McDerney Continuation have tried to get me to use a calculator and even a computer, but those gadgets only frustrate me and make my brain twitch.

"If you'd like, I can call my buddy, Chuck, over at Chuck's Wreck and Salvage to haul everything away," Chett Biffmann says before taking a sip from a twelve-ounce aluminum can that I assume contains root beer, except now I notice that the word *root* isn't on the can, and it's almost as if his chubby thumb has rubbed off those four letters, and now I cross my arms, and I can feel my body temperature rising from the inside, because Chett Biffmann shouldn't be drinking beer while he's guarding my truck parts. "I'm sure Chuck would give you a pretty penny for that ol' heap of junk—and don't worry, I would barely get any commission at all."

I write another note, fold it in half, fling it over to Chett Biffmann, and take a step back.

I'm going to put the Chevy back together all by myself by the time I get my driver's license.

"Suit yourself, Larry."

3

It's From Zeke

I leave Biffmann Self-Storage and race-walk to the bus stop, making sure one of my feet maintains contact with the ground at all times.

I race-walk whenever I'm in a hurry, which is mostly all the time. Race-walking makes it easier for me to keep track of the number of steps I've taken, which helps me to calculate the arrival time at my destination.

I make it to the bus stop forty-nine seconds before the bus pulls up.

I know all the bus drivers by name because I've been riding since I was thirteen years and twenty-eight days old. That means I began riding the bus on the 4,777th day of my life. That was the most sevens I could assemble together without waiting another three thousand days to buy my first bus pass.

"What's the good word, Lawrence?"

That's Rigoberto, who wears a neatly pressed bus driver's uniform and works weekends and always asks me what the good word is.

Based on the bus schedule and the fact that it's Saturday, I figured Rigoberto would be my driver. I never speak to him, but I always arrange in advance to hand him a folded-up note that has my good word for the day written on it in pencil.

"Mars!" Rigoberto shouts to me over his shoulder as I move down the aisle past fourteen strangers to the unoccupied seventh row and slide into the window seat. "That's a real good word, Lawrence. *Real* good. The Red Planet, fourth rock from the sun. No one has ever journeyed to Mars. Maybe someday, but not anytime soon."

Mars is my go-to good word for Rigoberto. That's because my life's goal is to be the mathematics flight specialist on NASA's first-ever manned mission to Mars.

And nothing is going to stop me, except maybe NASA, the independent agency of the U.S. federal government that's responsible for the country's civilian space program.

I've overheard kids at McDerney saying NASA won't allow someone with autism, high-functioning or otherwise, to climb aboard a Mars-bound spacecraft.

But that doesn't matter to me, because I'm superdetermined to be selected for the mission, even though it won't likely happen for at least another twenty-five years.

I exit the bus at 5:23 p.m., and I race-walk my normal 868 steps to 26488 Laszlo Lane. When I arrive, there's a brand new 2006 black four-door Dodge Stratus sedan parked in front of the house.

And there's a strange man wearing dark sunglasses sitting behind the wheel.

My brain doesn't recognize the man, or the car, which

makes me nervous and causes me to breathe harder than I usually do after race-walking those 868 steps.

The sedan has tinted windows and a strange radio antenna mounted on top of the trunk.

And it also has white federal government license plates with blue letters and numbers. My brain determines that the sedan is a NASA vehicle because its license plate has the letters NA, followed by a dash and then four numbers that are neither four sevens nor 1046, which comes as a relief, but only a brief one.

And the sedan isn't blocking the mailbox, which I also take comfort in. My dad lets me get the mail because he thinks I should have certain responsibilities around the house, especially ones that don't involve numbers.

The thing is, the U.S. postal system is run almost entirely by numbers, but I never mention that to my dad because he has enough stuff to think about, like his job as an architect, and my dead mom's forty-nine boxes in the garage.

And I know that our mail carrier, Bernadette, delivers our mail Monday through Saturday between 3:26 and 4:41 p.m., so I'm relieved that it's already 5:36 p.m., and I don't have to hand her a folded-up note when she wants to talk about the weather, which makes me nervous, even though Bernadette is always nice to me, except when it's raining and she just wants to deliver the mail and then keep driving.

I open the mailbox, and I find a promotional coupon for two dollars off a large pepperoni pizza at Mike's Pizza.

And a package.

Normally, the only packages Bernadette delivers to the Tuckerman residence contain drafting supplies for my dad.

But this one has a return address from Lawrence, Kansas, where the University of Kansas is located.

It's from Zeke.

And it's addressed to me.

4

I Wonder Whether This Nightmare Will Ever End

I'm excited. And I rock from side to side.

Zeke has sent me a jumbo manila envelope with $6.58 worth of postage stamps on it, which I estimate to be a bargain for a package that traveled 1,603 miles, but then I shake it a few times, and I notice it isn't as heavy as I think. At $0.0041048 cents per mile, I conclude that it's a fair deal for both Zeke and the United States Postal Service.

And I turn the package over, and there's a handwritten note stuck to the back of it. I discern that the note was written with a pen, not a pencil.

> *Dear Lawrence,*
>
> *Early this morning, I noticed this package sitting on a shelf in the back of the warehouse. Seems like it's been there for a couple of months. There was seven cents postage due. I'm guessing one of the mail sorters put the*

package there with the intent to deal with it later and then maybe forgot about it. I covered the seven cents for you as a way of apologizing on behalf of my boss, the U.S. Postmaster General.

Have a nice day.

Bernadette

My brain thinks about double-checking my cost-per-mile calculation to ensure its accuracy, but instead, it decides to focus on what might be inside the package.

I dig out my key ring from my backpack, and I slip my house key into the front door's deadbolt, and then I swivel the key precisely one-quarter turn to the left.

And when I open the door and walk inside, I hear my dad talking with two people, a man and a woman whose voices I've never heard before, which causes my brain to twitch the way it always does around complete strangers.

And I slam the door, which is my way of telling my dad I'm unhappy, or I'm angry, or sometimes both at the same time, which is the case right now. And then I walk past the living room without looking to see who's in there, because it doesn't matter, because with strangers, either they're there, or they're not.

And I make it as far as the hallway when my dad says, "Hold up, Sherman, there are a couple of people here I'd like you to meet."

That freezes me in my tracks. I've been trying hard to do all the things my dad asks me to do, but this time it involves two strangers—not people I know, like Dr. Tidewater or Rigoberto or Bernadette, or even Chett Biffmann.

I take out my pad, and I write my dad a note. And then I fold it in half, and I walk over to where he's sitting, and I hand it to him, being extra careful not to look at the two strangers.

NO!

I write the word in capital letters, and then I add an exclamation point for extra emphasis.

My dad forces a smile, but it doesn't disguise his look of disappointment. He folds the note back up and sets it onto the coffee table next to a couple of business cards with the letters SFC printed on them.

And I wonder whether the two strangers somehow figure out what I've written, and that the word is constructed in all caps, and that there's auxiliary punctuation.

The man clears his throat, and it's super loud, which makes my brain twitch again, only harder this time, so hard that I think maybe it grazes up against the inside of my skull.

"Sherman, my name is Flint Garrison. I'm a retired Air Force brigadier general. And this is Lydia Murakami. Lydia is a doctor, a developmental pediatrician, if you will."

Flint Garrison's use of the phrase *if you will* is short for *if you will allow me*. I figure he says it because he's reluctant to tell me that Lydia Murakami is a doctor, because he thinks it will make me nervous.

I've been to so many doctors in my lifetime—twenty-eight up to this point—that it doesn't matter anymore, but Flint Garrison's use of that language makes me trust him less than I already do.

He's wearing a gray business suit with a narrow-collared white shirt and a flaming scarlet necktie affixed to his shirt by a gold tie clasp with the letters SFC on it. And now my brain is beginning to sense a pattern. And there's a black leather briefcase at the man's side. And he speaks in a gruff, low voice that sounds like someone doing long division on an abacus made of rocks.

"We're here to speak with you about an urgent matter of national importance." Flint Garrison clears his throat again after he says that. And by now, I'm familiar with his throat-clearing method, so it makes me incrementally less nervous than when he did it the first time.

I write my dad another note.

The answer is still no.

I don't think it's necessary to capitalize the word *no* or add punctuation again, because I know my dad will get the message.

"General, you'll have to excuse my son. He's a better listener than a talker."

I hear Flint Garrison make a grunting sound under his breath. And then out of the corner of my eye, I catch a glimpse of Dr. Murakami writing notes in a journal before she closes it and takes a sip from a glass of water.

"That's all right, Mr. Tuckerman," Dr. Murakami says. "We can come back another time when Sherman isn't quite so busy. We wanted to speak with him about the planet Mars, but I'm sure it can wait."

Good, because I need to get to the kitchen to prepare my

dinner, which is my nightly astronaut training meal of freeze-dried chili mac 'n' beef. I can't do that as long as there are two strangers sitting in our living room, even if they're here to talk about Mars, which strikes me as odd, not because of the topic, which certain mathematics flight-specialists-in-training have a keen interest in, but because they want to talk to *me* about it.

I stand like a statue, waiting to find out what'll happen next.

"Lawrence—can I call you Lawrence?"

I don't like it when people ask me questions.

And the one Flint Garrison asks makes my brain twitch again.

"Lawrence, did you know that in Roman mythology, Mars is the god of war?"

Of course I know that.

I wonder whether this nightmare will ever end.

5

Go Away, I'm Busy

"Ahem."

Flint Garrison clears his throat for a third time. That's unprecedented in my experience. And unwelcome.

My brain notes that on an anatomical basis, his throat-clearing sound takes place at the back of his throat when he constricts his laryngopharyngeal tissues and vibrates his palatoglossal arch and vocal cords while exhaling through his nose.

It makes me wonder whether he might clear his throat another four times before he and Dr. Murakami leave, which I hope will happen soon—the leaving part, not the throat-clearing part.

I still have Zeke's jumbo manila envelope in my hands. I squeeze it. What's inside feels like the size and shape of a stack of standard 8½-by-11-inch paper, which is mathematically twice the size of my writing pad. And there's also something vaguely lumpy inside the package.

"Lawrence, if I may speak bluntly, the good doctor and I

are here to talk to you and your father about a Mars sample-return mission—a *manned* mission."

Flint Garrison places heavy emphasis on the word "manned," which everyone knows won't happen for at least another twenty-five years into the future, given the current state of the U.S. space program, coupled with the projected limits of near-future technology.

I continue down the hallway toward my bedroom, but I stop just short of the door so I can hear what everyone is saying.

"Mr. Tuckerman, we've heard good things about Sherman from Professor Bellwether at NASA's Jet Propulsion Laboratory at the California Institute of Technology," Dr. Murakami says. "Professor Bellwether was Sherman's supervisor during your son's summer internship. The good professor thinks Sherman is a prodigy and a mathematical genius, the likes of which he has never seen before."

Professor Bellwether is a senior research scientist whose main responsibility is to define the open scientific questions related to a Mars sample-return mission.

During my internship orientation, Professor Bellwether described the mission as a future spaceflight that would collect rock and dust samples from Mars and return them to Earth. But he said it was *unmanned*.

Professor Bellwether and I spent most of our time together performing mathematical calculations in support of his advanced theories on the gravitational pull of Mars—specifically, the amount of action the planet would exert on an object that was leaving its orbit, which the professor believes is inversely proportional to the square of the distance between the object and the center of Mars.

Math stuff.

And now I'm getting hungrier by the second, but by a narrow mathematical margin, I'm more curious than hungry.

"Mr. Tuckerman, we'd like to speak with you about securing Sherman's services for a *manned* sample-return mission to the Red Planet." Flint Garrison emphasizes the word *manned* again, but twenty-five years is a long way off, so I conclude that I have enough time to open the envelope Zeke sent me.

I race-walk the rest of the way to my bedroom, and I inch the doorknob one-quarter turn to the right, and I step inside, and then I slam the door behind me. The slamming-the-door part is my way of communicating to Flint Garrison and Dr. Murakami and even my dad that the Earth mission I'm on in this moment is of far greater importance than whatever they're talking about.

And I grab hold of the metal letter opener I keep in my desk drawer, and I carefully slice open the top of the envelope. As I suspect, there's a heap of paper inside.

And I notice a folded-up piece of paper sitting on top of the stack. Written in pencil on it are the words:

to Lawrence from Zeke

From the heaviness of the graphite and the width of the letters, I can tell that the note was written with a No. 2 pencil.

And I recognize Zeke's handwriting, which is easy to read, with letters that are straight up and down, unlike mine, which are slanted hard to the right and often written with more emotion, which sometimes includes anger, and I have found

| 22 |

that writing my words is a more useful and less destructive way to express my anger than, for example, slapping someone.

Also written on the folded-up piece of paper are these instructions:

Open this letter first.

Zeke knows me well enough to understand that I operate best when I have an understanding of the game plan, which is the basketball term Zeke uses to describe how his team prepares to play against a worthy opponent—or an unworthy one.

I unfold the note. It's a letter from Zeke. I know that I need to read the letter before I can move on to the stack of papers.

Dear Lawrence,
After I arrived at KU, I decided to handwrite the en-closed record of all the time we've spent together since we met at McDerney. Jeepers, talk about writer's cramp!

Just then, I hear a knock on my bedroom door. The person's knuckles land on the door seven times. I know it's my dad because that's how I ask him to knock. That way, I know it's him and not some different guy.

Zeke always knocks three times, and there's a brief pause after the first two knocks, which I assume he does for emphasis, so that I know it's him and not my dad.

Nathan, who is normally enraged, pounds his fist on my

bedroom door so hard that the framed poster of my hero, astronomer and planetary scientist Carl Sagan, goes crooked, and I have to use my tubular spirit level instrument to recalibrate it before I let Nathan in.

And just as in the advanced theories on the gravitational pull of Mars that Professor Bellwether and I worked on over the summer, I have observed that there's an inversely proportional relationship between how hard Nathan pummels the door and the number of times he strikes it.

My dad is speaking to me through the door. And the tone of his voice is gentle but firm. "Lawrence, the general and the doctor would like to know how long it will be before you come out of there and rejoin us in the living room."

Technically, I haven't actually *joined* them in the living room yet, so my brain concludes it's not mathematically possible to *rejoin* them.

I peel a sheet of paper from my pad, and I write my dad a note, and then I fold it in half, and I slide it under the door.

Go away, I'm busy.

6

Flint Garrison Clears His Throat Again

I hear footsteps fading down the hallway. I bring my attention back to Zeke's letter.

> *I wrote what might look from a distance like a pile of paper as thick as one of your math textbooks because I wanted you to know how important your friendship is to me. I didn't want to leave anything unsaid, so I think you'll find this written record to be as comprehensive as it is thick.*

Zeke always tries to relate to me through mathematics, which I consider to be the universal language of truth. Zeke is a way better writer than he is a mathematician, so I appreciate his extra effort.

> *I know how essential rules are to you. I'm going to*

impose one on you myself. You must not read this story until you are en route to Mars.

It means I'll have to wait years and years to read Zeke's written record. I'm prepared for that, but at the same time, I suddenly feel a tightness in my throat, and I clench my jaw until it hurts a lot, and then I rock from side to side, and then I keep reading.

I figure my observations will help you to pass the idle time in between conducting critically important experiments in space for the good of humankind.

If it comes to pass that you're selected as the mathematics flight specialist on the first-ever manned mission to Mars—and I REALLY like your chances—you have my permission to read the enclosed words during your journey. This story will be yours to keep forever, and you may do with it whatever you wish.

Thanks for being my friend.

Zeke

I rip open the door, and I race-walk back down the hallway. I'm hoping Flint Garrison and Dr. Murakami are still in the living room with my dad, because I have questions for them, starting with the obvious one.

"I'm glad you've decided to rejoin us," Flint Garrison says.

My brain elects not to point out to Flint Garrison the obvious mathematical error in his use of the word *rejoin*. I had never *joined* them to begin with, and 0 + 1 = 1, not 2. Instead, I write him a note, and I hand it to my dad.

"General, my son is asking why you and Dr. Murakami are here to discuss a manned sample-return mission to Mars that couldn't possibly take place for a very, *very* long time, another two and a half decades, at the earliest."

I glance at Flint Garrison, being careful not to make eye contact.

I notice that he has a push-broom mustache and a flattop haircut. His flattop is so flat that if I write him a note that says his haircut makes my brain twitch, and I rest the note on the top of his head instead of handing it to my dad to read, the note would sit precisely level, parallel with the surface of the living room carpet.

Flint Garrison adjusts his tie, and then he clears his throat for the fourth time, and now my brain considers placing its throat-clear counting process on pause, because it's more important that I concentrate on Mars and the reason why the general and Dr. Murakami are taking up space in the living room.

"Sherman, what if I told you that everything you've ever been taught in school about the history of space travel to Mars was, shall we say, a bit inaccurate."

That sounds vaguely like a question, but whether it's a real one or a fake, what the general is saying is not possible.

I've studied every single American mission to Mars, beginning with Mariner 3, which launched on November 5, 1964, all the way to the most recent mission, the Mars Reconnaissance Orbiter, which launched a year ago on August 12, 2005. Both spacecraft took off from Cape Canaveral in Florida.

There were other Mars missions during that time period that were conducted by the Soviet Union and the European

Space Agency, but I'm an expert on U.S. missions, and I'm familiar with the conventional wisdom that space-travel technology has not advanced far enough for there to be a Mars sample-return mission until at least the year 2031.

And that first sample-return mission would be *unmanned*. And it would launch at least twenty-five years after the moment when Flint Garrison and Dr. Murakami had planted themselves on our living room couch, apparently unwilling to leave.

I glance at my watch. It's fourteen minutes past the time for my nightly astronaut training meal of chili mac 'n' beef. And I know that my training meal takes priority over having a conversation about a mission to Mars that doesn't make any sense.

I write a quick note, and I pass it to my dad. And he reads it aloud.

Not possible.

"What's not possible, Sherman?" I glance at Dr. Murakami when she says that, being super careful not to make eye contact.

She's wearing pants and a blazer the color of the sky on a clear day, and she has a matching blue hat resting atop her long, silver hair, and she has smooth, light-brown skin. Her name, Dr. Lydia Murakami, is etched onto a shiny gold nameplate pinned to her blazer.

I send another note to my dad, who reads it to Dr. Murakami.

It's not possible to go to Mars until I'm at least forty years old, and I can't wait that long to have my nightly astronaut training meal of chili mac 'n' beef, so goodbye.

Dr. Murakami smiles. And Flint Garrison clears his throat again, and I take note that it's number five.

And my dad opens his mouth to speak, but he's interrupted by a knock at the front door—a knock I don't recognize because it's not comprised of any of my approved knocking patterns.

7

Fact or Fiction?

M y dad springs from his easy chair to answer the door, while I plant myself in my spot on the living room carpet, and I study the tops of my shoes, taking note that the ends of the laces on my left shoe beyond the knot are of un-even length, with one I estimate to be one and three-quarter inches longer than the other. I file away a mental note in my brain to recalibrate them after Flint Garrison and Dr. Murakami finally leave.

The general and the doctor are throwing off my routine. I cross my arms in front of my chest and stiffen my posture, hoping they will get the hint, but it doesn't work.

They only sink deeper into the couch, even though it's cov-ered in stiff, clear plastic, and I worry that Flint Garrison's and Dr. Murakami's butt indentations might take an eternity to unindent after they finally leave, and then I think their actual leaving might also take an eternity.

And I hear the front door creaking open. I know it isn't the

Mike's Pizza delivery guy, because we only have pizza cut into seven slices on Tuesday, and it's Saturday.

"Hey, Mr. T." I recognize the voice. It's Curtis Short, one of Zeke's three best friends. "Me and Stretch are looking for *the Dude*. Está en casa, amigo?"

Curtis has a total of seven nicknames for me. *The Dude* is empirically the most common, and therefore probabilistically the most likely, followed in sequential descending order by:

2. Bro

3. LT

4. The Calculus Kid

5. Dude Duderson

6. The Sultan of Square Root

7. Sharduhl the Magnificent

Curtis has called me that last one only once, which is a relief, because my brain knows it carries a lot of responsibility that has little to do with math.

Curtis played on Zeke's basketball team at Jefferson, even though Curtis's real love is surfing, which is why he uses the word *dude* a lot.

"We need to speak with Lawrence about an important automotive matter." That sounds like Stretch, Zeke's teammate and best friend number two.

And I know *I* am Zeke's third and final best friend, because he once told me so.

I have two friends, Nathan and Zeke. I have defaulted them to best-friend status because the math allows for it, even though I've only known Zeke for two years, and there have been times when Nathan's best-friend status could be called into question for reasons related to his anger during our chess matches, depending on his readiness to defend against tactics like the Annihilation of Defense, Demolition of Pawns, or even Space Clearance, which is not at all about outer space.

Stretch's real name is Roland Puckett. He acquired the nickname Stretch because he's taller than just about everyone. He works for Puckett Painting, the family painting business, but his life goal is to be a private investigator.

I feel comfortable around Stretch because I can just stare at his shoulder. I'm glad I don't have to worry about avoiding making eye contact with him. The last time I saw him, he was seven feet, four inches tall, and he was playing in the Southern California regional basketball championship, when Jefferson won the title on a last-second miracle shot by Brock Decker, who helped me to disassemble Zeke's pickup truck, but I still can't remember why we took the Chevy apart, and I'm getting angry all over again just thinking about not being able to re-member why.

"Sherman, there are a couple of young fellas here to see you."

I'm glad to leave the living room. I would prefer to go to the kitchen to prepare my astronaut training meal, but in-stead, I race-walk the short distance to the front door, where I see the Puckett Painting van parked in front of the house, across the street from the black sedan.

"Hey, bro." Predictably, Curtis chooses one of his more common nicknames to start our conversation, presumably to help me feel more at ease, which isn't necessary, because when I'm around Curtis and Stretch, they make me feel like it's okay to be myself.

"Hey." I whisper the word rather than write it down, because I feel safe enough to pretend to be one of the guys.

"Zeke called to tell us you might need some help getting the old Chevy roadworthy again. Fact or fiction, Swami?"

I'm not prepared for Curtis to introduce an eighth nickname into the mix. I ignore it and instead take out my pad and pull a pencil from my pocket protector as my dad goes back to the living room to rejoin Flint Garrison and Dr. Murakami.

I scribble a note, and then I fold it in half, and I hand it to Curtis.

"Cool, I love fan mail," Curtis says. I know he's trying to make a joke, but I don't understand it, which is awkward. I don't react, which is normal for me, and I don't know whether Curtis figures I'm playing it cool, or he thinks I simply didn't hear what he said.

"Just read it, man," Stretch says. "I've got to get the van back to the warehouse before my dad notices it's missing."

"Back off and scratch it, landlubber," Curtis says. "We're guests at the Tuckerman residence. I'm respecting LT's highly specialized communication workflow." Curtis studies the note and hands it to Stretch, who studies it some more and then hands it back to Curtis.

Fact AND fiction

"How about you break that down for us," Stretch says. I write a follow-up note.

Fact: Yes, I might need some help getting the old Chevy roadworthy again.

Fiction: Neither one of you guys knows anything about internal combustion vehicles beyond how to borrow one without asking for permission. Am I right, dudes?

8

Where Is He Going?

"Bro, I may not be handy with a socket wrench," Curtis says, "but I could tell you about the post–World War II societal influence of car culture in Los Angeles in the 1960s while you do most of the work."

Stretch bends his knees so that I can see his chin and part of his nose through the doorway.

"Yeah, and if any of the paint got chipped when you were reducing Zeke's prized possession to scrap metal," Stretch says, "I could show you how to repair it, for a nominal fee."

I think about their offer to help and how I've considered expanding my circle of friends to include Curtis and Stretch, even though they wouldn't be in the best-friend category, at least not right away, and how my existing group of two friends can't technically, by definition, be considered a circle, because mathematicians define a circle as a round plane figure whose boundary, or circumference, consists of points equidistant from a fixed point, or center. A triangle can't be a circle, basically.

"Sherman, we shouldn't keep our guests waiting," I hear my dad say.

I write out another note, and I hand it to Curtis.

See ya.

That's how Zeke always says goodbye to Curtis and Stretch. I do it too because it makes me feel, at least in the moment, like I'm one of the guys, which I'm not, at least according to my friendship calculations up to now.

And then I slam the door—a light slam, but a slam, nonetheless—so Flint Garrison and Dr. Murakami know I've concluded my business, and I'm ready to call into question everything they say.

"Hey, what just happened?" I hear Stretch say through the front door. "We drove all the way here to try and help out the kid. What are we going to tell Zeke?"

"Chill, bro. If LT needs our help, I'm sure he'll let us know," Curtis says as his voice fades away.

And then I return to the living room. I locate my shoe indentations and retake my spot on the living room carpet to hear what Flint Garrison and Dr. Murakami have to say about how the history of space travel to Mars is inaccurate.

"We're sorry for the interruption, General." My dad is trying to get the conversation back on course, but all I can think about is the astronaut training meal I'm not preparing in the kitchen. "I believe that my son is keenly interested in hearing more about your theories on Martian space travel."

Flint Garrison releases a thunderous sixth throat clearing. It's like he's using the phlegm in his throat to express disapproval of the interruption caused by Curtis and Stretch who, in a gesture of friendship, have offered to help me, even though the gesture was only symbolic. Possibly.

"Are you familiar with this country's Mars Observer mission?"

Isn't everyone?

The Mars Observer mission is also known as the Mars Geoscience/Climatology Orbiter, a robotic space probe that was sent to Mars on September 25, 1992 aboard a Titan III/TOS launch vehicle from Cape Canaveral Air Force Station in Brevard County, Florida.

"The spacecraft was lost three days before it was scheduled to achieve Mars orbit, or at least that's what was, *ahem*, reported in the press."

Flint Garrison studies my reaction to what he has just said. I'm careful not to move any muscles in my body while I assess whether to count his brief *ahem* as an official throat-clear. I decide to play it straight, increasing my running tally to seven.

And then I scribble out another note, and I fold it in half, and I hand it to my dad. He looks it over and hands it to Flint Garrison.

"I believe this is for you, General."

Flint Garrison reads my note silently.

> The loss of communication with the robotic space probe was never fully explained. It was most likely caused by a ruptured fuel tank that made the spacecraft spin out of control and lose contact with Earth.

"Yes, I am familiar with this theory," Flint Garrison says as he sets my note onto the coffee table. "It is, however, not what actually happened to the spacecraft."

With that news, I pivot on my left heel and race-walk down the hallway toward my bedroom.

"Where is he going?" I hear Dr. Murakami ask as I reach for the doorknob.

My dad doesn't hesitate to respond. "I think he went to get more paper."

9

None of This Is News to Me

Out of the corner of my eye, I catch a glimpse of Flint Garrison glaring at me as he strokes his bristly goatee with the fingertips of his left hand.

It sends his shirtsleeve several inches up his arm, revealing a gold wristwatch with the Air Force insignia beneath the crystal, and I'm careful not to let myself be distracted by a shiny object that isn't the cellophane packaging of a freeze-dried astronaut training meal.

And then Flint Garrison startles me by exhaling so hard through his nose that the note he had set down on the coffee table takes flight. The sheet of paper appears to defy gravity transiently before nestling vertically between strands of the light-green shag carpet. It stands up on its end, at a distance I estimate to be forty-nine inches in front of my shoes.

And I stare at the note, wondering whose job it is to pick it up. I've never been in this situation before. It makes my brain twitch. I freeze, because I never make important decisions until after the twitching stops.

"Let me get that for you, General," my dad says as he rises from his easy chair.

"No, Mr. Tuckerman, let's just leave it there for now." I wonder if Flint Garrison is testing me. Maybe he thinks that my note resting vertically in the light-green shag carpet will somehow unnerve me, but all I can think of is, if I were the person receiving my notes, I'd want to pick it up so I could continue to collect the full set.

Dr. Murakami confirms my suspicion. "Sherman, how do you *feel* about that piece of paper being on the carpet rather than on the table?" she asks, pen in hand, ready to make an important journal entry as her body sinks deeper and deeper into the plastic-covered couch cushion.

I write another note, and I hand it to my dad.

I don't like Flint Garrison, and I'm starting not to like Dr. Murakami.

My dad flashes a micro-smile and slips the note into his shirt pocket for safekeeping.

"General, my son is hoping we can move this conversation forward at a faster pace."

Flint Garrison gets the hint. "Dr. Murakami and I are interested in learning how Sherman normally deals with moments of high stress, but we can come back to that. Right now, it's time to put our cards on the table." He doesn't appear to have a deck of cards with him, but if he does, there is now plenty of room on the coffee table to put them down. "Sherman, can I trust you?"

I'm not sure if it's a trick question, especially since I don't think I can trust him, but I suspect it's best if I answer yes, since that will likely get me to the kitchen sooner.

And I write my dad another note.

I'm REALLY hungry. So, yes, he can trust me.

"General, my son says you can count on him. Now, you were saying something about how the news media had a different understanding of the Mars Observer mission from what might have actually taken place?"

Flint Garrison reaches inside his briefcase and pulls out a thin stack of 8½-by-11-inch white paper. The stack is stapled, I calculate, at a forty-*two*-degree angle in the upper-left corner with a standard-size one-quarter-inch staple, which can fasten together anywhere from two to thirty standard-weight pages at once and is designed to fit any standard-size stapler.

I wonder whether the general is testing me yet again, because stapling documents at a forty-*five*-degree angle was the first task I was taught by Professor Bellwether when I began my internship at NASA's Jet Propulsion Laboratory over the summer. The professor had explained that precision stapling is a foundational skill of scientists who work at NASA's field center in Pasadena.

And when I notice that Flint Garrison's staple placement is off by three degrees, I attempt to appear to ignore him while I secretly angle my head by those same three degrees to determine whether he notices that I notice, but when he beats me to the ignore, my brain concludes that Professor Bellwether has never offered instruction to Flint Garrison on the

JPL's precision stapling protocol, and I resume my original rigid stance.

Flint Garrison discharges a combination grunt and throat-clear noise that sounds as if it escaped from somewhere deep within him as he mumbles something about needing to refer to his notes because the information he's about to impart is highly scientific in nature.

And then he puts on a pair of reading glasses while I adjust the official throat-clear count to eight.

"The Mars Observer was the initial voyage of the Observer series of planetary missions, designed to study the geoscience and climate of Mars." Flint Garrison glances at me after he says that, possibly to gauge my reaction, of which there is none, because I already know those basic facts, so there's no purposeful reason for me to react to them. "The mission's primary scientific objective was to determine the global elemental and mineralogical character of the planet's surface material."

Flint Garrison says that the mission was also tasked with defining the topography and gravitational field of Mars, as well as establishing the nature of its magnetic field and atmosphere.

Again, none of this is news to me. I stifle a yawn. And then my dad shifts around in his easy chair, which causes me to wonder if he notices that I might soon lapse into a boredom coma.

"That's all quite interesting, General," my dad says, and I recognize his tone of voice, which often indicates that consequences might follow. My brain concludes that my dad is pressing Flint Garrison into getting to the point, which I hope will eventually lead me to a bowl of chili mac 'n' beef.

10

I Can't Contain Myself

"As I said before, we lost contact with the Mars Observer shortly before it was scheduled for orbital insertion, and we were unable to reestablish contact. Then the unexpected happened." Flint Garrison suddenly has my attention. "What I'm about to tell you, Sherman, is a matter of national security. I need your assurance that it will remain within the four walls of this room, with the four of us."

My brain finds the general's use of *four* twice in a single sentence to be mathematically intriguing.

"If it were to leak out," he continues, "I'm afraid the consequences would be, shall we say, *dire*."

Up to this point, I've only heard the word *dire* used in gangster movies, like when a mob boss threatens an underling who is reluctant to *play ball*, and he isn't talking about a basketball, or any other type of round object used in sports competition.

And then I feel my brain twitch again, but I'm able to get it under control, at least temporarily, when I rock from side to side. I manage to rock almost imperceptibly. I don't think that Dr. Murakami notices, even though she makes a burst of notes in her journal when it happens, and her writing hand is maneuvering in cadence with my rocking motion.

And I write my dad another note.

I understand. Tell him he doesn't need to get worked up.

"General, my son says you can surely count on him."

"Good, because this is when I inform you that after I retired from active duty with the Air Force, I joined a top-secret government agency known as the SFC."

"Wait, there's no such thing!" I surprise myself by blurting out those words.

I don't believe Flint Garrison, and the feeling of disbelief runs so deep inside me, all the way down my body to my feet and back up again, that I can't contain myself, and the words lurch out of my mouth before my twitching brain can put the brakes on them.

Dr. Murakami flips over a filled-in page of her journal, revealing a blank page beneath it, and she gets to work filling in that one too.

And Flint Garrison's posture shifts. I wait for him to clear his throat again, but he doesn't. "Oh, but there is such an agency, Lawrence," he says. "May I call you Lawrence?"

I blast out a note, and I shove it to my dad.

No!

"General, I think it's best you get to the point of your visit."

"Yes, of course. The SFC is the Strategic Federation Council. It is loosely affiliated with NASA in that we share many of the same resources, as evidenced by the vehicle parked out front. The SFC's mission is to use space travel to advance the trajectory of modern medicine. Simply put, the council exists solely to help doctors combat disease. Dr. Murakami is a developmental pediatrician who heads up our 2e program and coordinates resources with families whenever we align the organization with twice-exceptional gifted students and other promising neurodiverse candidates"—he turns to face my dad—"especially those with intellectual superpowers, like your son."

11

If It Is
Somehow True

Dr. Murakami sets her journal onto the coffee table. "Professor Bellwether told us certain things about you—your preference for solitude and your dislike of changes in your surroundings, for example. These are some of the special attributes you possess that lend themselves well to the proposal the general intends to make this afternoon."

If he ever gets to the point.

This is the first time anyone has come looking for me because of my diagnosis. All the other times, it made people move in the opposite direction.

Everyone in the living room, including my dad, is waiting for my response. The silence is shattered by my watch's alarm, which beeps to indicate that the intrusion into our house and my routine is no longer happening in the afternoon, because it is now 6:00 p.m.

I had set the alarm during the bus ride home to remind me

that my 5:45 p.m. astronaut training meal is supposed to be over now, because it's not allowed to last longer than fifteen minutes.

Now malnourished and slipping into semiconsciousness, I scribble a quick note to my dad.

Need sustenance. Stat!

"Sherman expresses his thanks for the background information, Dr. Murakami. He would like General Garrison to conclude his summary of the Mars missions."

My dad has just put the intruders on notice that the Tuckermans collectively want Flint Garrison to get to the bottom line.

The general dispenses with his customary throat-clear, presumably in the interest of saving time, while I hold firm in my position on the carpet, resigned to the consequences of his encroachment into our home and the resultant shattering of my astronaut training regimen.

"Months after NASA lost contact with the Mars Observer, we realized that the spacecraft had actually followed its automated programming, because it began to send faint signals back to Earth," Flint Garrison says. "The SFC secretly took command of the mission when the orbiter identified the presence of certain chemical compounds that are thought to have vast potential in the field of medicine."

I have no reason to doubt he's telling me the truth beyond my lack of trust in him and my suspicion that he's only divulging the bare minimum of what he thinks I need to know.

"This leads us to the Mars Global Surveyor mission, which

left Earth on November 7, 1996, and—*allegedly*—reached Mars on September 12, 1997."

I notice how he pauses when he says the word *allegedly*. I know from watching TV crime dramas that lawyers often use the word to convey that something is claimed to have taken place although there is no proof. And that makes me mega-suspicious of the general.

"The Global Surveyor spacecraft used a revolutionary new method of aerobraking and counterthrust to convert its original elliptical capture orbit into a nearly circular two-hour polar orbit."

I have a feeling Flint Garrison is about to tell me more stuff about the Mars Global Surveyor mission I already know.

"The scientific goals were to study the planet's gravity and topography, the weather and climate, the composition of the planet's surface, and the evolution of the Martian magnetic field."

I make a brief, barely audible snoring sound in the back of my throat. Flint Garrison's hearing is apparently better than I thought, because when I do it, he looks around the living room, then directly at me. Of course, I don't make eye contact with him, but I notice the sudden appearance of creases in his face.

"Did you say something, Sherman?" he asks as the creases deepen.

"That's all quite interesting, General," my dad says, possibly in an effort to lay down some strafing ground cover for me.

I think it's best to answer Flint Garrison by not moving a single muscle in my entire body until he gives up waiting and continues.

"NASA publicly told the media and, for that matter, the world, what the Mars Global Surveyor's objectives and time-line were, but the real situation was very different. The SFC had secretly taken over this mission from the outset, implementing the agency's revolutionary rocket propulsion science and advanced telemetry to accelerate the spacecraft's arrival by seventy-seven days—to June 27, 1997."

My brain takes a moment to process the general's new information, which sounds fishy at best, and preposterous at worst, and it's the second time he has offered a theory about the Mars missions contrary to common knowledge and the beliefs shared by avid followers of the Martian space program, like me.

But if it is somehow true, which is highly unlikely, then I can see how the pieces of the puzzle might come together, as evidenced by the SFC directing the Global Surveyor to enter Mars orbit exactly one week—seven days—prior to the landing of the Mars Pathfinder mission on July 4, 1997.

I glance at my watch. It's 6:07 p.m. I'm curious and hungry. I use my brain to analyze the math. I conclude that my curiosity overrides my hunger by a margin of 51% to 49%. I hold my position on the living room carpet, and I burrow in.

Flint Garrison continues. "All of this leads us to the Mars Pathfinder. The mission's primary objectives were to—"

Bam, bam. BAM!

Just then, the general is interrupted by a loud banging noise at the front door that shakes the house and likely moves it off its foundation by a fraction of a millimeter.

I recognize the rhythmic pattern and barbaric ferocity of the pounding.

Curtis and Stretch, it isn't.

12

I Know What's Coming Next

"Excuse me for a moment, General."

My dad leaps from his easy chair again. And that leaves me standing at the crossroads. Should I guard my spot on the living room carpet or accompany my dad to the front door?

If the living room were a spacecraft bound for Mars, and if I were wearing a spacesuit, the general's glaring eyes surely would be burning through the garment's neoprene-coated nylon and five layers of aluminized Mylar.

This effectively tilts the scales in favor of following my dad, who grips onto the doorknob with his right hand and turns it precisely one-quarter turn to the right.

"My goodness, Nathan, is everything all right?"

"Yeah, I'm cool. Why?"

"You were knocking on the door with a certain degree of intensity," my dad says. "I thought something might be wrong."

"This is my usual state of mind, sir. Lawrence knows I'm constantly worked up about something. If I knocked like a normal person, he might think I was in trouble and call the police."

For all of Nathan's impatience and fury, I know him to be a clear thinker, especially when it comes to door-knocking patterns, law enforcement, sporting goods, and chess.

My dad shakes his head, cracks a weak smile, and retreats to the living room, which allows me to have some one-on-one time with one-half of my best-friend posse.

"What's with the agent-provocateur vehicle out front?" Nathan says. "Is that your probation officer behind the wheel?"

Nathan and Zeke are the only two people besides my dad I normally speak with, and even then, I usually communicate through my notepad because it's easier, and I think by this point in my best friendship with Nathan, he expects it, and I don't want to let him down.

I write him a note, opting for the direct approach.

What's up?

"Ever since Zeke left Chip's Sporting Goods to pursue his basketball dream at the University of Kansas, business has picked up significantly. Chip thinks it's just a coincidence, but I'm not so sure."

Nathan's beating around the bush prompts me to use up another sheet of paper.

Get to the point. We've got company.

"Right. G-man sedan out front with tough-guy driver behind the wheel. Here's the deal. Chip gave me the green light to hire a part-time trainee sales clerk. You're the first person I thought of. All you need to do is apply for a work permit and get fitted for a Chip's Sporting Goods employee polo shirt. What do you think?"

What I'm thinking is, *Questions!*, but Nathan is enthusiastic about the prospect of us working together, and I have a whole lot going on with my junior year at McDerney, plus I need to put the pickup truck back together so I can drive around after I get my license, which will require money for gas and maintenance and insurance, so having a part-time job makes sense, but I know I can't make this kind of critically important and possibly life-altering decision without first checking with my dad, so I go back to the beginning of my original thought process, and I think about how enthusiastic Nathan is, and so I stare back at him, but not directly.

"I need a decision."

I write Nathan another note.

> *Tell Chip his assistant store manager is pushy.*

"Did I mention you can use your rookie employee discount to buy chess gear?"

Yet another question from Nathan. I decide to let it go because I already know from Zeke that the rookie employee discount Nathan is referring to is identical to the regular Chip's Sporting Goods employee discount, except that it gives Nathan an extra opportunity to call a new employee a rookie.

I write him another note.

I'll think about it.

"Better get on that. Competition for an opportunity to work alongside me is tight. Would-be rookies showing up to apply for the job are practically taking a number at the door."

I write Nathan another note.

See previous note.

Nathan extends his fist, but I pull back, then stare in the general direction of his fist without moving a muscle.

"Don't leave me hanging here, Lawrence. Pound it."

I don't like to touch people unless there's good reason to slap them, in which case I make an exception. My brain weighs the circumstances and decides to take a compromise position: it instructs my hand to slap Nathan's hand away. Which I do. Nathan looks only slightly more annoyed than usual. And then I write what I hope is my final note on the subject for the day.

There can be no bumping of fists until the mission is accomplished. And even then, it's unlikely.

My note isn't referring to Nathan's recruiting mission in particular. Instead, I mean it as a statement about fist bumps in general and how I reserve them only for missions that are fully and completely accomplished, meaning almost never.

"Suit yourself," Nathan says as he turns and walks away.

As soon as Nathan disappears from view, I wish he were still standing with me on the front porch, because I know what's coming next: Flint Garrison is going to tell me the reason why he and Dr. Murakami interrupted my astronaut training meal, and I'm not looking forward to it.

13

I Don't Like Loud Noises

"Where was I?" Flint Garrison asks.

The last time I checked, he was making deafening throat-clearing sounds while going on and on about a top-secret government agency's role in missions to Mars that had questionable outcomes.

"General, I believe you were about to tell young Sherman about the Mars Pathfinder," Dr. Murakami says.

"Yes, of course. Thank you, Lydia. The Pathfinder mission was launched from Cape Canaveral on December 4, 1996 aboard a Delta II rocket. It consisted of a lander and a six-wheeled robotic rover named Sojourner."

Again, it's information that even the most casual of Mars followers already knows.

My brain recalls that Pathfinder landed on Mars on July 4, 1997. I learned from watching the nightly network news on TV when I was six years old that the mission's primary objective was to explore the feasibility of low-cost landings on, and exploration of, the planet's surface.

The spacecraft had entered the Martian atmosphere without first inserting itself into orbit. It set down on the planet's surface with the help of parachutes, rockets, and airbags.

"The Pathfinder landed at Ares Vallis, an outflow channel in a region called Chryse Planitia, which is in the Oxia Palus quadrangle of Mars. The Sojourner rover explored the terrain there until NASA lost communication, for reasons unknown, on September 27, just eighty-five days after the spacecraft landed."

Then Flint Garrison drops a bombshell, or so he obviously thinks.

"There's more to the story than what was reported in the mainstream media."

Here we go again with the general's clandestine theory of reality. I'm getting more and more impatient. I write another note, and I hand it to my dad.

> I suppose he's going to claim that the SFC arranged for the Global Surveyor to enter Martian orbit 77 days earlier than the general public was aware so the orbiter could redirect the Pathfinder to Ares Vallis, because that was the location of the chemical compounds identified by the Mars Observer.

My dad pauses for a moment, and then he reads an edited version of my note aloud.

"You must be a mind reader, Sherman," Dr. Murakami says as she sets down her journal.

And then Flint Garrison weighs in. "I think you're beginning to see the bigger picture, young man."

No one has called me *young man* since my bus driver, Rigoberto, caught me putting my feet up on the seat in front of me on the way back from the JPL during my summer internship. I remember that Rigoberto's words made me feel embarrassed, because I got caught doing something I shouldn't be doing. But when Flint Garrison says it, I wonder if he's trying to gain an advantage over me in some way, and that makes me feel uncomfortable, and then my brain twitches, and I rock from side to side to get my feelings under control, but I'm so hungry, it's not working.

And then my body shakes, and then a sound escapes from the back of my throat that I don't recognize as one of the seven accredited noises I utter whenever I'm communicating that I'm having a problem.

And then my dad jumps from his easy chair, and he hustles me off to the kitchen.

"Excuse us, General."

And I catch a glimpse of Flint Garrison frowning and crossing his arms as my dad rushes me across the living room carpet. And then I take my seat at the kitchen table.

My dad measures fourteen ounces of water, and he pours it into the tea kettle on the stove before turning up the gas to high.

"Son, I'm sorry it took us so long to make dinner. I know how important your astronaut training meals are to you. Goodness, I've known it for a long time."

My dad's face is wrinkled. I've stopped rocking, but I'm

still shaking. I take out my pad, and I write an itemized note, and I hand it to my dad.

1. I'm okay.
2. I'm just REALLY hungry.
3. Flint Garrison knows about something weird that happened on Mars.
4. I don't know what it is.
5. I can't tell if I don't believe him, or I don't WANT to believe him.
6. I'm still REALLY hungry.
7. What kind of name is FLINT, anyway?

There's a lot of information in that note, and it isn't particularly well-organized, and my handwriting is nearly illegible, but that's what happens whenever my regular routine gets disrupted, and the shrill sound coming from the tea kettle is a welcome relief, until it isn't, because I don't like loud noises.

And then my brain distracts itself from hunger by remembering that the piercing sound coming from the tea kettle happens when steam travels up the kettle spout, where it pulses against the spout lid as it tries to pass through the spout hole, and that pulsing action causes the escaping steam to form vortices as it exits, which produces sound waves in the form of a whistle.

It's not as complicated as Professor Bellwether's advanced theories on Martian gravitational pull and inverse proportionality, but science is science, and it means my astronaut training meal is almost ready, and I will soon be a step closer to possibly fulfilling my life's goal of being the mathematics flight specialist on the first manned mission to Mars, whenever that will be.

My dad cuts off the top of the chili mac 'n' beef package, and then he pours the contents into my favorite bowl—the one that's decorated with an illustration of Phobos and Deimos, also known as the moons of Mars—and he covers everything with exactly one and three-quarter cups of boiling water. And then he stirs it with my training regimen metal spoon, and he pushes the bowl across the table toward me.

"Here, son. This should square you away."

I wait my usual thirty-five seconds for the meal to cool down, and then I dive in.

The familiar savory texture rakes across my taste buds, and the squishy mixture of twenty-one ingredients slides down into my stomach, which makes my brain stop twitching, and then the shaking stops, and now all that's left is the uneasy feeling that invades my midsection whenever strangers breach security at the front door.

I'm ready to hear the rest of what Flint Garrison has to say about missions to the planet Mars, as well as the reason why he's choosing to say it exclusively to me rather than any of the other 6,623,517,838 people who inhabit planet Earth.

14

His Larynx Might Be
Making a Run for It

"I apologize for the sudden interruption. My son and I have been working on coordinating the timing of his astronaut training meals. I should have done a better job of keeping him on his set schedule."

"That's all right, Mr. Tuckerman," Flint Garrison says. "It actually helps me to get a better sense of your son's priorities and level of focus—and I must say, I like what I'm seeing."

I make a secret wish in the secret-wish sector of my brain for the general to immediately tell us the reason for his visit and then leave, taking Dr. Murakami with him.

"As I said before we were interrupted, the SFC used the Mars Global Surveyor's instrumentation to identify the exact location of the mineral discovery made by the Mars Observer. However, it took us much longer to interpolate the Observer's data into our previous findings than we had originally anticipated, which was why we needed to accelerate the Mars

Global Surveyor's orbital insertion by seventy-seven days. We needed the Global Surveyor to tell the Pathfinder exactly where it needed to land. And that landing point was Ares Vallis. Are you still with me, Sherman?"

I am, and it's clear my wish hasn't been granted. Flint Garrison's complexion grows ruddier than when I first saw him, and now he's drumming his shiny black shoes against the carpet in a rhythmic pattern I don't recognize.

"I will remind you, Sherman, that this is a matter of national security," he says. "If the information I'm about to disclose were to leave this room in, shall we say, an unauthorized manner, then calling the consequences *dire* would be an understatement as vast as the Oxia Palus quadrangle itself."

I don't think anyone in the living room notices me taking a massive gulp, even though the creases in my dad's forehead deepen, and Dr. Murakami's note-taking speed accelerates, and Flint Garrison's nostrils flare.

"Sojourner actually had a more important mission than the general public and the news media were aware of," the general says, "and Pathfinder's task went well beyond conducting experiments on the Martian surface. It actually served as the initial leg of a top-secret, classified sample-return mission."

No way. I know that type of mission can't and won't happen for at least another twenty-five years, because space travel technology hasn't advanced nearly enough for Pathfinder to have the capability to carry it out.

I write my dad yet another note, and I dot the second *i* in *impossible* hard enough for the tip of my No. 2 pencil to poke through the sheet of paper and make a pencil mark on the sheet beneath it.

That's impossible!

"It's safe to say that you have Sherman's interest, General. He's asking for additional details."

"After the Mars Observer made the mineralogical discovery that research scientists believe would enable them to develop groundbreaking advances in medicine, the SFC brought in a team of the world's greatest scientific minds to conceive and execute an accelerated sample-return mission." Flint Garrison pauses to pull a handkerchief from his jacket pocket. He uses it to blot the shiny beads of sweat that are accumulating on his ample forehead. "Once the Global Surveyor calculated the exact coordinates of the discovery, the SFC got to work advancing Pathfinder's mission to include sample return."

And he goes on to explain that the Sojourner rover drilled forty-two core samples—each about the length and diameter of a stick of chalk—and extracted them from the area where the key chemical compounds were thought to reside. The general explains that the rover dropped the core samples onto the Martian surface where it had drilled them, then awaited further instructions from Earth.

And then he startles me with another thundery throat-clear, this one his ninth, and now it sounds as though his larynx might be making a run for it.

"The news media reported that NASA had lost communication with Sojourner for unknown reasons on September 27, which was nearly three months after it landed on the surface of Mars," Flint Garrison says. "But Sojourner was in fact still fully functional. The SFC secretly took control of the mission, leaking the false story of the rover's demise to the press."

I wonder how it's possible that everything I've ever learned about the exploration of Mars is not real. My near-total disbelief in the general's newest assertion causes me to write my dad what I hope will be my final note of the day.

I'm tired.
I want to go to my room.
Now.

15

More Stuff I Already Know

My dad stares long and hard at my note. Then he refolds it and slips it into his shirt pocket.

And then he nods at Flint Garrison.

And he smiles at Dr. Murakami.

And he looks at his wristwatch.

And then he glances up at me.

And now he squishes his eyebrows together and makes his face scrunch up the way he always does whenever he's preparing to deliver unpleasant news to my guidance counselor at McDerney.

"General, I'm afraid your interesting theories on the Mars space program have been a bit much for my son. It's getting late, and he's tired. Perhaps it would be best if we picked up this conversation another time."

Flint Garrison's throat-clear this time is measured and deliberate, and I note that the tally has reached double figures at ten.

"Mr. Tuckerman, I don't think you understand. None of this

is theoretical. We've got a real situation up there. Your son has expressed to Professor Bellwether at the JPL a keen interest in being a part of this country's Mars space program. And dare I say, we need his involvement—and we need it *right now*."

I write my dad a fresh note.

People don't usually need me for anything. I guess I could have my dessert now and listen to the rest of what he has to say.

I pop a sweet wedge of Bazooka Joe bubblegum into my mouth, and then I back it up with a second wedge, and then a third.

"General, my son feels that we should continue, and he only asks that you move it along at a much brisker pace."

Dr. Murakami leans forward and tosses her journal onto the coffee table. And when she lifts her head, I can see the cords of her neck standing out.

And Flint Garrison's complexion reddens even more. "Yes, of course. Moving right along, this leads us to the Mars Odyssey mission."

Here it comes, more stuff I already know.

Flint Garrison confirms Mars Odyssey's launch from Cape Canaveral atop a Delta II rocket on April 7, 2001, its arrival in Mars orbit on October 24, 2001, and its mission, which was to use its spectrometers and thermal imager to conduct a mineralogical analysis of the planet's surface from orbit, enabling JPL scientists to attempt to determine whether the Martian environment was ever conducive to life as we know it here on Earth.

"Mars Odyssey was also tasked with serving as a relay for communication with *future* surface explorers," Flint Garrison says. "But what the general public never knew was that the Strategic Federation Council was covertly brought in to reestablish contact with Sojourner, which, of course, was generally thought to have gone silent four years earlier."

The general says that the SFC radioed Mars Odyssey, commanding the orbiter to instruct Sojourner to assemble its forty-two core samples together on the Martian surface for later unmanned retrieval.

"All of this takes us to NASA's Mars Exploration Rover mission and the program's two rovers, Spirit and Opportunity," Flint Garrison says, "and that will lead us directly to the reason for our visit today."

16

Here We Go Again

I detect an inversely proportional relationship governing the information Flint Garrison has provided up to this point: the more details he offers, the less credible any of it sounds.

He takes out his handkerchief again, and he wipes away the new round of perspiration forming on his forehead, and then he loosens his tie and clears his throat for the eleventh time.

"General, could I get you a glass of water?" my dad asks.

"That would be most appreciated."

My dad exits the living room for the kitchen, leaving me standing there all by myself with Flint Garrison and Dr. Murakami.

"Lawrence—would it be all right if I called you Lawrence, as your friends do?"

Here he goes again.

He speaks directly at me, and my dad isn't sitting there to serve as *the blocker*, and it makes me wonder how he knows that my two best friends call me by a different name than almost everyone else, and then I wonder what else he knows about me.

"Say, how is that chili mac 'n' beef, anyway?"

Aaaaaaargh! More questions! Now he's *really* invading my space.

"I understand it has twenty-one grams of protein per serving, is that correct?"

I close my eyes, hoping that when I open them again, I'll be at the space travel section of the public library instead of standing on my living room carpet being walloped by a barrage of questions.

And then I open my eyes. It didn't work. Flint Garrison is still there.

I wonder if he's trying to distract me by estimating the protein value of a single serving of chili mac 'n' beef using a hypothetical number of grams that's divisible by seven.

And then I wonder how long it can possibly take for someone to pour a glass of water.

"Have you ever tried it with ketchup?" the general asks. "I'll bet that would make it even tastier."

I solve a series of parametric equations in my brain as I wait for my dad to finally return to the living room with Flint Garrison's glass of water. This way, I can pretend to be thinking about the general's question about ketchup, and formulating a thoughtful response to it, which I'm not doing, and then I wonder what Dr. Murakami is thinking, because she stopped writing and is instead staring at Flint Garrison, and then I wonder whether he's sweating again because Dr. Murakami is staring at him, or because he's just naturally sweaty, and then my dad walks back into the living room with the general's glass of water, and I exhale a sigh of relief that I don't think anyone notices, even though Dr. Murakami reaches for her journal again, and Flint Garrison tries to smile, but the corners of his mouth refuse to go along, and then my dad hands him the glass of water before handing me three more wedges of Bazooka Joe, which means I'll soon have a total of six pieces of bubblegum in my mouth while I wait for the general to make up stuff about the Mars Exploration Rover mission.

And then Flint Garrison burps.

And then it gets quiet in the living room.

And then I solve a different series of parametric equations inside my brain, this time to describe algebraic varieties of higher dimension, until he clears his throat again, and now the total is at an even dozen, and I'm hoping he's now ready to talk about the Mars Exploration Rover mission.

"Pardon me," Flint Garrison offers. "As I was saying, Mars Exploration involved two rovers, named Spirit and Opportunity, both of which were launched from Cape Canaveral. Spirit left the launchpad on June 10, 2003, and Opportunity lifted off twenty-eight days later." I take note that he uses another number divisible by seven. "The two spacecraft parachuted down onto the surface of Mars at separate locations in January 2004."

Common knowledge.

I work all six wedges of Bazooka Joe into a colossal wad, and then I blow a massive bubble that explodes all over my face as I wait for Flint Garrison's alternative viewpoint.

And I pick pieces of bubblegum off my chin as the general explains that the spacecraft were equipped with a battery of scientific instruments to validate the surface observations made by the Mars Reconnaissance Orbiter, and to figure out if the potential for life ever existed on the planet.

"The rovers were sent to analyze the mineralogy of rocks and soils to determine the processes that created them," the general says. "NASA targeted Spirit to the Gusev Crater, which is quite possibly a former Martian lake. Opportunity landed on the opposite end of the planet in a plain known as Meridiani Planum—or at least that's what was reported in the mainstream media."

Here we go again.

17

There's No Way Any of This Is True

And now my brain has the job of figuring out if it can believe anything Flint Garrison says.

And now I wonder how it can be possible that so much of what I've learned about space travel to Mars, in science class at McDerney, and throughout my summer internship at the JPL, is no longer valid.

Flint Garrison's face turns wrinkly, the wrinkliest it has been since he and Dr. Murakami set up base camp on the living room couch an hour earlier.

"I need you to take a leap of faith, Sherman, because what I'm about to tell you may not seem real at all."

There's no need for him to ask me to take such a leap, because I already took one when he said at the outset of his visit that he wanted to discuss an immediate *manned* sample-return mission.

I write my dad another note.

> *If it means that Flint Garrison and Dr. Murakami will finally leave afterward, and our living room can get back to normal, including the couch cushions, then yes, I will take the leap of faith.*

"General, my son says he's looking forward to finding out where this conversation is finally headed, and to please continue with great haste."

"First, I must tell you that Opportunity did not land at Meridiani Planum, as was reported by the press. The spacecraft actually set down onto the Martian surface just a hundred feet or so from where Pathfinder's six-wheeled Sojourner rover allegedly went silent back on September 27, 1997."

That means, at least according to Flint Garrison, and using my brain's built-in terrestrial planetary distance calculator, that Opportunity stuck the landing at Ares Vallis in the planet's Oxia Palus quadrangle within the Chryse Planitia region, which was 5,397 miles off course.

Or was it secretly *on course*?

I hit the start button on my brain's leap-of-faith clock.

"Sherman, I'm going to *read you in* on the rest of what actually happened up there."

I know from watching spy movies on TV that Flint Garrison will soon share critically important space-program secrets with me. And since confidential government data is often compartmentalized—meaning it is separated into parts that are not allowed to mix with other parts—the general will surely tell me only what he thinks I need to know.

"As I've already explained, Mars Observer, Global Surveyor, and Pathfinder all worked together in glorious harmony to enable Sojourner to collect and assemble core samples of the mineral discovery the SFC believes will lead to revolutionary advances in medicine. From there, our top scientists and engineers got to work developing the final phase of our accelerated sample-return program."

With that, Dr. Murakami closes her journal. "I'm afraid this is where things are going to take a bit of a turn. I want to make sure you're able to continue with this conversation. How are you feeling right now?"

I scribble out a quick note to my dad.

I think I'm going to need that seventh piece of Bazooka Joe.

"My son says he's pleased to learn that the conversation is finally reaching what appears to be its welcome conclusion."

And then Flint Garrison grunts before clearing his throat for the thirteenth and hopefully final time. Though I do note that if he aces throat-clear number fourteen, the total would be a satisfying multiple of seven.

"Our team was able to accomplish in seven years what would otherwise have taken three decades. We outfitted Opportunity to be an interplanetary sample retrieval lander. Specifically, the spacecraft landed on Mars with the rover, but it also carried a cutting-edge rocket to serve as an ascent vehicle."

I am so stunned by this news that I'm unable to write my dad a note that says: *There's no way any of this is true.*

Instead, I wriggle my shoes even deeper into the living room carpet, hoping it will somehow help me to brace for what Flint Garrison says next.

18

The Bottom Line

"If we are to move forward with this conversation, young man, there will be no turning back."

My brain determines that this statement sounds more serious than the sum total of all the other serious things Flint Garrison has said up to this point, and I begin to apply a formula to precisely calculate and compare the cumulative prior total seriousness with the seriousness of this most recent sentence, but then I stop midway through when the general says forty-two more words, which my brain notes is the same number as the amount of core samples drilled by the Sojourner rover, and it's also a number divisible by seven.

"Sherman, the Strategic Federation Council is prepared to deputize you today as a nonaffiliated associate submember of the council. That is the highest civilian ranking that the SFC can bestow on someone with your qualifications and stature within the interplanetary exploration community."

Nonaffiliated associate submember. *Huh*. I've never heard of that title before, but that does not strike me as unusual because, after all, I'm dealing with a top-secret government agency, and even though the title is noticeably contrived, I think it might impress both of my best friends.

I write my dad another note.

Better get me that 7th piece of Bazooka Joe—and hold the comic.

And now my dad is bouncing his right leg a lot, just like he does whenever we're sitting in Dr. Tidewater's waiting room, especially those times when he makes an appointment after I lose my temper and lock myself in my bedroom for a long time, and by a long time, I mean when the total number of days I'm in there is divisible by seven.

And Flint Garrison continues with the reason for his un-announced interruption of my evening astronaut training meal. "The Opportunity rover drilled the material from stromatolites that Sojourner previously identified on the Martian surface."

My brain recalls from science class at McDerney that stromatolites are layered sedimentary formations created on Earth some 3.5 billion years ago by photosynthetic cyanobacteria, which everyone knows are a type of bacteria capable of photosynthesis, meaning they can use sunlight to synthesize food from carbon dioxide and water.

Science stuff.

And then my brain recalls that stromatolites, which look like low, rounded, sort of mushroom-shaped rocks, represent the earliest known life form on Earth, but I don't know why the ones found on Mars are so important to the SFC.

Flint Garrison explains why.

"Our researchers have concluded that certain forms of bacteria might have infinite longevity. They believe that the Martian stromatolites could be of immeasurable scientific value because they were capable of resting in suspended animation for unlimited periods of time."

He says the SFC's analysis of Sojourner's spectrometer data revealed that the Martian stromatolites could possibly lead to sweeping advances in medical science, including, for example, the development of new treatments for antibiotic-resistant bacterial infections.

"After that, the Opportunity rover loaded the forty-two core samples aboard the ascent-vehicle rocket, and the rocket fired and lifted off from the Martian surface. The ascent vehicle's mission was to place the sample container into orbit around Mars. To give you an idea of what we're dealing with here, that container is about the size of a basketball."

"A *basketball*?" Yep, I say that aloud. Those two words escape from my mouth before my brain can intercept them and scrub the mission.

"Yes, Sherman, a basketball," the general says. "We sent that container into orbit around the planet while we concurrently worked to build an unmanned return orbiter that could travel to Mars two years from now to rendezvous with the container and bring it back to Earth."

And now my dad's bouncing right knee is gaining speed. "This is all quite interesting, General, but I don't know what any of it has to do with my son."

"I'm glad to say we've arrived at that point of the conversation," Flint Garrison says. "The bottom line is we encountered a problem. The rocket misfired during launch, causing it to place the sample container into an extremely shallow elliptical orbit, and not the intended spherical orbit that would have been at a safe distance from the Martian surface. According to our calculations, the planet's gravitational pull will cause that container to crash back onto Mars exactly seven months from the moment we rang your doorbell."

Dr. Murakami sets her journal back onto the coffee table and looks directly at my dad. "And if that happens, sir," she says, "the Martian stromatolites, the very ones that could possibly change the course of medical history, will be lost to humankind. And it would be years, perhaps decades, before we could even attempt to replicate this critical, potentially life-saving mission."

19

The Mission Is Doomed to Failure

Dr. Murakami makes it clear that time is of the essence, but I still don't know why she and Flint Garrison are confiding in me.

That changes.

"We had planned to send an unmanned spacecraft to intercept the core samples and bring them back to Earth," Flint Garrison says, "but our technology has not advanced to the point where we could attempt to capture the container with any degree of certainty while it's in such a precarious elliptical orbit around Mars. And we've already learned from the seven crewed moon missions—especially Apollo 13, the one that didn't make it to the moon—that we'll have a much better chance for success if we have, shall we say, a sure hand at the wheel."

And now my dad's knee-bouncing accelerates even more, and the creases in his forehead deepen as the general discloses additional details of the SFC's dilemma.

And my brain twitches as I grow more and more impatient waiting for him to get to the point.

"WHY ARE YOU HERE?"

The words explode from my mouth. And I don't know whether my brain was unable to stop them, or it had simply stepped aside and waved the words on ahead.

And then Dr. Murakami jolts her body ramrod straight, and she whirls her head toward Flint Garrison, who appears undeterred.

"The retrieval mission has to be a *piloted* round-trip operation, and the SFC's flight plan requires a deft hand at the controls," he says. "The flight engineer we've selected for the mission will have to utilize the Martian gravity and atmosphere to facilitate a delicate deceleration maneuver to capture the container. But he cannot do it all by himself."

I figure the SFC needs me to run mathematical calculations from Mission Control at Cape Canaveral in Florida. And then I wonder how I can possibly do that and still keep my weekly chess match at the rec center with Nathan here in Los Angeles.

"The SFC has built a top-secret spacecraft code-named Ares Pilgrim for a classified manned mission to Mars," Flint Garrison says. "We hadn't planned to deploy it this soon, but out of necessity, it is now gassed and parked on a launchpad at Vandenberg Air Force Base."

Which I know is in a remote section of central-coastal California, exactly 154 miles north of where I'm currently standing.

Even with the news that the SFC's spacecraft is housed in California and not 2,562 miles away in the easternmost reaches of Florida, I still worry about keeping my weekly chess match with Nathan.

"Mr. Tuckerman, I'm afraid this is where things get a bit technical. I will do my level best to explain them in basic scientific terms. Of course, Sherman will know exactly what I'm talking about."

My dad knows a whole lot about architecture, but space travel isn't an area of expertise for him the way it is for me.

"The outbound transit time from Earth to Mars is one hundred and eighty-two days," the general says. "And there are two different types of return-to-Earth inbound trajectories—opposition and conjunction."

Professor Bellwether taught me about opposition and conjunction return trajectories in the early days of my summer internship at the JPL.

I know that an oppositional return mission would fly most or all the way around the sun, swinging into the inner solar system with a flyby past Venus in order to increase speed. This type of mission has higher propulsion requirements. After reaching Mars and intercepting the sample container before it crashes onto the Martian surface, the Ares Pilgrim would have to orbit the planet for twenty-eight days before a 434-day return trip to Earth. That means the oppositional return mission's total flight time would be 644 days.

By contrast, on a conjunctional return mission, the Ares Pilgrim would circle Mars for 553 days after gathering the core samples, then depart its Martian orbit for the 182-day return flight home. Such a mission would last a total of 917 days.

I note that all the calculations are divisible by seven, which calms me down, but the moment is fleeting because with either return trajectory, the flight engineer and anyone else aboard the Ares Pilgrim would be forced to endure prolonged and potentially life-threatening exposure to zero-gravity and radiation.

And I won't even mention how taxing all of that would be on the spacecraft's life-support systems, the reliability of which would be supremely compromised.

I analyze all this data inside my brain while Flint Garrison discharges another window-rattling throat-clear.

And now my brain has only three conclusions left to draw:

1. The SFC's secret mission is doomed to failure.

2. Flint Garrison's throat-clear tally stands at fourteen.

3. The general needs to see an ear, nose, and throat specialist.

20

I Tell My Brain to Make It Stop

Unless Flint Garrison has up his sleeve what my best friend Zeke Archer calls a half-court buzzer beater, the only thing left to do is pop another wedge of Bazooka Joe while attempting to feel sorry for the Ares Pilgrim's flight engineer, who is about to embark on a suicide mission.

I write my dad another note.

> *Ask him which of the two flight paths the SFC has chosen for its deep-space mission to oblivion.*

"General, my son is curious as to the mission's trajectory, given the inherent limitations and perceived perils of each."

"You have good reason to inquire, at least based on what the astronomical community believes about oppositional versus conjunctional space travel. But all of that changed this week."

Flint Garrison pauses after he says this, which causes me to glance at him, which causes him to wink at me, which causes me to look away but not quickly enough to avoid seeing him wink, which causes me to wonder whether seeing him do that will scar me for life, and I reach into my pocket to search for more Bazooka Joe, but I come up empty, so I stare at the tops of my shoes and calculate a potentially more efficient way to tie my laces than the loop-swoop-and-pull bunny rabbit method my mom taught me when I was four and she was still alive.

The general continues: "Our scientists used advanced computer modeling to identify an extremely rare Transfer Orbit Trajectory Vortex Anomaly within the relative rotations of Earth and Mars."

I'm familiar with all of those words individually, but I've never heard them used in that exact order in the same sentence before.

"General, can you break that down for us."

"Simply put, the opposition and conjunction trajectories will soon merge as one, but only for the briefest moment, allowing for a six-month outbound journey, followed by a swift and efficient sample-container recovery operation, then an identical six-month free-return trajectory—all made possible by the Ares Pilgrim's radically advanced, hypersonic nuclear thermal rocket propulsion system, which has up to seven times the exhaust velocity of a chemical rocket."

I learned about nuclear thermal propulsion from Professor Bellwether, who taught me that rockets propelled by this type of fuel are designed solely for space exploration, not for use on Earth.

The professor explained that the system works by pumping a liquid propellant such as hydrogen through a reactor core, where uranium atoms split apart, which releases heat through fission, which heats up the hydrogen and converts it to a gas, which is expanded through a nozzle to produce thrust.

Space exploration stuff.

"General, just how rare of an event is this so-called vortex anomaly?"

"Our scientists have calculated that this type of astronomical phenomenon occurs a little less frequently than once every eight million years or so."

A wave of frustration ripples through my body as I reach for my pad, but my dad waves me off, and then his right knee stops bouncing.

"General Garrison, as you know, my son has a thing for numbers. I believe he's looking for you to be more specific than that."

"Right. This newly discovered Transfer Orbit Trajectory Vortex Anomaly occurs once every 7,777,777 years. Dare I say, we found it to be scientifically amusing that there were so many sevens in our calculation."

I'm not amused by this information, scientifically or otherwise. I know it means something super important. I ask my brain to figure out the significance, but it gives up after the seventh try.

Good grief, more sevens.

I reach for my pad again.

Assuming he isn't making all this up, what does he need me to do?

"General, my son wants to know how he can be of service—but before you answer that, I must remind you that Sherman is a fifteen-year-old high school junior with a standing weekly chess match and a list of important chores to do at home."

I'm not sure if my dad is looking out for me, or he's secretly making certain his workload around the house remains manageable.

Flint Garrison's posture turns rigid. "In order for the Ares Pilgrim to successfully pass through the vortex anomaly, we would have to launch it from Vandenberg Air Force Base exactly seven days from now."

The general tells us that for reasons of cost and technical feasibility, it is essential that the SFC keep the size of the crew to an absolute minimum. Then he describes the team his scientists have in mind for the mission:

1. Flight engineer: to pilot the spacecraft and serve as the mission's chief mechanic

2. Field scientist: with expertise in geology and biology, to serve as the mission's communications analyst and chief medical officer

3. Mathematics flight specialist: to perform mission-critical calculations

I feel an immediate call to duty. And then I feel myself rocking from side to side. I tell my brain to make it stop, but it doesn't work.

21

I Hope You Can Understand

The living room grows quiet.

Out of the corner of my eye, I notice Dr. Murakami staring at Flint Garrison, and that makes the palms of my hands sweaty, and then I see that he's staring directly at me, and that propels a wave of nausea across my stomach, and now I think I might have to—as the new astronaut recruits used to say during my summer internship at the JPL—*jettison the chunky cargo.*

"I'm going to spell it out for you, Mr. Tuckerman. We want your son to be the mathematics flight specialist on the world's first-ever manned mission to Mars."

And there it is.

Flint Garrison's bottom line and my life's goal are one and the same.

I'm frozen solid in my spot on the living room carpet.

And my dad's knee bounces, but this time it's the left one, and it's going up and down at an even more rapid clip than before.

"General, how safe is this mission?"

Flint Garrison is quick to respond.

"Our scientists and engineers have made what the SFC believes is an intelligent compromise between the Ares Pilgrim's top speed and its safety-system redundancies. The result, I'm proud to say, is a cutting-edge spacecraft that was built with what we feel is a high degree of reliability."

"A high degree?" The wrinkles in my dad's forehead are rippling in slow motion. "What exactly does that mean, General?"

"Mr. Tuckerman, there are no illusions here. No matter how many contingencies and abort options we've designed into the mission, we should both understand that the SFC would potentially be putting your son and two other individuals in harm's way. And that is the reason why, from a moral point of view, the size of the crew is so small."

"Does the SFC have a backup plan if my son is unable to go?"

"Of course. We've identified six other viable candidates for the mathematics flight specialist position, but we're sitting here today because Sherman is far and away our obvious first choice."

And now my dad turns to me. "Son, can you please go to your room for a few minutes while the general and I conclude our discussion."

"No."

I say the word out loud rather than write it down because I want everyone in the living room to know I have the right to be present whenever important decisions about my life, especially those relating to space travel, are under consideration.

And then my dad gives me *the look*. He gives me that look whenever I refuse to do something he asks me to do. I'm familiar with the look because he gives it to me a lot.

"No."

I repeat my previous statement of refusal to comply, even though in the eyes of the law, as well as those of the SFC, I'm only fifteen, which means that whatever my dad says, goes, which is super unfair, but I know that my dad has my best interests in mind, even though I'm watching helplessly as my life's goal is slipping through my fingers.

"General, it seems as though my son wishes to participate in discussions about his future. I guess he's growing up faster than I had realized."

After hearing those words from my dad, my body stands a bit taller, and it might also be a bit stronger too. And I instinctively raise my chin, and then I thrust out my chest and pull back my shoulders.

This must be what pride feels like.

"It's certainly one of the reasons why we like him for this mission," Flint Garrison says, "especially after our data scientists found that the spacecraft's computers won't function properly in the vortex anomaly because the floating-point registers will constantly bit-flip when bombarded by cosmic radiation. We tried adding extra shielding, but it didn't solve the problem, so we concluded that nothing would work better than a brilliant human mind running the math."

"General, if I may speak frankly, you're asking a teenager to go on what amounts to a possible death mission."

My dad's words erode my confidence and send a shudder

through my body. And my heart beats faster, and my legs wobble.

"We've looked at everything, sir, starting with reducing the mission launch mass and maximizing the reliability of the spacecraft's life-support systems. Our scientists have also calculated the proper allocation of consumables like food, water, and oxygen for a mission of this length and complexity."

Flint Garrison waits for a reaction from my dad, but there is none. My dad simply stares at him without saying anything.

I know from my time as a summer intern at the JPL that there's additional information the general has yet to cover.

All eyes are on him, except for mine, which are flying everywhere else around the living room.

And then my dad breaks the silence. "Is there anything else, General?"

"Yes, there is. Perhaps most importantly, our scientists have formulated a way to minimize Earth reentry deceleration forces on both the spacecraft and the crew. This will significantly decrease the risk of a misaligned reentry, so the Ares Pilgrim doesn't burn up or skip out of the atmosphere and strand the crew in interplanetary space."

And the room goes silent again.

And then I glance at my dad, and I recognize that look because I've seen it on his face before. He's processing information the same way he does when he's at his drafting table designing a building and suddenly realizes he's backed himself into an architectural corner.

My dad probes deeper. "Anything else, General?"

"There is. Normally on a mission of this magnitude, the

mathematics flight specialist would already have a degree in applied mathematics from a prestigious research university like Caltech in Pasadena. The specialist would also have to pass the SFC's Class II space physical to be certified for spaceflight."

I already know those requirements. I'm planning to meet them right after I graduate from McDerney.

"You said *normally*, General?"

"Yes, that's right. But in Sherman's case, and in view of the urgency of this mission and its time sensitivity, we're prepared to make an exception."

All eyes are on my dad, except mine, because I'm looking at where the cushions used to be, since they're no longer visible because Flint Garrison and Dr. Murakami have sunken so deeply into them that all I can see is their knees and the front part of the couch.

I start to write another note, but before I can finish it, my dad breaks the silence.

"General, I'm afraid that—"

I interrupt my dad by wadding my sheet of paper into a lumpy ball and flinging it at him. It caroms off his forehead, and then it lands on the light-green shag carpet directly in front of Flint Garrison.

My dad's face progresses through several shades of red until it settles on flaming scarlet, which is the exact same color as the general's necktie.

"Please give us a moment," my dad says. And he's no longer smiling. He lifts himself from his easy chair, and he motions me to the hallway leading to my bedroom.

And now anger engulfs my brain, making it twitch. And I

feel like I want to hit someone, but at the same time, I know it's a superbly bad idea, especially since if I slug Flint Garrison, he would probably slug me back a lot harder, and if I sucker-punch Dr. Murakami, she would probably react by writing notes in her journal that wouldn't be favorable, and smacking my dad isn't a great option either, because the last time I did that, he grounded me for a century, and it wasn't really one-hundred years, but it might as well have been, because it took a long time before I could play chess again with Nathan, who said he was okay with the long sabbatical from our weekly match because the cause was rooted in anger, something he said he understood, so I shuffle my feet across the hallway carpet and follow my dad to my room, where I slam the door behind me, and it's the kind of door-slam that sends an obvious message and rattles my lone bedroom window.

"Really?"

I don't know whether my dad is asking a question, or he's expressing disappointment, but the look on his face says it's both.

Off in the distance through my bedroom walls, I can hear Flint Garrison speaking. His voice is faint, but there's no mistaking what he says.

"I told you this was a waste of time, Lydia. We need to review our list of backup mathematics flight specialists on our way back to base."

Dr. Murakami says something in response, but her voice is so soft, I can't make it out.

I pull my pad from my back pocket, but before I can extract a pencil from the stash of seven in my pocket protector, my dad stops me—with his words.

"No, Sherman."

A big vein in my neck pulses. I know, because I can feel it. I take note of its rhythm, which is swift and unyielding. I flex my fingers because I don't know what else to do with my hands.

"Sherman, to the best of my knowledge, you and I have two methods of communicating with each other, not three. We either speak, or we write. We don't exchange ideas by throwing things at each other. Isn't that correct?"

The Tuckermans have a house rule that whenever my dad asks me a question, and there is no one else around, I must answer him by speaking, not writing.

I choose not to write a response to him, and I certainly don't throw anything at him. Instead, I opt for a variation of speaking: I don't say anything, which in itself signals my implied agreement.

"This whole mission-to-Mars business sounds dangerous. I know that the general is asking you to climb aboard the Ares Pilgrim in the interest of advancing medical science, which would be noble of you, but I can't knowingly put you in harm's way. It's just not something fathers do. I hope you can understand."

22

I Might as Well Be Dead

I take out my pad, and I pull out a pencil, and then I write my dad a note, and I fold it in half, and I hand it to him.

My dad sets the note onto my desk, next to the envelope from Zeke.

"It's just you and me in here, son. How about we talk this out instead."

My brain reminds me that when my dad says he wants to *talk something out*, it means he will talk and talk and then talk some more until he gets his way and nothing changes.

I pick up my note and hand it back to my dad, who exhales loudly enough for me to wonder whether Flint Garrison and Dr. Murakami can feel the air moving in the living room.

"Read it." I compromise by saying those words to my dad rather than writing another note telling him to read my previous note.

And then my dad changes the subject.

"What did Zeke send you?"

"It's personal."

"I'm not asking you to betray your best friend code of ethics. I'm only curious about what's inside the envelope."

My brain determines that my dad is not opposed to note-reading. Instead, he's temporarily more interested in Zeke's package than my note. I fish Zeke's letter out of the envelope and hand it to my dad, and I watch his eyes as they scan Zeke's letter. I'm able to watch my dad's eyes move because he's not watching me watch him.

And when he finishes reading the letter, he exhales, and then he makes a nonstandard noise that I don't recognize as one of his established, dad-type noises. He folds the letter in half and puts it back into Zeke's envelope.

"Interesting."

Zeke's letter is a lot of things. *Interesting* is certainly one of them.

"Yes."

It's the only word I can think of to say in response.

And now I'm in a conversation with my dad. I remove the top layer of palm sweat by rubbing my hands against my pant legs.

"I wish I knew how to help you understand," my dad says. "I can't take a chance on losing you."

And now my dad's eyes are moist. The last time his eyes looked like that was at my mom's funeral 959 days ago, which I note is a number evenly divisible by seven.

"Are you going to read my note?" When I ask my dad the question, I try not to sound agitated, which I am, so it doesn't work.

My dad closes his eyes. And a single teardrop glistens as it rolls down his cheek. I study the curvature of the clear, wet streak it leaves on the side of his face. And then I take note that it looks more like a transcendental curve than an algebraic one.

And then my dad picks up my note.

Calling

"What does it mean, son? Do you need me to call Dr. Tidewater?"

My dad doesn't get it. I peel off another sheet of paper. Even though it's my dad, it is easier for me to write what's in my brain right now than it is to say it to him.

> *Calling*
> *My friends and my best friends all have one.*
> *Curtis's is to surf.*
> *Stretch's is to work as a private detective.*
> *Nathan's is to achieve grandmaster status, the highest title a chess player can attain.*
> *Zeke's is basketball, whether as point guard at the University of Kansas, or coaching, or refereeing, or writing about basketball as a sports journalist someday.*
> *My calling is to be the mathematics flight specialist on the first-ever manned mission to Mars.*
> *That's why I was born.*

I glance at my dad. I notice that his eyes are moister than before.

> If I die while pursuing my calling, then
> at least I will have lived in the math.
> I will have lived the truth.
> My truth.
> If I don't at least try, I might as well
> be dead.

23

I'll Put That in Writing, If You Prefer

"Give me your pad, and hand me one of those pencils."
I figure my dad is going to answer my note with one of his own. In doing so, he's invoking mathematician and scientist Sir Isaac Newton's third law of motion: For every action, there is an equal and opposite reaction.

My brain recalls from math class at McDerney that Newton's statement means in every interaction, especially the one I'm having with my dad, where my fate as a potential future astronaut is uncertain, there are two forces acting on a pair of interacting objects, and the magnitude of the force on the first object equals the magnitude of the force on the second, but in the opposite direction.

It is one of the world's greater mathematical truths.

My dad doesn't write me many notes. Whenever he does, he always uses seven words to get his point across.

The last time he put pencil to paper was 273 days ago,

which my brain notates is a number divisible by seven. At the time, my dad wrote to tell me he would be working late at the architecture firm and might not be home in time to help cook my astronaut training meal.

I don't need my dad's help to prepare my chili mac 'n' beef anymore, but it's easier to let him help me than it is to tell him to stop.

He uses his shirtsleeve to blot the moisture from his eyes. I know that all my dad's shirts are one-hundred-percent cotton, so his sleeve is highly absorbent and does an effective job.

My dad scribbles something onto the piece of paper, and then he rips the sheet from the pad, and he folds it in half and hands it to me:

I love you, son. You can go.

I fling open my bedroom door and race-walk back to my spot on the living room carpet. My dad arrives a moment later, and he sits down in his easy chair.

"Are you all right, Sherman?" Dr. Murakami asks. I don't answer her, but I hope she interprets from my non-answer that I'm all right, but I'm only all right if my dad tells Flint Garrison that I have his okay to go on the mission.

"My son is feeling fine, Dr. Murakami."

I fine-tune my position on the carpet, being careful not to widen my shoe indentations, because the current side-support is mathematically suitable.

"Do you have any questions?" Flint Garrison doesn't waste time getting the conversation back on track.

My brain notes that a question about questions could be considered a question squared: q^2.

"Just one, General. Can you guarantee my son's safety on this mission?"

Flint Garrison begins his response with a nondescript, uneventful throat-clear, his fifteenth.

"As you might imagine, Mr. Tuckerman, this type of long-distance spaceflight does carry some inherent risk. Nevertheless, I guarantee you that I am highly confident this mission will be a resounding success. And I'll put that in writing, if you prefer."

24

I Can't Make the Trembling Stop

"There's not a moment to lose," Flint Garrison says as he pulls a manila folder from his briefcase and hands it to my dad. "We just have one minor administrative detail to take care of. I'll need you to sign this parental release of liability and nondisclosure agreement."

My dad spends a lot of time dealing with paperwork, in his job as an architect and with his responsibilities as my dad, especially when I transfer to a new school, and he has to fill out enrollment forms as well as legal documents that release the school from civil damages should I slap someone really hard, or worse.

My dad removes the stack of paperwork from the folder, and he squares the pages in his hands, and the wrinkles in his forehead deepen with each page he flips.

"General, there's quite a bit of legalese here. Would you mind giving me the bottom line?"

"Not at all. Basically, you're signing away your right to sue the Strategic Federation Council should anything happen to your son, which, as I indicated earlier, is highly unlikely. The agreement also precludes you and your son from discussing the mission with anyone unless and until the SFC grants you the official authority to do so."

"Official authority?"

"Yes, Mr. Tuckerman. It's standard protocol when dealing with the SFC in interplanetary matters."

And now the creases in my dad's forehead are pulsating. Without his signature on that agreement, the closest I'll ever get to Mars will be standing in my backyard gazing at it through my telescope.

"There are some words in here I'm not familiar with. Perhaps I should have our attorney look it over."

"There's no time," Flint Garrison says. "We need to run Sherman through a week of intensive training before we can strap him into his crew seat on the Ares Pilgrim. I'm afraid the spacecraft will launch in seven days regardless of whether your son is aboard or not."

My dad puts Flint Garrison's papers back into the manila folder, and he sets it on the coffee table. And then he takes the kind of deep breath he normally reserves for making decisions about my well-being or rescuing me from detention at McDerney.

"Son, would you mind handing me a pencil?"

I yank one from my pocket protector. I don't want to vacate my post on the living room carpet, and I can't reach my dad from where I'm standing, so I fling the pencil toward my dad. He catches it in midair with his right hand. The pencil's sharpened and beveled point is facing downward.

"You'll need to sign the agreement with a pen," Flint Garrison says.

"You'll have to make an exception this time, General. Here in the Tuckerman household, we only write with a pencil."

And then my dad signs the agreement, and he places it back into its protective folder, and he hands it to Flint Garrison.

And for the first time in my life, I believe I'm actually going to Mars.

"We must be on our way," Flint Garrison says. "You should pack your things, Sherman, but as you might imagine with this type of critically sensitive mission, weight is a factor. Whatever you decide to take with you has to fit inside a standard backpack and cannot weigh more than three pounds. And you won't need to bring a laptop computer. We'll provide one for you."

Mr. Appleton, my math teacher at McDerney, once made me use a laptop in class, and it caused my brain to twitch super hard, so I threw the laptop on the ground, and then I jumped up and down on it, which got me in a bunch of trouble with the Vice Principal, and then my dad had to drive our Ford Crown Victoria station wagon to school to explain that I don't need a laptop, because I do all my calculations in my brain.

"General, I would suggest that the laptop you assign to my son not be an expensive one."

Flint Garrison grunts. "Mr. Tuckerman, I hope you and

Sherman can appreciate that everything on this mission costs a fortune."

I shift my focus away from the laptop issue, and I make a list in my brain of all the essential stuff I'll need to take with me on the yearlong journey:

1. Pads of paper.
2. Pencils.
3. Bazooka Joe bubblegum.
4. Magnetic travel chessboard with chess pieces.
5. Travel abacus.
6. Clean underwear.
7. Zeke's package.

I leave chili mac 'n' beef off my list because my brain concludes there will be a sufficient supply on the spacecraft.

And then my brain makes spatial math calculations to determine whether I can cram all my things into my Mars-themed standard backpack while staying within the requisite weight limit. My brain estimates that there's likely enough room, and that I can adjust the amount of underwear downward if there's only enough space for the more critical items.

I vacate my spot on the living room carpet and race-walk to my bedroom. My dad follows close behind.

Once inside, I'm careful not to slam my bedroom door, mainly because I don't want my framed poster of Carl Sagan to get crooked, because there isn't enough time to use my tubular spirit level instrument to recalibrate it, because I need to pack. But I also don't want my dad to think I'm upset about having to limit what I take on the spaceflight.

"I guess all those astronaut training meals are finally going to pay off."

I note that my dad doesn't ask a question, so I don't respond. His shoulders are drooping, and he's using the thumb and index finger of his right hand to rotate the gold wedding band on his left ring finger in a counterclockwise direction.

The last time I saw him do that was at my mom's funeral.

I gather the items from my list and place them in the center of my bed. The final item I put in the pile is Zeke's envelope.

"I guess the only reason you decided to go to Mars was to read Zeke's diary." My dad wiggles his eyebrows when he says that.

I remove all the math textbooks from my backpack, and I place them alphabetically by author into the mathematics section of my bookcase. Then I quickly rearrange them alphabetically by subject. Then I load my travel items into the backpack.

The last thing I pick up is Zeke's envelope. When I squeeze it, I feel something lumpy at the bottom. I dump out the envelope's contents onto the bed to see what it is.

Zeke's non-lumpy letter comes out first, then his hefty stack of papers, and then two miniature square-shaped orange basketballs, like fuzzy dice, connected together by a string, which I confirm to be the lumpy evidence.

My brain recalls Zeke saying that his nosy neighbor, Mrs. Fenner, gave him the fuzzy basketballs the night before he left for the University of Kansas. Zeke told me that Mrs. Fenner said it would bring him good luck.

It makes me wonder if that's why Zeke included it in his envelope.

And then I wonder how much luck I'll need on the journey to Mars.

And then my hands get clammy again.

And then my lips and chin tremble, and I can't make the trembling stop.

25

My Lips and Chin Tremble All Over Again

A knock at my bedroom door distracts me. It makes the quivering stop.

"Sherman, it's Dr. Murakami. Vandenberg Air Force Base is a bit of a drive, and we have much ground to cover once we arrive."

I ignore Dr. Murakami and instead do a quick calculation in my brain. I determine that my house at 26488 Laszlo Lane is 154 miles from Vandenberg Air Force Base. I take note that the mileage is divisible by seven.

It's Saturday evening. L.A. traffic will be light to moderate. I estimate that my dad can drive us there in two hours, forty-eight minutes in our Ford Crown Victoria station wagon.

I shove Zeke's package into my backpack, and I secure the zipper.

And then I tie up loose ends by making a list in my brain of all the things I need to do when I return home from Mars:

1. Eat Mike's pepperoni pizza every Tuesday with my dad.

2. Play chess at the rec center every Thursday with Nathan.

3. Put the pickup truck back together while avoiding Chett Biffmann as much as possible.

4. Get my driver's license.

Then I remember the last thing I wrote to Nathan as he was pestering me about coming aboard at Chip's Sporting Goods. I told him I would think about it, so I add three more items to the list:

5. Apply for a work permit.

6. Tell Nathan my polo shirt size is medium.

7. Work at Chip's so I can afford to pay for gas and maintenance and insurance.

I need to let Nathan know I've decided to accept the position. I sit down at my desk, and I write him a letter while my dad looks over my shoulder.

Dear Mr. Freeman:

Since it's a formal business letter, I choose to address Nathan more formally.

I'm writing to advise you that I have decided to accept your offer of employment as a part-time trainee sales clerk. I trust that the offer still includes the Chip's rookie employee discount for purchasing chess gear at a favorable discount. I propose to start with your firm one year and one week from the date of this letter.

"Remember, son, I signed the general's nondisclosure agreement. The SFC certainly has not granted you official authority to discuss your mission with Nathan."

My dad's reminder prompts me to provide Nathan with just enough information to secure the position at Chip's without disclosing confidential details.

> In case you are wondering why there is a lengthy delay in my projected start date, it's because I need to take care of a pressing matter. And since it is highly confidential, I am unable to disclose whether or not it has anything to do with space travel.
> Sincerely,
> Sherman "Lawrence" Tuckerman

I give the letter a triple fold, place it into an envelope from my desk drawer, and address it to Nathan, in care of Chip's Sporting Goods.

"Would you like me to put a stamp on that and mail it for you?"

Questions. But I figure my dad is only trying to help, so I let it go and hand him the envelope.

"Sherman, we do need to get going," Dr. Murakami says through the door.

That makes my lips and chin tremble all over again.

26

It Won't Be Possible to Break Protocol

I slip my backpack over one shoulder. My dad opens the bedroom door.

"I trust you have everything you'll need," Dr. Murakami says.

That makes me wonder whether I've packed enough paper and pencils and Bazooka Joe for the mission. Then I calculate that if I print my numbers and letters smaller than usual, and if I conserve my bubblegum supply by only popping a wedge into my mouth in times of ultra-high stress, I should have enough of everything I'll need on the journey.

When Flint Garrison notices me reentering the living room, he bounces up from the depths of the couch, and for the six-teenth time he clears his throat, and I'm hoping it's the last time he does either of those things, though I might just be willing to cut him enough slack for five more times, to get to twenty-one.

"I think we can still make it to the base before they decide to send out a search party," he says.

"Sherman, I have one more question before we leave," Dr. Murakami says, and I think by now she would've figured out that I don't like it when people ask me questions. "Professor Bellwether has told us about your life's goal of being the mathematics flight specialist on the first manned mission to Mars. It certainly is a noble and lofty goal. Can you tell me about your motivation behind it?"

No one has ever asked me that question before, and Dr. Murakami is invading my space with it, and I only have two choices, to answer her truthfully, or ignore her altogether, and now my lips and chin are trembling, because no matter which option I choose, I know there's a chance it will disqualify me from the mission, and now I'm standing at a crossroads for the second time today.

And then my brain does the math, determining by the narrowest of margins that I'm better off being an active participant in my own life rather than a victim of it, which is something Zeke taught me.

I swing my backpack off my shoulder and dig out my pad, and I pull a pencil from my pocket protector, but before I can write a note, my dad takes a step forward and waves me off.

"My son was born with boundless curiosity, Dr. Murakami. He understands that bringing home evidence of ancient microbial life on Mars will help astrophysicists construct new theories on how life might be present everywhere in the universe, and not just limited to Earth."

Dr. Murakami smiles. "Thank you for that lucid explanation. We'd also like to hear what Sherman has to say on the matter."

I put pencil to paper and write more furiously than I've ever written before.

In order for us to wisely take care of the planet, it's essential that we understand how other planets in our solar system have evolved. And Mars is the optimum starting point because it offers the best possibility for self-sufficiency during exploration, given our current level of technology.

I fold my note in half, and I hand it to Dr. Murakami, who reads it silently. And then she opens her journal to a book-marked page, and she clicks her pen and makes a notation. "Is there anything else?"

"Yes," I say before my brain can stop me. "My life's goal is a peripheral mathematical subset of my overall fundamental goal—to understand perfect order in the universe."

And Dr. Murakami squints.

And Flint Garrison grunts.

And my dad fumbles for his car keys. "I assume we'll be caravanning to Vandenberg?"

Flint Garrison's response is instantaneous. "I'm afraid not, Mr. Tuckerman. Top-security mission. You'll need to say goodbye to your son right here, right now."

I reach for my pad, and I scrawl out a note and hand it to my dad.

Tell him I only ride in a car with you or Zeke. I don't ride in a car with Nathan, because he doesn't have one. He takes the bus everywhere.

The last part about Nathan isn't relevant to the dilemma I'm facing, but I write it anyway so my dad can have the full and complete breakdown of my established driving options.

"General, my son and I are wondering whether you might make an exception in this case."

"It won't be possible to break protocol. Security is supremely paramount at the Strategic Federation Council. You'd better say your goodbyes now."

My dad turns to me and smiles. There are tears in his eyes again, and I wonder if he will blot them with his cotton sleeve, which he doesn't. Instead, he asks me a question.

"Can I hug you?"

I hope it's the last question anyone will ask me before I blast off in the Ares Pilgrim.

"No."

I choose to say the word rather than write my dad another note because I need to conserve paper, and I don't like to be touched.

27

I Have Less Anxiety, at Least for Now

I race-walk ahead of everyone, through the entry hall, out the front door, across the lawn, all the way to the black four-door Dodge Stratus sedan parked in front of the house.

The strange man sitting behind the wheel is still wearing a pair of dark sunglasses, even though the sun went down an hour ago. He gives me a weird two-finger wave as I approach. I ignore him.

I yank the front passenger door handle, and I slide into the shotgun position alongside the man, and then I slam the door. I set my backpack onto the floor, and I grapple for the seatbelt as Dr. Murakami approaches.

My window is up. The man pushes a button to roll it down. I push my button to roll it back up, but the man lowers it again.

"I see you've met Ryker," Dr. Murakami says through the window. "He's quick on the trigger."

The car's power window button is a tiny chrome switch that's activated by pushing it forward and back with a finger. It doesn't look like the trigger of any pistol I've ever seen in TV crime dramas. I conclude that Dr. Murakami is attempting to make a joke, but I don't think it's funny, and Ryker isn't laughing either.

"Ryker prefers that General Garrison ride in the front seat, which will give us an opportunity to get to know each other better on our way to the base."

I already know Dr. Murakami as well as I want to. I need to think up something to do on the drive that doesn't include listening to her talk.

I get out of the front seat, and I climb into the backseat directly behind Ryker, because I don't want to risk looking at his face again, because he makes me nervous.

Flint Garrison takes his place in the front seat. Dr. Murakami gets into the backseat next to me. I hope everyone will leave me alone on the way to Vandenberg Air Force Base.

I look past Dr. Murakami, and I see my dad standing on the front porch waving goodbye. Now that I'm traveling to Mars, my dad will have more chores to do and less paper and fewer pencils to buy.

Flint Garrison clears his throat. That's number seventeen—a number that at least includes a seven, graphically—and it sounds louder than any of the throat-clears in the living room, mostly because I'm physically closer to him in the sedan than I was in the house.

"The base, Ryker, and step on it."

Ryker maneuvers the sedan through the streets of my neighborhood and onto Chamberlain Drive, the main thoroughfare. I'm familiar with the route to Interstate 10. The westbound on-ramp is 2.1 miles ahead.

"Sherman, you never did tell me where you got the nickname, *Lawrence*." Flint Garrison doesn't ask me a question, so I don't respond. "Is it a family name? A distant relative, perhaps?"

More questions.

"General," Dr. Murakami says, and I welcome the interruption. "I think we should—"

"Young man, I understand you're an excellent chess player. Where did you learn how to play?"

More questions! I ignore Flint Garrison by reviewing in my brain the principles of the Pythagorean Theorem, a mathematical proposition that isn't self-evident, but instead is proven by a chain of reasoning, meaning it is a truth that is established by means of accepted truths.

I intend to use the theorem to perform navigational distance calculations on the journey to Mars. However, sitting in the backseat of the sedan next to Dr. Murakami, the only truth I've established by means of accepted truths is that Flint Garrison will continue to ask me questions, because he has never stopped asking them.

"I understand you like to order takeout from Mike's Pizza over on Broadhurst Parkway. What kind of toppings do you like? What do you think goes better with pizza, orange soda or root beer? Have you tried the garlic bread?"

"Aaaaaaaaaaaaaaaaaaaaaaaaaaaaaaaaaaaaaaah!" I scream.

And Ryker jams on the brakes, putting the sedan into a four-wheel lock skid as nearby sedans swerve to avoid slamming into us.

And then the two tires on the passenger side thump against the concrete curb, causing the car to lurch sideways, which causes Flint Garrison's head to career off his window, which wouldn't have happened if Ryker had left the window down.

And I see the veins of the left side of the general's neck bulge as white smoke billows in all directions.

He mutters, "What in the world . . ." before his voice trails off.

I wonder if he is momentarily confused by the smoke. I rip my pad from my backpack, blast out a quick note, and drop it onto the bench seat between Ryker and the general.

> Intense heat from the abrasive spinning action of the tires oxidized certain chemical compounds within the rubber. The oxidized amalgamation was subsequently vaporized and released into the air as white smoke.

Flint Garrison reads my note, and then crumples it into a wad and flings it onto the floor. And then he exits the car and waves Dr. Murakami out to join him, leaving me in here with Ryker, which makes my palms sweaty. I can't hear what they're saying outside because Ryker still has the front passenger window rolled up.

And the general does a lot of shouting and additional vein popping.

And Dr. Murakami listens and nods, and her veins seem normal.

And then they get back in the car.

And neither of them is smiling.

And Ryker restarts the engine.

"Sherman, we've got a long drive ahead of us, and General Garrison would like Ryker to be able to concentrate on the task at hand. Can you take a deep breath for me and try to relax?"

And even though Dr. Murakami asks a question again, it doesn't bother me as much this time.

I think about saying something to her, but since my pad is already out, I write her a note instead.

Yes

I take a deep breath.

I exhale.

I have less anxiety, at least for now.

28

And My Palms Get Sweaty All Over Again

I take deep breaths for nearly three hours while Ryker speeds along the network of highways leading to Vandenberg Air Force Base.

I spend the entire time solving rational polynomial equations in my brain, in particular, equations that contain at least one fraction whose numerator and denominator are both polynomials, and while it may not be entirely rational to board a spacecraft destined for Mars, what with the danger and all, I know these brain pushups will help me on the journey when I apply Newtonian mechanics to calculate fuel expenditure, exhaust velocity, and Mars insertion trajectories.

Plus, it helps me to block out Flint Garrison's persistent questions and throat-clearing.

Ryker steers the sedan off a desolate stretch of Highway 1 and guides it down a tree-lined gravel road. The noise of the tires crunching over pebbles drowns out the sound of my heart hammering against my rib cage.

It's dark outside, except for the sedan's headlights, which illuminate a wooden security guard shack with a red-and-white striped barrier arm blocking the entrance. I determine that the barrier arm is more of a formality than an actual security measure, as Ryker could easily drive around it, or even right through it.

Wait a second. I remember seeing photographs of the main entrance at Vandenberg Air Force Base during my internship at the JPL.

This isn't it.

Vandenberg's main entrance has a rock wall with the name of the base on it in steel letters, and there's a concrete-and-glass, tile-roof building with a uniformed armed guard manning the post.

A man in a gray pinstriped business suit and dark sunglasses exits the guard shack, and I wonder whether the SFC issues a pair of those sunglasses to all its employees.

The man does a Ryker-style two-finger wave as he approaches. I notice a shiny metal object resting inside what looks like a holster attached to the belt beneath his sports jacket.

I stiffen my shoulders.

And Ryker rolls down his window.

And when the man leans in, I catch a whiff of his cologne, so my brain concludes it's important to smell good while working as a security guard at SFC headquarters.

The sudden, unexpected smell unlocks a sector of my brain I haven't visited in exactly sixty-three days. The scent reminds me of the cologne Brock Decker was wearing when we took apart Zeke's 1965 sea-foam-green Chevrolet Fleetside short-bed pickup truck. I try to remember the reason why we did it, but the man shatters the silence, breaking my concentration and making my brain twitch.

"It's good to see you again, Ryker. You too, General."

I hover my left index finger directly over my power window button so I can react instantly in case Ryker lowers my window. Instead, Ryker hands the man a red folder.

The man examines the documents inside the folder, and then he walks back to the guard shack, and he picks up a phone receiver and engages in a conversation, possibly about cologne, but more likely about the four of us in the car, and then he hangs up.

"They're waiting for you in Central Command, General."

"Thank you, Wolf," Flint Garrison says, and my brain gets twitchy all over again when I ponder whether Wolf is the man's actual name, or a nickname he picked up for exhibiting aggressive behavior, or worse.

"Dr. Murakami, this must be Master Tuckerman, the mission's mathematics flight specialist."

It's the first time anyone has ever called me Master. I know from watching TV crime dramas that a person uses the term to express authority over a boy who is too young to be called Mister.

My brain weighs the suitability of Wolf's decision to apply the term to a fifteen-year-old male youth who is seven days away from boarding a spacecraft bound for Mars. And then my brain shifts gears, concluding that it's the first time any-one has ever called me by my Ares Pilgrim Mars mission title, which causes my right knee to bounce up and down—just like my dad's knee, only faster.

Dr. Murakami doesn't respond to the man. Neither does Ryker.

But Flint Garrison does.

"Thank you, Wolf. You can step back now. We'll be on our way."

The man retreats to the guard shack and raises the barrier arm. Ryker returns the two-finger wave and puts the sedan into drive, and my brain makes a mental note to work on perfecting my own two-finger wave in case I ever need to blend in, should a critical situation call for it.

Ryker rolls up his window and passes the guard shack. And we crunch our way down a winding, dimly lit road for 4.9 miles until we round a turn, and an immense white building comes into view.

And next to it is a brightly lit rocket parked on a launchpad. The words ARES PILGRIM are painted in black letters on the white crew capsule that caps the rocket.

And my palms get sweaty all over again.

29

Is This a Joke, General?

The white building is three stories high. All the windows have a reflective, mirrored coating of some kind. It's impossible to see what's going on inside.

And there's a satellite dish mounted atop the building. I note that it's pointing toward the constellation Cetus. I remember from world literature class at McDerney that Cetus is the sea monster from the Greek myth about Andromeda, who is a princess and the daughter of a king.

In the myth, Andromeda is sacrificed to Cetus as punishment for her mother's boastfulness. It makes me wonder if my mom—if she were still alive today—would brag about me going to Mars. I don't wonder whether she would be punished for bragging, though, because the Andromeda story is only a myth, and my mom is already dead.

Instead, I focus my attention on the satellite dish's primary reflector structure because it carries an SFC logo that matches the one engraved onto the general's gold tie clasp.

Everyone exits the sedan but Ryker and me. I don't know

the exact reason why Ryker is staying behind, but maybe it's because he's in charge of the car. I remain in the backseat because my calculations tell me it's safer here than inside the white building.

Dr. Murakami knocks on my window with the knuckles of her right hand. Her knocking pattern is similar to Nathan's, but her knock is not as forceful.

"Sherman, you need to come out of there. We shouldn't keep the mission director waiting."

I feel my own hands curling themselves into fists. I know I can't write notes with my hands like this. I straighten them out, and then I lift a pencil from my pocket protector.

I write Dr. Murakami a note, and I hold it up to the window.

I need time to think.

"What's the problem, Lydia?" Flint Garrison says, and his voice is loud.

My brain ponders whether I can blast off to Mars from the backseat of the sedan all by myself, which is a favorable idea in the moment, until I realize that the car's propulsion and life-support systems are woefully inadequate, but then I remember there's a subsector of my brain that likes to play tricks on me when I'm scared, as it's doing right now.

I command my brain's primary sector, the one in charge of my brain's secondary sectors, to take control of the rogue subsector.

And then I grab hold of my backpack, and I climb out of

the sedan. I slam the door behind me so hard that the steel hubcap on the left rear wheel falls off.

It rattles around in a circle on the pavement for seven full rotations before coming to a stop.

And I can see the full moon reflecting off the hubcap's shiny metal.

And I write Flint Garrison a note.

That's going to leave a mark, bro.

That's a saying I learned from Curtis when he was playing basketball at Jefferson with Zeke and the guys, the time Stretch took an elbow to the nose, and it drew blood.

I decide not to give the note to Flint Garrison. Instead, I do a test run of my two-finger wave, aiming the experimental gesture toward Ryker as I walk away from the vehicle.

Ryker doesn't respond, which causes me to wonder if he doesn't see it, or sees it but ignores me because I lost my sole opportunity to be a member of the Two-Finger Wave Club when I didn't respond to his initial two-finger wave back at the house, and then I wonder if the club only has two members, Wolf and Ryker, and membership is now closed, or if maybe Ryker is unhappy about the hubcap, or the door possibly being out of alignment after I slammed it.

The chilly night air makes my skin tingle. My nose, which is indirectly connected to my brain, picks up the scent of fresh pine needles. For a moment, I forget where I am. And I am no longer scared.

"This way," Dr. Murakami says as she and the general

walk toward the security door at the entrance to the white building.

And the palms of my hands get sweaty all over again.

"Hey, kid." It's Ryker. I pivot on my heel.

"Hey." I speak the word rather than write it because I'm trying to conserve paper.

"Be careful up there," he says. "We've got your six."

I know from watching TV crime dramas that if someone's got your six, it means they've got your back. I wish Ryker had said he's got my *seven* instead, even though I know that's not the official expression. It makes me consider Ryker as a possible non-best friend, putting him in the same friendship category as Curtis and Stretch, but not Brock Decker.

I want to tell Ryker thanks, but I don't, because it's easier for me to turn and walk away.

Flint Garrison punches a seven-digit code into a keypad next to the door. The lock makes a *click-thump* sound. Dr. Murakami pulls the door handle, and she walks inside. And then me. And then Flint Garrison.

There's a woman sitting behind a reception desk. The plaque on her desk says TRINIDAD. My brain works to determine whether Trinidad is her name, or it's where she's from, or both.

"They're waiting for you inside, General."

"Thank you, Trini," he says, and my brain freezes momentarily as I realize that it failed to anticipate a fourth Trinidad option: the word is the woman's name, *and* it can be shortened into a nickname. And I conclude that if anyone ever tries to call me Sherm or even Law, I will probably slap them really hard.

Flint Garrison takes us down a long hallway leading to a door with a placard on it that says CENTRAL COMMAND. And my stomach churns and gurgles. And Dr. Murakami stares at me. And I pretend not to notice she's staring, and then I wonder whether she notices me pretending not to notice her.

I don't know whether I'm hungry, or I miss my bedroom, or I miss my dad, or I'm afraid of doing something stupid in Central Command that will screw up my chances of going on the mission.

I hear voices coming from inside the room. Flint Garrison swings open the door, and we step inside. And when the door closes behind us, the hollow door-close echo sound seems to orbit Central Command.

And then a voice inside the room drowns out my stomach before making it sink.

"Is this a joke, General? He's just a kid."

30

You Can Count on Me

Flint Garrison crosses his arms. "That's less than helpful, Stone."

I do a quick headcount in my brain. There are thirty-one people sitting in black leather chairs that surround an enormous oval conference table. The man Flint Garrison calls Stone is sitting at the head of the table at the far end of the room.

"C'mon, Flint, he doesn't even look old enough to drive," says the man whose name is Stone.

I extract a wedge of Bazooka Joe from my backpack and pop it in my mouth. Ordinarily in similar circumstances, I would go for a double wedge, but I need to conserve my supply.

Flint Garrison's annoying throat-clear, his eighteenth, recaptures everyone's attention: "Stone, if we're going to get this mission off the ground, there needs to be—"

"I have my learner's permit." Those words escape my mouth before my brain can reverse thrusters.

I don't make eye contact with anyone, but my brain determines there's a mathematically high probability that everyone is staring at me, because all of their heads swivel toward me at the exact same moment.

And that makes my cheeks feel hot, and tears are welling up in my eyes, and when I wipe them with my sleeve, I conclude that my shirt is not one-hundred-percent cotton like my dad's, because my sleeve doesn't blot the moisture as effectively as his does.

"Kid's got some *moxie*," Stone says.

That word jars my memory.

Stone is Stone Godfrey.

I remember reading years ago in a back issue of *Astronaut Quarterly* that Stone Godfrey was the one with moxie because of his force of character and nerves of steel under pressure.

Ace test pilot.

Wounded Iraqi war veteran idolized for his courage on the battlefield.

Innovative and respected Space Shuttle astronaut.

Family man.

PGA golfer on the pro tour.

American Sailing Association Yachtsman of the Year.

National hero.

And then, a sharp fall from grace.

Alcoholic.

Gambler.

Drug abuser.

Washed-up has-been.

The last time I saw an article on Stone Godfrey in *Astronaut Quarterly*, he had checked himself into a rehab facility to avoid a jail sentence. The story reported that he was going through a messy divorce, and his two kids had stopped talking to him.

I wonder whether I would've stopped talking to my dad if he'd done all those things that Stone Godfrey did.

"Stone is the Ares Pilgrim's flight engineer," Flint Garrison says, looking directly at me, probably because everyone else in the room already knows Stone Godfrey's title. "I don't think you could find anyone more qualified at zero gravity than this pillar of a man."

I glance at Stone Godfrey, being careful to avoid eye contact. I take note that he hasn't shaved in several days, and his gray hair is messy, and his eyelids are puffy, and there are two fleshy layers of extra chin beneath his original one.

I conclude that Flint Garrison has more confidence in Stone Godfrey than I do.

"And why isn't our field scientist here?" Flint Garrison says. "Where is Maya Jupiter?"

Hold on a minute. Field scientist Maya's last name is the same as one of the eight planets in our solar system?

I don't include Pluto in my planetary summation because fifty-six days earlier, which I note is a number divisible by seven, the International Astronomical Union downgraded Pluto's status to *dwarf planet* because it didn't meet the criteria the IAU uses to define a full-size planet.

I didn't like the decision at the time, and I still don't like it now, especially since Pluto has met all the IAU's criteria, except one: It has not cleared its neighboring region of other objects by achieving gravitational dominance, which is a technicality I can relate to, and not in a good way, because I'm not always able to isolate myself from strangers, like, for example, right now in Central Command.

And some day, when I become a member of the International Astronomical Union, I will unearth new data, and I will apply that data using advanced mathematical theories to prove the IAU wrong, and then I will work to reverse its decision and restore Pluto to full planethood.

I also note that the word Jupiter consists of seven letters.

A man wearing a gold name badge that says PAX BOOKER, FLIGHT DIRECTOR replies. "General, our field scientist is in the restroom. Maya has been in there for a while now."

My brain notates that Pax Booker has a friendly smile, and the pale color of his hair and beard is kind of inversely proportional to the dark tone of his skin.

And then my brain recalls that in physics, black and white are not colors because they don't have specific wavelengths—white light contains all wavelengths of visible light, and black is the absence of visible light—which makes them outcasts that have been shunned and rejected by color-spectrum society, which is something I can relate to because of my autism.

Flint Garrison's face tightens. "Dr. Murakami, can you please look in on her?"

"Of course, General." Dr. Murakami rushes from Central Command, leaving me standing there with Flint Garrison and thirty-one strangers.

I take advantage of the delay by analyzing the conference table, and I note that Pax Booker is sitting at the table's co-vertex rather than at its vertex, where Stone Godfrey is sitting. That means everyone has a marginally better view of the person in charge of the mission than of the one in charge of flying the spacecraft.

"We're not blessed with an abundance of time to prep for spaceflight. We might as well get started without her," Pax Booker says. "Why don't you take a seat, Sherman, and we'll begin the debriefing."

I'm standing behind four empty chairs grouped together at the opposite end of the conference table from Stone Godfrey. The math obviously supports these chairs being reserved for Flint Garrison, Dr. Murakami, Maya Jupiter, and me.

I choose an end chair rather than one of the two in the center of the grouping, because it decreases my odds of sitting next to Flint Garrison.

And I can tell that all eyes are on me, especially Pax Booker's.

"Maya has already met the team," Pax Booker says. "While we're waiting for her to join us, I think it would be a good use of our time to introduce you to everyone."

Off in the distance, I hear the faint sound of someone throwing up. It's followed by a lot of murmuring in Central Command, and then by the noise water makes when it rushes through overhead plumbing after someone flushes a toilet.

Flint Garrison grunts and exits Central Command.

"I don't expect you to remember the names and functions of everyone here," Pax Booker says, "so I'm going to go around the room swiftly with these introductions."

I want to tell Pax Booker not to be concerned about my ability to recall data, but communicating this message would require that I take time to write him a note, because I don't want to speak to him, or anyone else.

I let it go. Instead, I take out my pad and a pencil, and I draw an elliptical circle on the page identical in shape to the conference table.

"Beginning to my left, we have our guidance engineering team, then the mission's EECOM manager, our electrical power systems personnel, and the Ares Pilgrim's flight dynamics scientist. You've already met Commander Godfrey. Going around the horn, to Stone's left are our CAPCOM technicians and the booster systems engineer."

Then Pax Booker introduces the rest of the team:

Guidance navigation and control officer.

Mission AECOM specialist.

Retrofire officer.

Flight surgeon.

Astrodynamicist.

U.S. Department of Defense liaison.

Flight activities specialist.

Operational planning team.

Integrated communications officer.

Mission director from NASA HQ in Washington, D.C.

Strategic Federation Council public affairs chief.

I use my elliptical layout to jot down all the names and positions Pax Booker identifies.

I learned from my Jet Propulsion Lab internship that mathematics flight specialists need to be prepared for anything and everything in outer space. I practice the JPL's directive by writing the data in ultra-small letters so that I don't run out of space on the page.

"Dr. Murakami, who I'm sure will be joining us any moment now, is a developmental pediatrician by trade, but Lydia will also serve as the mission's psychologist. And I believe that's everyone."

I add Dr. Murakami's name and pair of job titles to complete my roster of people and positions.

"I'm sure you're real zippy over there with that pencil, Sherman." Stone Godfrey's conclusion is accurate. My notes are always exhaustive and all inclusive. "I'm wondering if I can count on you up there in outer space when the chips are down."

I tear off the sheet of paper that has my elliptical organizational chart on it, and I set it aside. Then I write a fresh note to Stone Godfrey, and I fold the piece of paper in half and write his name on the outside, and then I set it on the conference table in front of the integrated communications officer to my right.

My note makes its way along the south side of the conference table until one of the CAPCOM technicians hands it to Stone Godfrey.

Stone Godfrey unfolds my note, and he reads it silently.

And then he reads it aloud to everyone in Central Command:

"'You can count on me, no matter what position the chips are in. And it's okay if you call me Lawrence. My friends do.'"

31

Yin and Yang

My brain recalls how Zeke once described courage as the quality of mind or spirit that enables a person to face difficulty, danger, or pain without fear.

I have no idea where my sudden burst of courage comes from, or even if it truly is courage, because I was frightened when I wrote my note to Stone Godfrey, and I still feel panicky, even as my brain debates the complex mathematical relationship between courage and fear.

And then I exhale when I realize I've stopped breathing.

And then I consider that my understanding of the nature of courage might come from my friendship with Zeke, in those times when I sat in the top row of the bleachers and witnessed his heroics on the basketball court at Jefferson.

And I wonder whether I also developed a sense of it from watching Nathan shove open the doors of a hostile community college gymnasium to go to battle against a more experienced and more highly decorated opponent at a regional chess tournament.

And then I gaze in the general direction of Stone Godfrey, and I see the corners of his mouth slide upward and the sides of his eyes scrunch up.

My brain concludes that he recognizes my courage. And then I exhale again, more deeply this time.

Stone Godfrey points his right index finger at me. "I'm relieved to hear that I can count on you on this mission, because both of our lives will depend on it."

"Yeah, mine too."

That voice comes from behind me. I swing my head around. There's a teenage girl entering the room through the door behind me. Flint Garrison and Dr. Murakami follow closely behind her.

My brain uses existing data to deduce that this must be Maya Jupiter, and now there are thirty-five people in Central Command, which I note is a number divisible by seven.

"I will call you Tuckerman," Stone Godfrey says, "and I have no interest in being your friend. I do, however, have an interest in being your commander, and I will expect you to carry out your responsibilities as mathematics flight specialist with great precision and care. Are we clear?"

I write another note, and I fold it in half.

Crystal

"And I won't need that note you're writing, because the one I'm holding in my hand is the last one you will write me. Understood?"

I nod.

I hope Stone Godfrey sees me nodding and then stops talking to me.

"Thank you for that moment of clarity, Stone," Flint Garrison says.

"There's one more thing, Tuckerman."

Turns out Stone Godfrey has more to say, and my brain twitches in anticipation of what it might be.

"Since you seem to like to write so much, I'm putting you in charge of the Captain's Log. It's a big responsibility, one that you seem eminently qualified to handle."

I nod again, less enthusiastically this time.

A welcome flash of relief hits me when Dr. Murakami takes the seat right next to me, and then Maya sits next to Dr. Murakami, leaving Flint Garrison with the chair farthest away from me.

The general clears his throat for the nineteenth time. "Sherman, I'd like you to meet Maya Jupiter, the mission's field scientist. As I explained back at the house, Maya has great expertise in geology and biology and will also serve as the mission's chief medical officer. But perhaps more importantly, she is our communications analyst."

I pretend to beat Maya Jupiter to the ignore before I turn and catch a glimpse of her out of the corner of my eye.

I notice the warmth of her bronze coloring next to Flint Garrison's pale skin. I swiftly scan her eyes. They're deep brown, and there's a kind of sparkle to them.

Maya's hair is even darker than her eyes. It's long and wavy and verges on black. My brain concludes that she's not much older than I am.

Maya Jupiter leans behind Dr. Murakami and toward me. "Hand me some paper, and give me a pencil from that thing-amajig in your shirt pocket," she whispers.

I don't normally lend out pencils from my pocket protector, but I want to trust Maya, so I make an exception.

"Maya, are you all right?" Pax Booker asks as arched wrinkles materialize on his forehead.

"Guess you heard me in the latrine calling Huey on the big white telephone. Guess I should have listened to Dr. Murakami and stayed clear of the sushi at the base diner."

Flint Garrison sits bolt upright in his chair. "Maya, you *know* that the Vandenberg dining facility is off limits to SFC personnel. We are guests on this Air Force base. What were you thinking?"

"You know me, Flint, always questioning authority."

Maya's comments are followed by the sound of muted laughter in the room. My brain considers that Maya addressing the general by his first name might be viewed as a sign of disrespect by members of the team, especially those who are giggling.

His jaw tightens. "Jupiter, this is the last time I'm—"

Maya interrupts the general by holding the palm of her left hand inches from his face. Then she blows a strand of hair away from her mouth while she scribbles something onto her borrowed piece of paper, and then she folds the note in half.

Maya reaches across Dr. Murakami and passes the note to me. Maya's note is written in a simple substitution cipher—she has replaced every plaintext character with a different ciphertext character, which offers next to no communication security, as the code can be easily broken, which my brain quickly does:

I'm a rule-breaker. My instinct is you're not. Yin and yang. We're going to get along just fine, friend.

I respond to Maya with a noncoded note of my own.

Can I have my pencil back now?

32

My Friends Call Me Lawrence

I remember the concept of yin and yang from the philosophy class I took at McDerney.

It suggests that all things exist in the world as inseparable and contradictory opposites—or more to the point, that equal opposites attract and complement each other and may actually be interconnected and interdependent.

I ask my brain to analyze the significance of Maya's yin and yang analogy in the context of the mission and, as a complementary matter, whether to consider her as a possible friend—not a best friend like Nathan and Zeke, at least initially, but more in the Curtis and Stretch and possibly Ryker friendship category.

Pax Booker interrupts my thought process.

"It's getting late, and we've got a grueling week of training ahead of us. Sherman, Dr. Murakami will be your primary point of contact from this point forward. Lydia, can you please show Mr. Tuckerman to his quarters?"

"Of course, sir."

Pax Booker appears ready to wind things down for the night. "Let's all meet here tomorrow at zero-six-hundred for breakfast, debriefing, and training assignments."

My hand goes rogue by raising itself, even though my brain doesn't authorize it.

"Yes, what is it, Sherman?" Pax Booker says.

"What about the countdown?"

"What about it?"

"I want to do it."

Muted laughter returns to Central Command, softer this time.

"There's no need to worry about that," Pax Booker says. "We'll have it handled in Mission Control."

"The countdown involves numbers. As the mathematics flight specialist, I'm uniquely qualified to perform the duty." And now I'm in another conversation with the flight director, and I can think of a gazillion things I'd rather be doing, starting with walking 154 miles back to my bedroom.

Dr. Murakami fidgets in her seat, and then she closes her journal and speaks softly to me under her breath: "Sherman, why don't we talk about this later, when we—"

"I need to do the countdown!" I feel heat escaping my body from the top of my head.

"Tell you what," Pax Booker says. "We'll figure something out."

I take Pax Booker at his word, and then I sling my backpack over my shoulder, and I follow Dr. Murakami to the door.

"You'll want to avoid the breakfast burrito at the Central Command debriefing tomorrow." I don't see who says that, but I already recognize Maya Jupiter's high-pitched, breathy voice and the way she places extra emphasis on some of her vowels. "Last time I had one, I ended up in the bushes by the side of the building doing the hoaky-croaky."

I don't respond to Maya, mostly because she doesn't ask me a question, but I take note of her expanded food-borne illness vocabulary.

"And don't worry about crusty ol' Stone Age," Maya whispers. "His spectacular cliff dive from a life of astronaut royalty has made him secretly humble. He feels the need to hide that from the people he meets, but he's a big softie once you get to know him."

I don't want to know Stone Godfrey any better than I already do, which is not well at all, and I'm not looking forward to spending twelve months in a spacecraft with him, and I'm also wondering how Maya already knows so much more than I do about the mission—and about Stone Godfrey.

"Seems you have three different names," Maya says. "Which one would you like me to call you?"

Maya asks me a question, which I don't like, but I'm weirdly compelled to answer her. "My friends call me Lawrence."

"Very well, Sherman Tuckerman. Lawrence it is."

33

Dr. Tidewater's Theory

I follow Dr. Murakami up a flight of stairs and down a long hallway. She leads me to a room with the number 252 on the door, which I note is a number divisible by seven.

It occurs to me that I'm suddenly surrounded by a consistent pattern of numbers that include seven or are multiples of seven, and it started when Flint Garrison and Dr. Murakami appeared on my living room couch earlier in the day.

"Here's your room key," Dr. Murakami says. "There's chili mac 'n' beef in the pantry and a hotplate in the kitchenette." I note that the SFC has done its homework regarding my astronaut training dietary requirements. "If you need anything, all you have to do is pick up the phone and call me at extension seven-seven-oh-seven."

7707! The extension number's divisibility by seven is satisfyingly self-evident. I close the door to my room, and I flip the latch to the locked position. And then I unlock and lock it six more times, just to make sure.

And then I open the curtains. The Ares Pilgrim is in plain

view through the window. Floodlights illuminate the space-craft's gleaming white surface and trio of bright-orange Delta IV rockets at the base.

And my hands are flapping.

And my body is rocking from side to side.

And I'm so tired that I'm no longer hungry.

And even though it is well past my bedtime, I must first unpack my backpack so that all my stuff can be safely tucked away.

I stick my paper and pencils into a desk drawer. I set my magnetic travel chessboard, chess pieces, and travel abacus on top of the coffee table next to the Strategic Federation Council Ares Pilgrim Mars Mission Operations Manual I find there. My clean underwear goes inside a dresser drawer.

When I open the closet door to secure my Bazooka Joe supply inside, I notice seven silver-and-red uniforms hanging from a wooden rod that stretches across the width of the closet. Each uniform has an SFC logo sewn onto the left sleeve. I presume there's a clean uniform for every day of the weeklong training program.

I set Zeke's package on my nightstand. And then I strip down to my T-shirt and underwear, and I slide under the covers.

I'm dead tired, but I can't sleep, and my eyes are wide open.

And now my brain realizes that for the first time ever, I'm going to sleep in a place other than my bedroom on Laszlo Lane, which ends my streak at 5,747 consecutive nights at home, but then my brain determines that the four-digit number has two sevens in it, and it's also divisible by seven, and now my brain couples this new data with my upcoming seven-day stay in this foreign bed, and it concludes that there is a sufficient enough quantity of sevens in the equation to equalize the unfamiliarity and loneliness.

I try to make myself sleepy by compiling a list in my brain of all the things I'll miss while I'm on the mission.

I start with my bedroom, because that's my obvious first choice, and then there's playing chess with Nathan at the rec center, and telling Rigoberto what the good word is, and waiting for Bernadette to deliver packages from Zeke, even though that has only happened once. I add three more things to the list, which puts me at a total of seven, but I'm still wide awake, so I give up.

And then I remember what my pediatric neurologist Dr. Tidewater says I should do whenever I'm too focused on sevens and unable to get to sleep. He says I should solve trigonometric equations in my brain.

I decide to put Dr. Tidewater's theory to the test. If I focus on determining unknown angles involving the maximum of six functions, with successive approximations for sine, cosine, tangent, cotangent, secant, and cosecant, it will take my mind off . . .

34

This Is Supposed to Be a Top-Secret Mission

Pax Booker handed out our training assignments during the breakfast debriefing in Central Command the morning after I arrived at SFC headquarters.

In the meeting, he told me that I'd be in charge of retrieving the basketball-size sample container that's orbiting Mars, and I would train for the task in the SFC's neutral buoyancy laboratory, a forty-foot-deep swimming pool that's the size of a football field and contains 6.3 million gallons of water, and it has a full-scale replica of the Ares Pilgrim's capsule resting at the bottom.

I learned about neutral buoyancy during my internship at the JPL. My brain recalls that the term refers to the equal tendency of an object to sink or float. The neutral buoyancy lab makes me equally and objectively weightless through a combination of weights and flotation devices, so I can hover underwater and manipulate tools much the same way as I would in the zero gravity of space.

NBLs are most commonly used to prepare astronauts for spacewalks, but SFC scientists are using it to teach me how to operate a practice version of the Ares Pilgrim's robotic arm, including how to adjust its angle to the required twenty-three degrees.

Three and a half days have passed since Ryker dropped me off in the parking lot, and now I'm floating at the bottom of the NBL, and I'm wearing liquid-cooled underwear inside a specially designed underwater spacesuit with lots of lead weights in it, and I'm surrounded by two safety divers.

I soon find out that the easy hand and body movements I once took for granted are more difficult when I'm wearing an underwater spacesuit with bulky gloves.

"Let's try it again, Tuckerman."

That's dive training officer Pfeffermann, speaking to me via the communications gear inside my helmet after I whiff on my sixth attempt to capture the mock sample container.

And now my brain imagines that Curtis and Stretch are the two safety divers, and Stretch says, "Nice hands, bud," after each unsuccessful attempt. And Curtis counters with, "Chill, bro, Dude Duderson here will soon be in a precarious orbit around Mars doing this for real while you're trying to decide between growing a couple more inches or ordering a large pizza with everything."

And then my two friends bump imaginary fists, and the imaginary fleshy *thump* noise brings me back to reality.

And on the seventh try, I snag the mock container.

CRAIG LEENER

"Good work, Tuckerman," officer Pfeffermann says. "Just remember to set the robotic arm angle correctly when you're doing this for real, and you'll be good to go."

The NBL team extracts me from the pool and helps me out of my underwater spacesuit. And then I wobble back to room 252 to prepare my nightly chili mac 'n' beef.

And I'm exhausted, and my body aches, and I'm homesick.

And while exactly fifty percent of my brain is excited that I made it halfway through the training program, the other fifty percent is telling me to jam all my stuff into my backpack and sling it over my shoulder and walk the 154 miles of highway back to my bedroom.

And then the phone rings, and I hope it's not Dr. Murakami, even though my brain thinks it might help to speak with her right now.

"Hello."

"Sherman, this is Trinidad in reception. I've got your father on the line. Can I patch him through?"

"Yes."

How does my dad know how to reach me? And is he calling because he somehow knows I'm struggling? And why doesn't Trinidad call herself Trini?

"Mr. Tuckerman, I have your son on the line."

And then I hear a click, and then I hear my dad's voice.

"Son, are you all right?"

"Yes."

"I'm relieved to hear that. I just wanted to check in and make sure."

"How did you find me? Flint Garrison said this is supposed to be a top-secret mission."

"Dr. Murakami left me her business card and said I could stay in touch prior to launch. I'm calling to tell you that Nathan came by the house this afternoon to drop off an employment application, so he must have received your letter."

"Okay."

"Nathan said you need to fill it out with a pen. I thought about clueing him in on our Laszlo Lane pencil policy, but I didn't want to agitate him, so I let it go."

"Okay."

"Anyway, I'm glad you're all right. Be safe. I love you, son."

"Okay. Goodbye."

35

Do You Think Stone Is Hiding Something?

I have survived training week. It is now one hour before the launch of the Ares Pilgrim, and I'm in my quarters, and my brain is buzzing, and every muscle in my body is aching.

I had thought I was in excellent physical condition heading into the weeklong training program because of all the race-walking I do every day, and all the times I climbed seven flights of stairs inside JPL Building 238 to deliver telecommunications data to the scientists and mathematicians during my summer internship, and all the weekends I spent at the rec center rebounding for Zeke when he was working on his perimeter jumper before he drove his father's pickup truck to the University of Kansas.

But my body was not ready for the time I spent floundering around underwater in the neutral buoyancy lab, or the hours of multi-axis training I had to endure as I was strapped and suspended in a chair inside three tumbling rings to simulate what an uncontrolled spin in microgravity would feel like.

I also rode with Stone Godfrey in a T-38 Talon supersonic jet trainer after Flint Garrison ordered him to brush up on his piloting skills.

I called shotgun when we boarded the aircraft, only to find out that the cockpit's layout required me to sit in the compartment directly behind Stone Godfrey, not to his right in the traditional shotgun formation.

But it worked out for the best, because I was able to peek over Stone Godfrey's shoulder as he flipped switches, turned dials, and flew the aircraft at seven times the force of gravity, which made it impossible to lift my hands to take notes. Instead, my brain committed everything to memory, and as a side benefit, I was able to conserve paper.

When we made it back to Vandenberg, Flint Garrison asked me to leave Central Command and go to my quarters so he could yell at Stone Godfrey about the barrel rolls he performed as we were buzzing the control tower.

I spent the last night sitting with Dr. Murakami while she asked me questions about my mom and dad, and my astronaut training meal regimen, and why I prefer to use my brain over a calculator and a computer.

And then Dr. Murakami showed me several pieces of white cardboard that had funny-shaped black inkblots on them. She told me it was something called a Rorschach test, which she said was a psychological evaluation she would use to assess my personality characteristics and emotional functioning, with my perceptions recorded and then analyzed using psychological interpretation, complex algorithms, or both.

I told Dr. Murakami that I didn't see the point of the test, because all the inkblots were in the shape of already-been-chewed wads of Bazooka Joe.

And that's when she hastily collected the white pieces of cardboard.

"If all of this is too much for you, Sherman, perhaps I should speak with the general. I feel it might be best if you stayed behind and we sent one of our six backup mathematics flight specialists on the mission instead."

And that's when I wrote her a note that said:

Perhaps it would be best if you got some new inkblots.

And then Dr. Murakami stared at me and shook her head, and neither one of us said another word after that.

And now the launch is seven minutes less than an hour away, and I'm in my quarters packing the critical supplies I'll need on the journey.

I jam all my stuff into my backpack, and I take one last look around my quarters.

The room is as stark and unfamiliar as it was when I arrived at SFC headquarters, except for the hotplate, which I have swiftly mastered.

I make a note in my brain to ask my dad to install one in my bedroom when I get home, because the prospect of never leaving there once I'm home again is appealing, and a bedroom hotplate would enable me to achieve that goal.

I step into the hallway, and I pull the door closed.

"Hey! Where ya goin'?"

Maya startles me. She's standing outside my room asking a question with such an obvious answer that my brain determines I can ignore her.

"Don't mean to go all Stone Age Godfrey on you, but I think we should *talk* to each other on this mission rather than pass notes. Might help us get to know each other better."

There's nothing in the SFC operations manual that says I'm required to get to know the field scientist on a personal basis, what with so many fuel expenditure and exhaust velocity calculations to carry out over the next twelve months.

And then my brain remembers what Dr. Tidewater taught me—that if I look for the good in strangers, I will surely find it, and then my brain determines that while Maya is currently a stranger, I have reason to believe I can trust her, and she might even turn out to be a friend after all.

"Hold this," I say as I hand Maya my backpack. I open it, and I extract my pad and a pencil, and I write her a note.

> Yes, we can talk with each other. And I'll need you to return this sheet of paper to me when you're done reading it so I can write on the back of it later. I'm trying to conserve supplies.

"Kind of a mixed message there, Mr. Sherman Tuckerman. You're a deep thinker. I like that in a cabin mate."

The precarious reality of spending a year in close quarters with someone who talks too much begins to set in. My chin trembles, but it goes away when I slump my shoulders and sigh.

Maya and I walk down the flight of stairs leading to Central Command for our final preflight instructions. When we swing open the door, I see Stone Godfrey in his usual spot at the far vertex of the conference table. He's wearing Ryker-style dark sunglasses, which is curious, because it's still dark outside, and the lighting in Central Command is subdued. The only other people in the room are Flint Garrison, Dr. Murakami, and the flight surgeon we met at the beginning of the week.

"This might feel a bit cold," the flight surgeon says as she slips the diaphragm of her stethoscope inside my shirt and presses it against my chest.

My brain reminds me that I don't like to be touched, but it also points out that if I don't pass the preflight physical, I'll be experiencing the Ares Pilgrim's launch from a window seat at the base diner.

I almost come out of my skin when the flight surgeon slips the cuff of her sphygmomanometer around my upper arm, but then my brain distracts itself by reminding me that the word *sphygmomanometer* is a fancy name for a device that measures blood pressure, and then the flight surgeon squeezes the bulb until my upper arm feels like it's being strangled.

"You're cool as a cucumber, Sherman," the flight surgeon says. "It's remarkable for someone about to board a spacecraft bound for Mars."

When she says those words, I notice an empty feeling in the pit of my stomach, and my hands get clammy. When I'm sure no one is looking, I wipe my hands on my pants.

The flight surgeon runs the same tests on Maya before

turning her attention to Stone Godfrey. "You're up, Stone. Let's take a look at your vitals."

"Not on your life!" Stone Godfrey bellows from across the room. And then he rattles off what might be a new indoor record for the number of clichés used by an experienced astronaut to express a single thought prior to boarding a spacecraft. "I'm going to take one for the team because the Transfer Orbit Trajectory Vortex Anomaly waits for no man. I'm your best hope to thread the needle, and it's not over until the fat lady sings, so let's get this show on the road."

All eyes drift toward Flint Garrison, who has the final say in all mission-related administrative decisions. The general's throat-clear is menacing, and it's his twentieth. "That's not good enough, Stone. I'm not going to endanger the lives of this crew while you take an unreasonable stance on some routine, preflight medical tests."

Stone Godfrey pulls off his dark sunglasses and slams them off the conference table. I notice that his eyes are bloodshot, a conclusion my brain draws even without making direct eye contact from the other end of Central Command.

"I've spent my entire career as an astronaut preparing for this moment," Stone Godfrey says. "I'm not letting some inconsequential medical tests stand in my way. I'm going to climb aboard that spacecraft if I have to scale the Delta IV rockets with my bare hands to do it."

Maya leans in and whispers into my ear. "Do you think Stone is hiding something, or he just likes messing with the general?"

Yet another question. My brain determines that Stone's motivation includes equal measures of both factors, and I think about writing Maya a short note to tell her so, but I don't want to waste paper unnecessarily. I ignore her, and I turn my attention to Flint Garrison, whose chalky complexion turns cherry red.

"Okay, Stone, we'll have it your way," he says, "but I'm going to be watching you like a hawk, every minute of every day for the next twelve long months."

36

Everyone Knows There's No Basketball on Mars

Stone Godfrey smirks and chuckles and puts his dark sunglasses back on.

"The three of you need to take the launch tower elevator to the preflight staging center on the seventh floor and suit up," Flint Garrison says as the normal pale color returns to his face.

Maya and I head down a long hallway to the elevator. I swivel my head and take note that Stone Godfrey is following several steps behind us. Maya hits the button, and the elevator door opens, and we step inside.

And we wait and wait for Stone Godfrey to enter the elevator, but the door grows tired of waiting and begins to close. With mere inches before the door slams shut, Stone Godfrey wedges his hand inside and forces it open.

"Seven, please," Stone Godfrey says. I look at the elevator panel and discover there's only one button on it, and it has the number seven etched onto it.

"Very funny, Stone," Maya says, but I don't see any humor in our elevator ride.

Stone Godfrey releases a deep exhale, and now the inside of the elevator smells like Chett Biffmann's breath when he's sitting behind the counter at Biffmann Self-Storage sipping from an aluminum can that has the word *root* missing from it.

Maya elbows me sharply in the ribs, which takes my mind off the gross smell, because now my ribs hurt. I think about elbowing her back, or even slapping her, but I'm distracted when the elevator door swings open, and Stone Godfrey steps out.

"What'd you do that for?" I yell at Maya in protest.

"*Shh*. Sorry. Just trying to get your attention."

"How come?" And now I'm in a conversation I don't want any part of.

"You think ol' Stone Age has been drinking?"

Ugh, another question. "How would I know? Maybe the same kind of stuff Chett Biffmann drinks, I guess."

"Who's Chett Biffmann?"

And then the elevator door closes again, with us inside.

"He owns the place where I store my vintage Chevy pickup truck, and he likes to drink a lot of what I originally thought was root beer, until I found out it wasn't."

"We'll get back to that root beer thing in a moment. How is it that you own a pickup truck, but you only have a learner's permit?"

"I can't drive the pickup because Brock Decker and I dismantled it, but I can't remember why."

"Who's Brock Decker?"

The elevator door swings back open, and the mission's flight activities specialist is standing there.

And his feet are planted wide apart.

And he's cracking his knuckles.

And he's glaring at us.

"Do either of you think it's productive to be playing in the elevator like children when you should be in the preflight staging center suiting up for the mission?"

My brain determines that the flight activities specialist's question doesn't require a reply, which comes as a relief, because notepaper is now officially in short supply, and I've already done more than enough talking for one day.

But Maya has more words left. "If you'd been in here with us, you would've seen that we were conducting a simulated, two-person confined-space study, using the elevator car as a replica of the Ares Pilgrim's flight deck. It's a routine preflight analysis. I'm surprised someone with your level of experience didn't recognize it as such."

Then Maya winks at me. I don't wonder whether her wink will scar me for life, like Flint Garrison's last week in my living room, but it makes me uncomfortable enough to extract a wedge of Bazooka Joe from my backpack and pop it into my mouth.

"What else have you got in there?" the flight activities specialist asks as he points to my backpack, the tone of his voice escalating.

"Nothing. Just some stuff."

He reaches for my backpack, but I pull it away and loop one of the straps over my shoulder so that the bag is now behind me, which means I'm putting up *the blocker* in case the flight activities specialist makes an unwanted second attempt.

"Wait right here. I need to speak to General Garrison about this."

I know what it's like to get in trouble, because it's a routine occurrence for me back home, and even though I'm exactly 154 miles due north of my living room carpet, my brain determines that being in trouble is the same no matter where I am.

The flight activities specialist disappears into the elevator and returns a minute later, with Flint Garrison in tow.

"Sherman, I understand there's evidence of an attempt to smuggle some sort of unauthorized contraband onto the spacecraft. Is that true?" Flint Garrison asks me yet another question, and by now I think I've hit my limit, and he doesn't clear his throat before he asks it, leaving me to conclude that the launch window is so close at hand, there simply isn't enough time.

"The only requirement you gave me was whatever I took on the mission had to fit inside my backpack and couldn't weigh more than three pounds." Great, so now I'm in another conversation, this time with the general. "And I didn't even pack any chili mac 'n' beef, because I figured the SFC had that covered."

"General Garrison, the clock is ticking," the flight activities specialist says. "Confiscate everything, and let's be done with this nonsense."

Maya Jupiter steps between the general and me. "Look, Flint, leave the kid alone. He's only trying to get on the spaceship, which he won't be able to do with all you people breathing down his neck."

I don't expect Maya to come to my rescue, but there she is, leading with her dark, dimpled chin.

"Jupiter, you're already in enough trouble, and if we decide to bounce you from this mission, you know where your next stop will be."

Maya scowls at Flint Garrison, but she doesn't say another word.

"Young man," he says as he extends his hand, "let's have a look inside."

I hand over my backpack. I haven't been this angry since back in my living room, when the general grilled me with question after question while my dad was in the kitchen taking forever to pour him a simple glass of water.

Flint Garrison drops to one knee and empties the contents of my backpack onto the hallway carpet, revealing my pads of paper, pencils, my twelve-month supply of Bazooka Joe, magnetic travel chessboard and chess pieces, travel abacus, and Zeke's package.

"What's in there?" the flight activities specialist asks, pointing toward the manila shipping envelope that contains Zeke's diary and his two miniature square fuzzy orange basketballs connected together by a string.

"Nothing, just a letter from Zeke, my best friend." I summon up whatever courage I have left after surviving the longest week of my life. "And a couple of mini basketballs. They're for good luck. And if I can't take that package with me on this mission, then you can tell Ryker to drive me back to Los Angeles right now, because I'm not going to Mars."

Flint Garrison's face softens. It might be his version of a smile, but I can't tell for sure, because I haven't seen him do that before. "Basketballs, huh? Egad, Sherman, you can't take those with you. Everyone knows there's no basketball on Mars."

37

The Room Grows Quiet Again

"I'm telling ya, Flint, the kid's got some moxie," Stone Godfrey says from the preflight staging center doorway.

Flint Garrison starts to return my travel essentials to my backpack, but I throw myself onto the carpet and shove away his hand.

"Stop! You're doing it all wrong!"

It's a calculated risk, because I don't like to be touched, and by extension, I don't like to touch others, and Flint Garrison is already so upset with me that I don't know how he will react, but by now, I need to have things my own way, or I'm going to go out of my mind, which, on an intellectual level, won't be in the best interests of the mission.

Flint Garrison recoils. "My apologies, Sherman," he says, "I was only trying to help."

"The best way you can help Lawrence is to get out of his way." Maya isn't giving up on defending me, but I wish she would, because even though my life's goal is to be the mathematics flight specialist on the first-ever manned mission to

Mars, and being aboard the Ares Pilgrim will make my life complete, Maya might have more to lose than I do if she's scrubbed from the mission, at least based on Flint Garrison's threat moments earlier.

"How about we all calm down and get suited up," says Stone Godfrey, emerging as the unexpected voice of reason.

Flint Garrison and Maya glare at each other while I repack my backpack exactly the way I will need it for the mission. And then we follow Stone Godfrey inside the preflight staging center.

The scent of isopropyl alcohol and disinfectant hangs heavy in the air. The bright fluorescent lights cause my brain to vibrate against the inside of my skull.

Twenty-one technicians, all wearing gloves and masks and white lab coats, break into a sharp round of applause as we enter the room. *Twenty-one*. Good.

The closest I've ever been to strangers clapping in my presence was when I sat atop the bleachers at Jefferson the night Zeke's team won the Southern California regional basketball championship on a last-second miracle shot by Brock Decker.

Thinking about that makes my brain explore the reason why Brock Decker and I disassembled the pickup, but I still can't remember, and by this point, it's officially driving me nuts.

I have no idea why all these technicians are applauding. I haven't done anything beyond making a lot of SFC officials upset with me.

Stone Godfrey smiles and waves to everyone. "I love this part," he says under his breath to no one in particular.

The twenty-one technicians break off into three separate mission preparation stations. Each station has an astronaut's name and title inscribed onto a brass plaque mounted on the wall. I spot mine.

ASTRONAUT SHERMAN TUCKERMAN
ARES PILGRIM MARS MISSION
MATHEMATICS FLIGHT SPECIALIST

The familiar call-to-duty feeling returns, making my hands sweaty all over again. And I rock from side to side. And I'm too nervous to stop. And I'm pretty sure none of my seven technicians notices.

And then my brain makes a mental note to ask for permission to take the plaque home after the mission, so I can mount it on my bedroom wall.

"Right this way, Astronaut Tuckerman," says a technician as she guides me over to my prep station. "We need to get you suited up. There's not a moment to lose."

And I stand there doing all I can to maintain my composure as seven sets of gloved hands prod and poke and squeeze me into my spacesuit. My brain tells me that I must endure this process in order to board the spacecraft, but it doesn't make it any easier.

"How are you enjoying all the attention, Tuckerman?" Stone Godfrey asks from across the room.

I'm not enjoying it at all. I ignore Stone Godfrey, and I hope he doesn't repeat the question, but if he does, I'm prepared to ignore him a second time.

"Can I have your attention, please," Flint Garrison says,

and the room turns to whispers before it dissolves into silence. "I want to thank all of you for your diligence and hard work in getting us ready for this landmark, deep-space mission. It truly has been a team effort, and I know that our three brave astronauts will benefit greatly from your monumental attention to detail. I am deeply moved by your thoughtful dedication."

"Hey, Flint, don't get all mushy on us now," Stone Godfrey says. "You've got a reputation as a first-class hard-ass to maintain."

The room grows quiet again.

Flint Garrison's face glowers in a collage of color, drifting from shade to flaming shade of red before it settles back into its usual pasty flesh tone.

The general squeezes his hand into a fist and shakes it in the air. "Stone, if I were twenty years younger, I'd—"

And then Flint Garrison breaks into ear-splitting laughter that sounds as though he is releasing it from the deepest, darkest part of his soul—presuming he actually has a soul.

And one by one, I hear people exhale what sounds like sighs of relief. And then everyone in the preflight staging center roars in laughter.

I don't laugh because my brain doesn't detect anything funny. Instead, I stick my fingers in my ears and wait for the noise level to return to normal.

And then Pax Booker walks through the door, and there's a hush in the air again.

38

Let's Light This Firecracker

"It's time, people," Pax Booker says. "The Transfer Orbit Trajectory Vortex Anomaly is upon us. Astronauts, to the gateway bridge."

My team of technicians makes final adjustments to my spacesuit and secures my helmet and gloves. Then, one-by-one, they wish me good luck on the journey.

I respond by giving each person a Ryker two-finger gloved wave which, by this point, I have quite nearly perfected after a full week's practice.

Stone Godfrey and Maya Jupiter and I meet together in the center of the room and walk toward the gateway bridge leading to the Ares Pilgrim.

I stop on the platform landing to size up the spacecraft. I count three enormous orange Delta IV rockets at the base. Steam is flowing freely from pressure valves at their sides. Above the trio of rockets is the second stage, then the Ares Pilgrim space capsule.

The space capsule is constructed in modules, beginning

with the rocket propulsion system at the base, the exterior of which is lined with silica tiles that comprise the spacecraft's heat shield, which will protect the Ares Pilgrim when we re-enter the Earth's atmosphere during the final phase of the mission.

Above the rocket propulsion system are Maya's quarters, which house the medical supplies and communications equipment she'll need.

Then there's my section. I'll be calculating fuel expenditure, exhaust velocity, and Mars insertion trajectories in the area above Maya's. I'll also be eating chili mac 'n' beef there, as well as rationing sheets of paper and wedges of Bazooka Joe.

At the top of the Ares Pilgrim is the flight deck, where Stone Godfrey will pilot the spacecraft and carry out his chief-mechanic duties.

Each of the three living compartments has a windowed hatch. Mine will slide open when it's time to use the Ares Pilgrim's robotic arm to capture the sample container. I'll also use it to observe both planets during the mission.

It's a tight fit inside the capsule, with every square inch of the spacecraft's interior accounted for. And there are hatches that connect the three living quarters, and they open by swiveling the metal handle precisely one-quarter turn to the right, the same way I turn the padlock key for space 1046 at Biffmann Self-Storage. That means I'm preprogrammed to open the hatches efficiently.

And if I had a say in where the mathematics flight specialist's quarters would be located, I would've chosen either the top or bottom section, because both of those have just one hatch leading to another person, whereas my area has two, which means I'll have exponentially less privacy than Stone Godfrey and Maya.

Maya crosses the bridge and enters the Ares Pilgrim first.

"Let's do this, Tuckerman," Stone Godfrey says as he nudges me from behind.

I hustle across the bridge, being super careful not to look down because of my secret fear of heights, which I haven't told anyone about, and then my brain pauses to think about the irony of that fear as I prepare to travel thirty-five-million miles above Earth.

I step inside the Ares Pilgrim and maneuver my way to my quarters. After I stow my backpack, I slide into my crew seat and wiggle into the five-point restraint harness. I adjust the straps and lock myself into position.

I take a look around. It's a lot smaller than my bedroom, and I don't have any of my usual stuff in there, like my desk, my math textbooks, and my Carl Sagan poster.

My cabin contains the Ares Pilgrim's airlock, a small, air-tight chamber I'll enter when it's time to retrieve the orbiting sample container. The airlock will equalize the atmospheric pressure before the exterior hatch window opens and I operate the robotic arm at a precise twenty-three-degree angle as we circle Mars.

When Maya and I trained together on the airlock's operation at Vandenberg, she told me that Flint Garrison said it's her job to make sure I don't accidentally float a No. 2 pencil out the exterior hatch, but if I do, then it's her job to make sure I don't wander out of the spacecraft to retrieve it.

I'm glad she'll have my back.

I notice a laptop computer strapped to the top of a utility platform. There's a label stuck to the lid that says FOR THE CAPTAIN'S LOG, but no one has told me I have to use it. I'm going to write the log using my pads of paper and my supply of No. 2 pencils.

"I asked Flint for the largest quarters because of all my communications equipment and medical gear, but I think your cabin is bigger than mine. Can you measure it for me?"

It's Maya, poking her helmet through the bottom hatch. By now, it should be obvious to her that I don't like it when people ask me questions, but it's not, and I'm not sure whether she really wants to know whose cabin is bigger, or she's merely being polite, or just plain nosy.

I think about writing her a note, but I've already put away my backpack, and I can't reach it because I'm strapped in for liftoff.

"They're exactly the same."

"You should consider a second career in politics. I only stopped by to tell you to hang on tight. It's going to get dreadfully bumpy in this slightly larger cabin real soon."

I try not to think about what Maya says because I'm afraid the palms of my hands will sweat so much that it will cause my interior glove circuitry to short circuit, which might cause the SFC to abort the mission, and I don't even want to think about what Flint Garrison would say.

And now I'm hyperventilating, and my knees are shaking. I tell my brain to practice solving logarithmic equations, which I note are used to calculate the intensity of earthquakes and sound waves. I figure I might as well contemplate an equation that has a practical application to the life-threatening predicament I'm about to enter.

"Flight deck to Tuckerman, come in." It's Stone Godfrey, speaking to me through the radio intercom in my helmet.

"What."

"The flight surgeon advises he's picking up an elevated heart rate and disproportionate respiration levels over there. Are you all right?"

I don't like it when people ask me questions, and I don't know what the correct answer is. I employ a stall tactic I learned from Zeke—answering a question with one of my own. Zeke says it's a tricky way to buy some time if I'm ever in a jam.

Like right now.

"Can you define *all right?*"

Stone Godfrey doesn't waste time answering. "Yeah, here's a definition for you: Quit stalling, or I'm coming over there to find out for myself, and I guarantee your heart rate and respiration levels will rise even more while I investigate."

Stone Godfrey threatening to invade my quarters makes beads of sweat form on my forehead.

Then I remember something Dr. Tidewater taught me that I've been reminding myself of all week: I take in three super-big gulps of air, and then I practice finding random square roots by prime factorization until my breathing stabilizes.

"I'm good, Stone. Let's light this firecracker."

39

I Just Want to Go Home

I have no idea what possesses me to say those seven words. Maybe it's something an astronaut is supposed to blurt out moments before he is catapulted to the cosmos strapped inside a tin can sitting atop a massive fireball.

And then my brain determines that I'm so nervous, certain words are flying out of my mouth that I've never said before. And since I haven't said many words in my lifetime, the likelihood of my saying something new in the seconds before liftoff, in purely probabilistic terms, is high.

"You hang in there, Tuckerman," Stone Godfrey says. "I've got the wheel. All you have to do is grind the numbers, and you'll be a math nerd at the JPL getting coffee and donuts for the scientists again before you know it."

I'm about to point out that I *am* one of the scientists and that I've never fetched refreshments for anyone, when I hear Pax Booker's voice come through the radio intercom in my helmet. "Ares Pilgrim, we are at T-minus five minutes and counting. We are go for launch."

I grip onto the padded arms of my crew seat. Even though I cannot see my knuckles inside my fancy space gloves, I know they're white.

"Hey, Lawrence, this radio intercom system enables any one of us to speak directly to another crew member aboard the spacecraft."

Maya's tendency to engage in needless conversation is ill-timed and unwelcome. "Shut up. I'm trying to concentrate."

"What if I told you I've hacked the intercom system. Heard your entire conversation with Stone Godfrey. Guy's ever so slightly full of himself, which I suppose is a positive trait for the person flying this thing."

"You hacked it?"

"Yeah, piece of cake. Hey, remind me to tell you the real reason why I was selected for this mission. It's kind of top secret, but I will grant you special dispensation to hear the details."

"Ares Pilgrim, we are at T-minus three minutes and counting. We are go for launch."

My brain makes a notation to avoid circling back with Maya for the details of her selection. And then I think about all the things that can possibly go wrong once the countdown begins.

Wait, the countdown.

Pax Booker never got back to me on my request to do the countdown.

I glance at the left sleeve of my spacesuit, where there's a tight grouping of radio intercom switches assembled in a circle at the top of my forearm. I push the button with the words Mission Control on it.

"Sherman Tuckerman to Pax Booker, come in."

"Tuckerman, what are you doing over there? We're less than three minutes till launch." It's Stone Godfrey, and he's pissed. My brain determines that the Mission Control button also transmits to the Ares Pilgrim flight deck.

"Hey, Lawrence," Maya says. "What's up?"

Apparently, it sends my voice signal to the communications analyst, as well.

"Sherman, this is Pax Booker. What's on your mind, son?"

I ask Pax Booker about the status of my request to do the countdown. "Remember, I'm uniquely qualified to perform this duty."

"Sherman, I'm afraid we're unable to accommodate your request." Pax Booker doesn't leave any wiggle room in his words.

"You told me you were going to figure something out."

When I say that, my voice is choked with tears, and now I'm in a conversation with the flight director again, and both my crewmates are listening in, and I'm hyperventilating for the second time, and my entire body is shaking, and I just want to go home.

"Why can't you understand? I NEED TO DO THE COUNTDOWN!"

40

Everything Is Up to Stone Godfrey

There is a long, uncomfortable silence before I hear a response from Mission Control.

"Ares Pilgrim, we are at T-minus two minutes and counting," Pax Booker says. "We are go for launch."

There's another pause, then Pax Booker adds, "We didn't forget about you, Sherman. I'm trying to work it out with the team. I need you to stand by."

There's no time to practice algebraic equations, or dwell on my friendship rankings, or recall any sage words from the writings of Carl Sagan. I need to sit and sweat and wait for a decision from the flight director.

Stone Godfrey breaks the silence. "C'mon, Pax, it's not that big a deal. Kid's got a ton of moxie to even ask. You geniuses need to let Tuckerman do the countdown, and then let's get this flying cigar tube off the ground."

More silence from Mission Control. Then Pax Booker's

voice cuts through the stillness: "Ares Pilgrim, we are at T-minus sixty seconds and counting. We are go for launch."

I'm not prepared for the disappointment of having my request to do the countdown denied, although Stone Godfrey coming to my defense is lessening the blow.

Pax Booker radios the Ares Pilgrim: "Sherman, we've worked it out. I'm going to give you the high sign at T-minus fifteen seconds. You'll take over the countdown beginning at ten seconds. Copy?"

"Copy."

I let go of a huge breath. Chalk up another life goal about to be met. If I could find a way to tell Zeke and Nathan right now, I would.

"Ares Pilgrim, we are at T-minus thirty seconds and counting." Pax Booker's voice is strong and resolute. "We are go for launch."

"Get ready, Lawrence. This is your moment to shine," Maya says, and I'm hoping she's only talking to me and not everyone else.

"Ares Pilgrim, we are at T-minus fifteen seconds and counting. We are go for launch. Astronaut Tuckerman, you take it from here."

I feel my crew seat vibrating as I count down the next five seconds in my brain before pressing the Mission Control radio intercom button.

"Ten. Nine. Eight. Seven. Six. Five. Four. Three. Two—"

Before I can complete the countdown, a thunderous, deafening roar invades my helmet.

And then the Ares Pilgrim bucks and soars to the heavens.

And my heart is racing. And I'm afraid it's going to explode.

And I can feel every square inch of my body trembling. I've never been so petrified in my entire life. My brain knows that going home isn't an option, but it can't keep me from screaming at the top of my lungs.

"Make it stop! I want to go home!"

And then I hear Pax Booker's voice cutting through the wall of unearthly sound. "Ares Pilgrim, you have cleared the tower."

"Aaaaaaaaaaaaaaaaaaaaaaaaaaaaaaaaaaaaaaaah!"

Seconds tick. My brain reminds me that the tremendous G-force I'm experiencing is due to the vector sum of all non-electromagnetic and non-gravitational forces acting against my freedom to move. And the harder my body presses back into my crew seat horizontally, the more my bones feel like they're being crushed from the inside.

"Breathe, Lawrence." It's Maya, no doubt trying to calm me down.

I feel the spacecraft perform a pitch-and-roll maneuver. It means Stone Godfrey's hands are at the controls, and it makes my hands feel less clammy.

Moments later, I sense the spacecraft decelerating, and then I'm thrown forward against the straps of my restraint harness, which shoves my stomach into my throat and plasters my nose up against the inside of my helmet. I know from the debriefings that it means the fuel within the first-stage rockets is depleted.

I hear an explosion coming from the second stage. It means

the bolts that attach the first stage to the second have deto-
nated, jettisoning the first stage from the Ares Pilgrim.

And then I hear the second-stage engines ignite. And then
the Ares Pilgrim is thrust even higher as it accelerates with
tremendous force now that the spacecraft is no longer bur-
dened with the dead weight of the first stage. It almost feels
as if another space vehicle has just rear-ended us as I'm
smashed back into my seat again.

The ride is choppy. My body is bouncing around like it's
duct-taped to the inside of a paint shaker.

I wish I could be with Nathan or Zeke right now so we
could sit together in silence and chew Bazooka Joe and stare
off into space. That always helps to calm me down back home
in Los Angeles, but it's not an option right now.

"Mission Control to Ares Pilgrim, come in." It's Pax
Booker. I hope nothing is going wrong.

"Stone here. Go, Mission Control."

"Commander, you are T-minus two minutes from entering
the Transfer Orbit Trajectory Vortex Anomaly. Copy?"

"Copy that, Pax. Time to bring this bucking bronco into
the barn."

I glance outside my hatch window. I can see the curvature
of the earth, and behind it, the inky blackness of the sky.
From this vantage point, I wonder why boundaries and bor-
ders matter so much to everyone. From way up here, everything seems interconnected.

I feel the spacecraft tilt slightly and alter its course.

"You're only going to get one shot at this, Stone. Make it
good."

"Copy that, Pax. It'll be like driving a golf cart to the nineteenth hole."

"Hey, ya think ol' Stone Age is overconfident?" It's Maya, coming over the radio intercom. Her timing is lousy, as usual.

"I hope I'm the only one you're talking to right now."

"Who's the communications expert around here?"

"Shut up. I need to concentrate."

"On what?" Maya asks. "We don't have anything to do until Captain Stoner steers us into the secret expressway."

Maya is right. The spacecraft's computers are doing most of the heavy lifting. At this point of the mission, Maya and I are like passengers on an ultra-fast-moving, noisy public transit bus. And Stone Godfrey, in the role of Rigoberto, only needs to react if something goes wrong.

"Ares Pilgrim, you are T-minus one minute from insertion."

"Jupiter, Tuckerman, enjoy the idle time while you've got it. Once we've entered TOTVA, you're going to be busy."

My brain notes that Stone Godfrey has just converted the Transfer Orbit Trajectory Vortex Anomaly to an acronym. I don't challenge him on it, but chances are if we all play a game of Scrabble during mission downtime, and Stone Godfrey tries to slip in TOTVA, Maya would reject it summarily out of hand. Realizing that we probably don't have a Scrabble set with us makes me also realize that I have no idea whether any of my fellow crew members know how to play chess. I may end up playing a lot of games against myself.

"Ares Pilgrim, you are T-minus thirty seconds from insertion."

"Hold on, you two. I honestly don't know what to expect here." Stone Godfrey's voice lacks its usual swagger when he says that.

I grip my hands onto the arms of my crew seat again. I know that my knuckles must be even whiter than before.

And I catch a glimpse of Earth through the hatch window, and it's a shade of blue I've never experienced before, and parts of the planet are covered by swirling white clouds whose patterns seem to be governed by a set of mathematical properties all their own, and now I can see the curve of the horizon, and beyond it, the blackness of space.

Pax Booker's voice cuts through the radio intercom, this time for the countdown. I don't ask to do it, and he doesn't offer me the opportunity.

"Ten. Nine. Eight. Seven. Six. Five. Four. Three. Two. One—"

And now everything is up to Stone Godfrey.

I hear a barely audible whooshing sound. And then everything goes quiet. And then the spacecraft quivers, and it gains speed.

"Hold on!" It's Stone Godfrey, issuing an unnecessary command.

Then all at once, the interior of my quarters goes dark, including my instrument panel.

If I were able to pry one of my hands from the arm of the crew seat and hold it in front of my face, I would not be able to see it.

There's not a single photon of light to be found.

41

I'm Beginning to Feel Like a Real Astronaut

The sound of the lower hatch opening breaks the silence. And then there's a shuffling noise, and I sense someone or something moving toward me.

"What's happening up here?"

I don't like it when people ask me questions, especially ones that serve no purpose and don't require an intelligent answer.

"Same as down there. Waiting for the lights to come back on."

It's too dark to see the radio intercom switches on the sleeve of my spacesuit, but I'm able to use my other hand to locate the buttons. I push them. Nothing happens.

"Protocol requires us to stick to our posts and await instructions from the flight engineer," Maya says.

"Then why are you in my quarters?"

"Two reasons. The communications gear is dead, and I like to question authority."

I loosen the crew seat restraint harness, and I reach my arm to the exact spot where I stowed my backpack.

I pull out a wedge of bubblegum and attempt to pop it in my mouth, but it bonks off the faceplate of my helmet. I don't hear the bubblegum hit the floor, which means we must now be weightless inside the spacecraft.

"I took off my helmet and gloves after we jettisoned the first stage." Maya must have heard my unsuccessful Bazooka Joe attempt. "The flight dynamics scientist covered it during training. Space travel knowledge comes from paying close attention during space travel college."

"There's no such thing as space travel college."

Just then, the spacecraft's lights flicker back on, and I see my Bazooka Joe wedge floating around the cabin. I unlatch my helmet and remove it, and then I take off my gloves, and I grab the errant bubblegum and remove the wrapper, and I shove the calming pink sweetness into my mouth.

I hear the upper hatch opening. In slides Stone Godfrey, and now we're about to have a three-person conversation in a confined space designed for one.

"Darnedest thing I ever saw," Stone Godfrey says. "When we entered TOTVA, the entire spacecraft shut down. All systems—everything, all at once. I had no ability to control anything. It was weird, but I wasn't worried because it was like someone or something was guiding the Ares Pilgrim into the vortex anomaly."

Stone Godfrey's words—those of a seasoned and decorated astronaut—cause my heart to beat faster. I feel sweat forming on my upper lip.

"Maybe we need to inspect the flight deck's water supply," Maya says.

I wait for Stone Godfrey to react, but he doesn't. Instead, he issues new orders.

"Jupiter, reestablish communication with Mission Control and get me Pax Booker on the blower. Then set up a series of back channels in case something else knocks us offline. I want options at my disposal."

"Aye-aye, Captain."

"Tuckerman, I need you to calculate the Ares Pilgrim's fuel expenditure to this point, then run a six-month projected sequence of exhaust velocity scenarios to assist us in maximizing fuel efficiency as we exit TOTVA and approach Mars insertion trajectory. Check?"

The SFC's training week has drilled the correct response in me. I don't even pause before responding: "Check."

"I've got to run some tests in the flight deck. Maybe I can figure out what happened to us back there."

Stone Godfrey makes his way back to his quarters. And then Maya slides back through her hatch and begins her work. And I pull paper and a pencil from my backpack and jot down the readings from the gauges on my instrument panel. And then I get to work crunching the numbers.

And for the first time since meeting with Flint Garrison and Dr. Murakami in my living room, I'm contributing to something greater than me.

I'm beginning to feel like a real astronaut.

42

Discretion Is My
Middle Name

I run my six-month exhaust velocity calculations. My brain is able to process the data efficiently, without assistance from my travel abacus.

I write my findings on a piece of paper from my pad, and I fold it in half. And then I push the flight engineer button on my sleeve.

"Yes, what is it, Tuckerman?"

"I've got the six-month projected sequence of exhaust velocity scenarios you asked for."

"Already? Bring it up."

I open the hatch to the flight deck, and I float in through the opening, and then I use the overhead handrails to grapple my way to Stone Godfrey's crew seat, where he's leafing through the Ares Pilgrim's operations manual.

I hand my piece of paper to Stone Godfrey. "Here's the data you requested."

"Wait, that's everything?"

Stone Godfrey is questioning my work. Did I run the numbers correctly?

"It's all there."

He examines my findings while I take a quick look around his quarters. The first thing I notice is that the main console has more instruments on it than mine. And there are personal items strewn about the cabin—a golf magazine and a picture of Stone Godfrey in a spacesuit standing alongside two young people who I presume are his children.

And there's an amber-colored pill container Velcroed to the top of the console. Stone Godfrey must see me staring at it, because he leans forward and secures the container inside a drawer.

"This is some good work, Tuckerman."

I don't respond to Stone Godfrey because he doesn't ask me a question.

"The schedule says we've got fifteen minutes until your next assignment. Go ahead and do whatever it is you math geniuses do in your spare time."

I return to my quarters, and I put all my stuff away so that everything is where it belongs, and then I pull Zeke's package from my backpack, and I reread the part of his letter that establishes his diary's principal guidelines.

I know how essential rules are to you. I'm going to impose one on you myself. You must not read this story until you are en route to Mars.

After everything I've witnessed over the past week—Flint

Garrison's obnoxious throat-clearing and improbable Mars mission scenarios, and Dr. Murakami's bubblegum-shaped inkblots, and Ryker's sunglasses, and Maya Jupiter's sudden possible friendship despite her penchant for talking too much, especially when over-describing her own intestinal illness events, and Stone Godfrey's mostly capable but sometimes shaky leadership—it's finally time to read Zeke's record of all the time we spent together since we met at McDerney.

I understand that the mission will become increasingly more complex after I retrieve the sample container, because returning safely from Mars is exponentially more challenging than it is to arrive there. It is therefore in the best interests of the mission that I complete my reading of Zeke's diary just prior to sample container retrieval.

So I count the total number of pages in the diary, and then I divide that number by 182, which is the number of days Flint Garrison identified as the outbound transit time from Earth to Mars, and that tells me precisely how many pages per day I can read.

And now that I've set the ground rules, I remove the two fuzzy orange basketballs from Zeke's envelope. And then I pull a roll of silvery gray duct tape from my utility drawer.

My brain recalls that duct tape has been stowed on-board every space mission since the Gemini program began in 1961, and now the Ares Pilgrim mission is a part of duct tape's space travel history.

I tear off a small piece of duct tape, and I fasten the two fuzzy basketballs to the ceiling of my cabin using the string that's interconnecting them. And now I have two square fuzzy basketballs bobbing around weightlessly in my quarters, which means I will have good luck for the remainder of the mission, at least according to Zeke's neighbor, Mrs. Fenner.

And now I'm ready to begin reading.

I flip past Zeke's letter to the first page of his diary.

> *I pushed open the cafeteria doors so hard, they swung back into me and knocked me on my butt.*
>
> *Great way to start a story about two friends, right? But that's exactly how it happened.*
>
> *Most kids in the cafeteria at Ernest T. McDerney Continuation School didn't notice my less-than-dignified entrance. The few who witnessed it snickered and went back to their lunches.*

I remember noticing Zeke's entrance. I was in the cafeteria eating a bowl of chili mac 'n' beef at the time. But I wasn't one of the kids who snickered.

"Are you measuring your cabin?" It's Maya again, poking her head through the bottom hatch. Her long hair sways above her head, dark and wavy and weightless.

"No, I'm being interrupted during my well-earned quarter hour of downtime assigned to me by the flight engineer."

"I like how you've decorated the place," she says as she nods her hair toward the ceiling. "What are you reading?"

"Zeke Archer's diary. Zeke is on the basketball team at the University of Kansas. He mailed me the diary shortly after he arrived on campus."

What just happened? Why am I offering up more information than Maya asked for?

"He's your best friend, right? He'd have to be to let you

read his diary. And wow, KU hoops. Zeke must have some serious skills on the hardwood."

I am not prepared to respond to Maya's observations, especially the part where she shows apparent knowledge of basketball. I consider drafting a list of my best friends and handing it to her to give her a sense of the bigger picture, but my brain rejects the idea because I'm not ready to introduce Nathan into our conversations, and also because that would be a questionable use of my limited paper supply.

So I ignore Maya instead.

"Hey, I've got an idea. Why don't we get Zeke on the phone?"

My brain instantly recognizes Maya's suggestion as a ridiculous idea, because it's impossible and also a violation of mission flight rules.

"Shut up."

"No, I'm serious. Let's get Zeke on the phone. I'm sure he'd love to hear from you, and you can tell him you're reading his diary."

I can't tell Zeke I'm reading his diary. If I did, I'd be disclosing that I'm en route to Mars, and since the Ares Pilgrim mission is top secret, that's not an option, and I'm also discovering that Maya can be excessively self-assertive.

I counteract her pushiness by returning to my established but less-than-effective method of dealing with her tendency to talk too much.

"Shut up."

"You don't have to tell him you're on a spacecraft bound for Mars. Let's just call him and say hello."

I'm so frustrated that I write Maya a note from my dwindling supply of paper.

> *It is simply not possible to place a phone call to Zeke's cell phone or the landline inside his dormitory from a spacecraft that is beyond Earth's atmosphere and hurtling toward Mars.*

"You're underestimating me again, Sherman Tuckerman. Are you remembering why I was selected for this mission?"

"No, because you never told me."

I'm totally out of ways to tell Maya no. I give up and jot down the number to Zeke's landline, because if by some miracle she can get Zeke on the phone, the connection would, I estimate, likely be better on his hardwired dorm room phone than on his cell.

"Here it is. Do you promise not to get us in trouble?"

"Discretion is my middle name."

I note that Maya's attempt to make a promise lacks any sort of legitimacy.

She returns to her quarters. And a moment later, I hear static drifting through the hatch, followed by a series of short electronic tones. And then her voice comes across the radio intercom on my instrument panel.

"Mr. Archer, please hold for Mr. Tuckerman."

43

Jupiter, This Has Your Fingerprints All Over It

"What, you have a secretary now? How much are they paying you at the JPL?"

Maya drifts back into my quarters. I can't believe she got Zeke on the phone. I'm so stunned that all I can do is stare at the instrument panel in disbelief.

"Lawrence, are you there? I don't have much time. I'm running out the door to the Fieldhouse training room to get my ankles taped. We're playing Tennessee State tonight, and I think Coach is going to insert me into the lineup in the second half to give our starting point guard a breather. Lawrence? Say something."

"It's a student internship. It's unpaid."

"There you are. I was only kidding about the secretary thing. Hey, who was that woman? And how come this line is so staticky? It sounds like you're calling me from the North Pole."

My brain recalls that the North Pole is the northernmost point on Earth, or more specifically, the point in the Northern Hemisphere where the planet's axis of rotation meets its surface. That means Zeke's North Pole reference, while no doubt made in jest, is conceptually somewhat vaguely accurate.

"I'm definitely calling long distance."

"What's up, buddy?"

I freeze again. I'm afraid to say anything, because I might accidentally violate the parental release of liability and non-disclosure agreement that my dad signed, which precludes me from discussing the Ares Pilgrim mission with anyone. One slip-up, and I'm done for. My dad, too.

"Lawrence, say something."

Maya is the pushiest person I know.

"Who's that woman?"

I panic. "It's not a woman, it's Maya Jupiter, and she's sort of a friend, and you may have noticed that her last name is identical to one of the planets, and we're not in an extremely shallow elliptical orbit around Mars or anything like that, and I really called to tell you that I received your diary."

Why am I always saying too much when I'm around Maya?

"What diary?"

"The one you sent me."

"I don't know what you're talking about, bud. I never sent you a diary. I don't even keep a diary."

"Don't you remember? It arrived in the same package with Mrs. Fenner's two miniature square fuzzy orange basketballs connected together by a string."

"Yeah, I remember sending you those. Mrs. Fenner told me

they'd bring good luck. I figured you might need some when you and that cement-head Brock Decker try to put the old Chevy back together. Maybe someday you'll tell me why you guys took it apart to begin with."

I still can't remember why Brock Decker and I dismantled the pickup truck, and by this point, I'm wondering if I ever will.

"Who's Brock Decker?"

I wish Maya would stay out of the conversation, but she seems incapable of minding her own business.

"Is that Maya Jupiter? Hey, what's it like hanging out with His Eminence, Lord of the Numbers?"

"Lawrence and I just met, but we've already become fast friends."

Fast friends? What in the world is she talking about? And now Maya has me asking questions inside my own head.

"Lawrence tells me you're on the basketball team at KU. I think that's fantastic! It must be awesome playing in such a storied venue as Allen Fieldhouse. I'm guessing Coach Worth has you guys working on your transition defense after the way last season ended, with that tough loss to Bradley University in the first round of the NCAA tournament. And I'll bet the Jayhawk mascot is fun to be around. When I played basketball in middle school, our mascot was a turtle—not nearly as cool, and it moved a lot slower, but I played point guard, just like you. Lawrence tells me you guys are best friends. I think that's great. I have lots of best friends, and we're always going out and doing fun stuff together, like going to basketball games and talking about space travel."

This conversation is getting away from me, and now I'm worried that Mission Control might be listening in, and it's only a matter of time before Stone Godfrey comes barreling through the upper hatch to read us the riot act.

"Anyway, I have to be going now," I say. "And thanks for sending Curtis and Stretch to help with the pickup truck."

"The guys said you turned down their offer."

"Scheduling conflict." Technically, that's true. "I've put the Chevy's reassembly back onto the docket for a year from now."

"A whole year? You must really like riding the bus."

I really do like riding the bus, and I'm glad Zeke doesn't probe further.

"Hey, when the truck is roadworthy again, why don't the two of you drive to Kansas for a game? I could leave you a couple of tickets at the will call window."

Good grief. That's not a good idea at all. "I'll make a mental note."

"If I get a triple double tonight, Maya, I'm dedicating it to you."

I've never heard Zeke dedicate anything to anyone. How did Maya get him to do that?

Maya pushes a button on my instrument panel, and then I hear a 2,000 Hz electronic tone, and then the phone line goes dead.

"Wow, a dedication. What an honor."

I ignore Maya, and then I decide to make my initial entry into the Captain's Log. I retrieve my pad and a pencil from my backpack to summarize the three things I've learned in the past four minutes:

Captain's Log—Ares Pilgrim Mars Mission, Day 1
1. Maya's level of skill as a communications analyst is off the charts.
2. Zeke not remembering that he wrote and mailed me a lengthy handwritten diary is weird and troubling.

I hope the observations I'm making are what Stone Godfrey had in mind when he assigned the Captain's Log to me.

I hear the upper hatch turning, and Stone Godfrey sticks his head through the opening.

"What are you two doing down there? Mission Control radioed to say there's been some sort of unauthorized activity going on with the communications system. Jupiter, this has your fingerprints all over it."

3. It's impossible to get anything past Pax Booker, or even Stone Godfrey.

44

Mars Was the Way
Better Option

We're in big trouble, I just know it. My body is shaking so much that my mouth is unable to form any words.

"I was performing a linear subcarrier bandwidth attenuation assessment," Maya says.

I have no way to verify the accuracy or truthfulness of her statement, which is just as well, because my brain tells me she's most likely making it up.

"It's a routine acoustic soundwave evaluation performed by professional communications analysts, Stone. I'll be sure to put it in my report."

Stone Godfrey shakes his head and returns to his quarters, slamming the hatch behind him.

"Later—got important research to conduct," Maya says.

I don't respond because she doesn't ask me a question. Instead, I stare at my instrument panel, pretending to be contemplating a mathematical calculation, like how many minutes will transpire before Stone Godfrey or Maya invade my quarters again.

She disappears through the lower hatch, and I'm glad she's leaving because as long as I'm *not* with her, my chances of getting in trouble with Mission Control are reduced dramatically.

But then her hatch opens again.

"Almost forgot to tell you why I was selected for the mission. Got a minute?"

My brain analyzes my three best options, given the circumstances of being cooped up with her inside a space capsule for the next twelve months, and then I make a quick log entry:

> Captain's Log—Ares Pilgrim Mars Mission, Day 1 (continued)
> 1. I can ignore Maya.
> 2. I can answer Maya's question by saying no and hope she goes away.
> 3. I can answer Maya's question by saying yes and hope that she's only curious about whether I have a minute to listen to her talk. After that, she will hopefully go back to her quarters to conduct research that doesn't include making any more phone calls.

Then I answer her. "I guess." I opt for a compromise position, a concept Dr. Tidewater taught me that bridges the gap between conflicting actions by means of mutual concession.

"Great," Maya says as she floats about the cabin. "Built

my first transistor radio when I was two years old. My parents wouldn't let me use a soldering iron, so the butler helped me."

"You had a butler?" And now I'm dragged into yet another conversation with Maya that I don't want to be in.

"Oh, yes. Jarvis was a wonderful man and an electrical engineering genius. His great-grandmother's next-door neighbor's second cousin's uncle was Mignani, butler to Guglielmo Marconi."

"Wait. *The* Guglielmo Marconi, the Italian electrical engineer who, at the end of the nineteenth century and with the help of his mysterious butler, Mignani, invented the first commercially successful radio transmission system? The man who held the patent rights for radio and went on to win the Nobel Prize in Physics in 1909?"

"Yes, the one and only—and the butler connection was obviously a strong one."

I'm fighting the urge to be fascinated by Maya's near-mythical connecting of the dots that serve as the foundation for her early days in radio communications.

"You were about to tell me how you were selected for the mission, remember?" I try to keep her on track so the conversation can end sooner than later, but now Maya has *me* asking a question, and I just want to be alone in my quarters, but I am strangely compelled to see where it all leads.

"When I was fourteen, my parents sent me off to Sorbonne University in Paris to study astrophysics and medical science under a high school foreign-exchange program arranged by the French government. A year later, I dropped out and hitchhiked across Europe with Émilie and Héloïse, two classmates who shared my keen interest in radio communications and teenage rebellion. While traveling through Luxembourg, we stopped in the city of Grevenmacher, where we constructed a pirate radio station and disguised it inside an abandoned hay barn on the outskirts of town."

Astrophysics and medical science as a high school student at the most prestigious university in all of France? A pirate radio station in a hay barn in Luxembourg? Is she serious? I'm wondering if it's possible that this story may never end.

"Then what happened?"

"We broadcast day and night, demanding that the prime minister's official residence and office in the Hôtel de Bourgogne be converted into a student-run youth hostel. That's when members of the Grand Ducal Police, which is Luxembourg's national police service, triangulated our position and arrested us for violation of the International Broadcasting Offences Act, an amendment to the Wireless Telegraphy Act of 1926. As you can see, my roots in the communications field run deep."

The next noise I hear is not Maya's voice concluding her story about how she was selected for the Mars sample recovery mission. Instead, it's my stomach growling, a reminder that I'm twenty-eight minutes late for my chili mac 'n' beef.

But her story is so intriguing—bordering on bizarre and outlandish—that I mentally set aside my hunger.

"Then what happened?"

"When word of our arrest made it back to the family compound in Beverly Hills, Father reached out to none other than Flint Garrison for assistance. Father and the general served in the Air Force together and have been old friends for decades."

That explains why Maya would occasionally refer to the general by his first name during training week. I'm hoping the story ends here, but my brain can't stop itself from forging ahead.

"What happened next?"

"Father and the general met up at Vandenberg and piloted a decommissioned Boeing C-17 Globemaster III Air Force military transport plane to Wiltz-Noertrange Airfield, then drove a rented Vauxhall Movano van to Grand Ducal Police headquarters to secure our release from custody, coincidentally on my sixteenth birthday. Obviously, cake and ice cream were out of the question."

That's unbelievable. My brain concedes that my life has been dull compared to Maya's, until now. And it leaves me wondering how we're ever going to get anything done when she's always jabbering. Half of me wants her to stop talking and go back to her quarters and not come out for several weeks, but the other half of me needs her to keep going.

"Then what?"

"I'm glad you asked. General Garrison succeeded in getting the charges dropped, but the arrangement was conditional, because at the same time that the Strategic Federation Council's plans for the Ares Pilgrim's launch were being finalized, the veteran military astronaut tabbed to serve as mission field scientist was run over by a runaway combine harvester in the middle of a cornfield in Kossuth County, Iowa."

Run over by a *what*?

"That really happened?"

"Absolutely. And that's when Father and the general reached an accord with the chief of the Grand Ducal Police that I would perform a full year of community service for the SFC, with the understanding that if I violated any part of the agreement, they would hand me back to law enforcement authorities in Luxembourg, and I would do hard time at the UNISEC, a juvenile detention center in nearby Dreiborn, until I turned eighteen. Needless to say, I've more or less stayed out of trouble since then, because Mars was the way better option."

Wow, what an amazing story, and told in such vivid detail. I can't believe Maya took me into her confidence like that. She must really trust me.

I decide to make another log entry:

Captain's Log—Ares Pilgrim Mars Mission, Day 1 (continued again)

Maya's decision to accept the mission makes total sense. I would have selected Mars over going to the slammer too.

45

Leave the Kid Alone

I'm sitting in my crew seat processing everything Maya has just told me, wondering how on Earth anyone can have such a wildly strange and exciting life.

And I'm at a loss as to how to respond, which is fine, because I've already said too much in our brief time together aboard the spacecraft, and I just want to get back to Zeke's diary.

"What about you, Sherman Tuckerman? How about you tell me why you were selected for this mission. Better yet, why don't *I* tell *you* what *I* heard through the grapevine."

My brain determines that Maya didn't hear something about me through a fruit-bearing vine. Instead, she's referring to the circulation of rumors and unofficial information, which is troublesome, because the only people who know the actual reason for my assignment are SFC officials and my dad.

"The grapevine?" And now I'm encouraging Maya to continue talking, and I'm afraid this conversation might not end until I excuse myself to deploy the Ares Pilgrim's robotic arm to retrieve the orbiting sample container six months from now.

"I heard from a reliable source that shortly before Carl Sagan died ten years ago, he amended the official charter of the Planetary Society, the organization he cofounded in 1980 to rally public support for space exploration and the search for extraterrestrial life."

What is she talking about? "Carl Sagan amended the Planetary Society's charter shortly before he died?"

"Yes, I know it sounds super crazy, but rumor is the famed planetary scientist and astrophysicist covertly modified the organization's written constitution to include what he referred to as the Tuckerman Clause."

"The *what*?"

"The Tuckerman Clause. It assigns to any member of your family, in perpetuity, first right of refusal to join the crew of any manned spaceflight to any planet in the solar system. Best I can tell, it alludes to a professional relationship Sagan had with an unknown member of the extended Tuckerman clan."

And now I think I'm on a mission to Mars with a crazy person. "That's not true!" I don't want to talk anymore, but Maya has it all wrong.

"Oh, really?"

"The Tuckerman family and Carl Sagan have never *ever* crossed paths. The SFC selected me for this mission because of the mathematical ingenuity I demonstrated throughout my student internship with the JPL. In fact, Professor Bellwether himself recommended me for the assignment."

How did Maya get me to say all those things? I've never told that to anyone.

"*Hmm*, must've somehow got it wrong. I stand corrected."

And with that, Maya retreats to her quarters, and now I have even more questions, but they will have to wait, because I need to read my daily allotment of Zeke's pages before she has a chance to peek her head through the hatch again.

I flip open the diary to where I left off.

The sound of activity erupting from a far corner of the cafeteria caught my attention. It came from Lawrence's table. This was a regular occurrence at lunch.

I'm interrupted again, this time by the sound of the upper hatch opening.

"What's all the racket down there, Tuckerman? I thought I ordered you to take some R and R."

Great, now Maya gets me in trouble again.

"I took it as more of a suggestion than an order." Maya's influence has me sticking up for myself for a change.

"Don't make me come down there again."

"Count on it, Skipper."

I return to the diary.

Lawrence was a fourteen-year-old junior. I figured he must've skipped a few grades prior to McDerney.

Zeke is right about that. I went right from fifth grade to middle school.

He arrived daily at the cafeteria carrying a metal

travel case containing a bowl and a spoon, a thermos of
hot water, and the kind of foil-wrapped food brick you'd
carry in your backpack while boarding the Space
Shuttle.

Zeke recognized my astronaut training meal regimen from
our early days together at McDerney. That's a true friend.

This made Lawrence a target for thugs and bullies,
meaning nearly the entire student body, especially McDer-
ney's very own cement-head, Brock Decker.
Brock was the sum total of the worst parts of all the
campus felons you never wanted to meet, bound together
by arrogance, faulty judgment, and an expensive haircut.

Zeke sure has an economical way of summing up Brock
Decker's finer qualities.

Brock was shouting at Lawrence. I sprang to my feet,
but Curtis blocked my path. "Bro, I've seen that look on
your face before," Curtis said, referring to the precise mo-
ment before I punched out someone at the city finals.

I was in the arena at the top of the bleachers when that
happened. Zeke's poor judgment cost him his full-ride schol-
arship to KU.

I moved Curtis aside and arrived at Lawrence's table
just as Brock was preparing to separate Lawrence from

his lunch. Lawrence's lips trembled, but he never looked up.

"Leave the kid alone," I said.

I remember that. It was the precise moment at McDerney when my best-friend sum total instantly shot up from zero to one.

46

My Life Hasn't Been the Same Since I Read It

I plunge myself deeper into the day's allotment of pages, taking in Zeke's observations and insights about basketball and life, until these words stop me dead in my tracks:

> Lawrence handed me a folded-up piece of paper. I opened it. His handwriting was measured and precise, the letters carefully formed and slanted to the right. I read the note silently:
>
> They're planning to take the game away.
>
> "Who is? What game?"
>
> "Basketball," Lawrence said. Yes, he actually said the word before writing me yet another note:
>
> The 7th Dimension, an interdimensional energy being. Says it was the force behind the creation of basketball on

Earth. Says it has decided to take the game away, and it's your fault. If you're planning to shoot around with your friends today, you'd better step on it.

The 7th Dimension. That has a familiar ring to it. I have a vague sense that it's important, but all I have in my brain are foggy memories.

And then my stomach reminds me that I'm late for my astronaut training meal, although it's not a training meal anymore, because I'm no longer in training. I'm a real astronaut.

Being weightless makes food preparation and consumption much more challenging than it is on Earth, but my survival instincts are strong.

My cabin has a galley that's specially equipped with a rehydration station, where I insert my package of chili mac 'n' beef and add hot water. Then I squish the food all around inside the package to mix it up, and then I cut off the top of it with a pair of scissors that are tethered to the galley wall, and then I eat my meal with a spoon, being careful not to let any of it escape into the cabin.

The soothing taste makes me homesick, but it passes quickly because I have additional pages to read today. I hope Zeke includes more info about the 7th Dimension.

Within a matter of hours, visible signs appeared that seemed to indicate the sport of basketball was ceasing to exist. First, there was Lawrence's crazy talk about the game being taken away.

I can see why Zeke drew that conclusion. My note sounds like utter nonsense.

Then the rec center basketball court's rims and nets vanished. After that, my prized leather basketball disappeared from its customary spot in my closet. When I asked Lawrence about it at school the next day, he offered this explanation: "Yes, I know. It's starting."

I remember saying those words, but I can't recall why. I turn the page.

"And you know this how?" I asked.

Lawrence didn't answer. He simply pointed to his pocket protector, the one with the seven No. 2 pencils, graphite tips pointing skyward like a row of tiny missiles ready for launch.

"So the pencils are telling you," I said, challenging my friend to stop being so cryptic and just spill the beans.

Lawrence wrote me another note:

I use my pencils to intercept and decode their communiqués. The 7th Dimension brought basketball to Earth in 1891. Now it has decided to take the game away forever. It will happen on the third Friday in April. And the voices are saying it's YOUR fault.

I guess there's no longer any need to wonder why I carry around seven pencils wherever I go. I have a vague recollection of using them as some sort of antenna device, but from there, my brain draws a blank.

After that, I learned that Chip's Sporting Goods had been burglarized, but the only stuff missing was some basketball gear. Store owner Chip Spears said the police think it was an inside job, because there was no evidence of a break-in, and the alarm never went off.

So many random weird things were happening to my best friend, and the weirdest part is, I don't remember any of it.

The next day, as I was riding my bike down Drexler Drive, I caught a glimpse of a bright, fiery object in the sky streaking diagonally toward Earth at a tremendous rate of speed. It appeared to crash into Chip's Sporting Goods. The thunderous explosion scrambled my eardrums. I didn't know whether it was some sort of space debris, or a missile, or worse.

When I got back to my apartment, I flipped on the radio to see if I could find out what happened. Sure enough, a local journalist reported that a meteorite had crashed into Chip's. Fire Department officials later told the news media that there were no fatalities, and the damage was confined to the store's basketball aisle.

A meteorite slamming into the basketball section at Chip's Sporting Goods? I think about calculating the odds of that happening, but I decide to keep reading instead.

I rode my bike to Lawrence's house to confront him

about all the weird things that were happening ever since he told me that basketball was being taken away. When I pressed him on the matter, he wrote me a long note, folded it in half, and handed it to me.

    And my life hasn't been the same since I read it.

47

Keep Your Pencils Sharp

The sound of the lower hatch opening breaks my concentration, which is okay because Zeke's cliffhanger paragraph concludes the day's quota of pages.

Maya's dark, wavy hair floats through the opening in advance of her head.

"Do I smell food? And you didn't invite me over to share? Some friend."

Maya's conclusion is misguided, but it establishes the fact that she now views me as a friend. I have no evidence to the contrary, beyond her knack for talking excessively and asking too many questions.

"The Strategic Federation Council's chili mac 'n' beef meal packets only come in single-serving portions, and I don't have enough to go around because my supply needs to last me the entire mission."

"That's all right. I prefer the pasta primavera. I'm a vegetarian—well, mostly, anyway. Hey, before we blasted off, the flight activities specialist confided in me that you told him you were considering converting to a strictly pescatarian diet. Fish only. I think that's fabulous—except, of course, for the fish."

Wait a second. I had never even met the flight activities specialist until he tried to confiscate my supply of Bazooka Joe as we were preparing to board the spacecraft.

I don't want to accuse Maya of flat-out making that up. Instead, my brain channels Dr. Tidewater by charting a diplomatic course.

"Are you sure he was talking about me and not Stone Godfrey?"

"Oh, you're right. Not sure how I got that confused. Hey, guess how much protein a package of chili mac 'n' beef has compared to beef stroganoff with noodles, chicken and dumplings, seafood chowder, sweet-and-sour pork, and turkey Tetrazzini?"

I would only be guessing. And I'd prefer to perform a comprehensive cross-comparison study of the protein levels rather than use the limited data I have at my disposal to speculate on them, but I can't, because I'm in the middle of thinking about Zeke's ominous last paragraph and the next day's page allocation.

"I'm busy doing a deep-dive analysis of Zeke's diary. Can we talk about this later?" And Maya has me asking her another question, and now I'm revealing what I'm doing during my personal, flight-engineer-mandated R and R time.

"Looks like a missed opportunity to me, Sherman Tuckerman, but I can take a hint."

Maya returns to her quarters, but before she closes the hatch, she pokes her head through the passageway again and bombards me with another question.

"I'll bet Zeke's diary is amazing. My life in the lower compartment is so boring. I could use some excitement. Anything in there you'd care to share with your cabin mate?"

Geometrically, the shortest distance between two points is a straight line. The Ares Pilgrim's path to Mars via the Transfer Orbit Trajectory Vortex Anomaly is a prime example of this principle. And so is my response to Maya on her request for me to share details of Zeke's diary.

"No."

Maya leaves for the second time. I close my eyes for a moment to honor Stone Godfrey's directive to relax.

I open my eyes. I'm aware that I fell asleep right after Maya left.

> Captain's Log—Ares Pilgrim Mars Mission, Day 2
> I feel groggy enough right now to think I've been asleep for at least 3 to 4 hours, but when I read the gauges on my instrument panel, I realized I'm a full day closer to completing the mission, which is why I identified this as Day 2 in the Captain's Log.

I open Zeke's diary again, but reading the day's allotment of pages will have to wait, because the upper hatch is turning, and Stone Godfrey is staring at me through the opening.

"Tuckerman, I just received a communiqué from Mission Control. They're getting some strange readings from the nuclear thermal fuel's containment gauges. Pax wants you to rerun the six-month exhaust velocity projections, and he also needs you to calculate fuel expenditure up to this point, and to project how it might change when we exit TOTVA and approach Mars' insertion trajectory, given the revised fuel levels. Copy?"

"Copy. I need a moment to run the calculations. Wait here." And now I'm giving Stone Godfrey an order, which causes my right knee to bounce up and down, just the way my dad's does whenever he's stressed.

"Tell you what, Tuckerman. How about you bring the calculations up to the flight deck when you're done. And let's not keep Mission Control waiting. There was a sense of urgency in the flight director's voice."

I don't respond to Stone Godfrey because I already answered his "Copy?" question with a "Copy" of my own, and since there are no remaining unanswered questions, I begin my work by peeling a sheet of paper from my pad as he returns to his quarters.

Before I can run the numbers, Maya's hatch opens, and she glides in through the opening.

"Permission to enter."

I don't know whether Maya is asking for permission, or she's telling me she has granted herself permission to infiltrate my personal space which, to my way of thinking, would be a mission infraction. I ignore her, and I begin my fuel calculations.

"I heard the flight director's conversation with Stone. Sounds like it might be serious. I came in to help."

"I'm the mathematics flight specialist on this mission. I'm busy working. Please leave."

"Sounds like someone woke up on the wrong side of the crew seat, but that's okay. I can take a hint," Maya says as she returns to her quarters, but I don't know what she means, because there was nothing in my words to indicate I was making an indirect suggestion to her.

When I run my calculations, I understand why Pax Booker is concerned. The Ares Pilgrim's fuel expenditure has exceeded mission capacity guidelines after only two days in space. The deviation is minor, but I know I'll need to monitor it closely and continuously.

And taking the irregularity into account, I modify my six-month exhaust velocity projections accordingly, and then I recalculate the projected insertion trajectory fuel requirements, and then I write down my findings on a piece of paper, and I take it up to the flight deck.

"Are you sure about these numbers?"

It's the second time Stone Godfrey is questioning the accuracy of my calculations, but I know my work is one-hundred-percent fact-based. I feel blood rushing to my face. And the skin around my eyes is tightening. I don't know how to respond to Stone Godfrey's lack of confidence in me. It reminds me of all the school administrators who questioned my mental competence before the last one transferred me to McDerney.

"Copy."

It's all I can think of to say. It would have been easier to write the word on that piece of paper I handed to Stone Godfrey, but there's no room left on either side.

"Copy? That's it? What exactly are you telling me, Tuckerman?"

"The truth. It's the only conclusion a mathematical calculation can have."

Stone Godfrey stares long and hard at me. I'm careful not to make eye contact with him for fear of . . . And I'm so rattled that my brain can't complete the thought, which is just as well, because my fear of the unknown is greater than my secret fear of heights.

"Keep your pencils sharp. We're not out of the woods by any stretch of the imagination."

48

Stone, We've Got a Problem

Stone Godfrey's words don't require a response. I return to my quarters and flip to the page where Zeke says I handed him a life-changing note.

> *I take a deep breath and a leap of faith as I prepared myself for Lawrence's words.*

And I take a parallel and corresponding deep breath, so I can be in sync with my best friend.

> *The 7th Dimension is an interdimensional energy being that's also known as the Entity. Its world headquarters are within the intertwined root system of a grove of trees that live adjacent to Allen Fieldhouse on the campus of the University of Kansas, in the city of Lawrence. The university is considered to be the birthplace of basketball.*
>
> *The 7th Dimension's secret emissary is James Naismith, a Canadian physical educator, medical doctor, and minister.*

Working through Dr. Naismith, the Entity brought bas-
ketball to humankind in the winter of 1891 as a means of
fostering peace and brotherhood on the planet.

The fog in my brain is lifting. My memory begins to
return.

My dad is an architect. There were always pencils and
drafting tools around the house. When I was four, I used
the ancient Greek geometric technique of neusis construc-
tion to develop a triangle on a piece of paper using a com-
pass and a marked straightedge. With those same tools, I
circumscribed a heptagon around the triangle, then laid
out seven precisely measured and beveled No. 2 pencils
over the heptagonal figure to create the exact seven-sided
antenna needed to intercept Entity communiqués.

Yes! I remember now! I unzip my backpack to make sure
my pencils are safe. And one by one, they drift out and into
the weightlessness of my cabin.

I don't retrieve them because having them surround me
gives me a sense of peace that I haven't experienced since
before Flint Garrison and Dr. Murakami showed up unan-
nounced in my living room.

I shift my attention back to Zeke's diary.

Basketball accomplished its intended purpose for de-
cades. But when humanity strayed from the path through
violence, greed, and corruption, the Entity concluded it
was time to terminate the experiment. The breaking point

occurred at the city finals, when you punched out a referee.

I was there! Brock Decker took a cheap shot at Stretch as Zeke's team was driving downcourt for the winning basket. Zeke was at the crossroads and decided to throw a punch at Brock Decker. But Brock Decker ducked, and Zeke clobbered one of the referees instead. And that was the beginning of the end for basketball!

Basketball will cease to exist tomorrow at midnight, and the 7th Dimension says there's nothing anyone can do to stop it.

Zeke needed to travel to 7th Dimension headquarters half-way across the country in Kansas to reason with the Entity on why basketball had to remain on Earth.

But the only way to arrive at 7th Dimension headquarters by the deadline was to borrow his brother, Wade's, antique 1965 Chevy pickup, which was parked inside space 1046 at Biffmann Self-Storage while Wade was serving in the Marine Corps in Afghanistan.

I'm suddenly interrupted by a short series of staticky tones blasting through my instrument panel, followed by Pax Booker's voice.

"Mission Control to Ares Pilgrim, come in."

Stone Godfrey responds on behalf of the crew. "Ares Pilgrim. Go, Mission Control."

"Stone, we've got a problem. We don't think it's a serious one, but we wanted to bring you up to speed."

"Roger, Pax. Go ahead."

The lower hatch opens, and Maya shoots through the opening.

"Whoa, cool, there's a floating pencil parade in your cabin."

I hold up my hand to silence her, taking note that Pax Booker's tone of voice is more serious than Maya's or Stone Godfrey's.

"We've taken a hard look at Sherman's calculations. They're dead accurate and align with what we're seeing down here in Mission Control."

No surprise there.

"Bottom line, Stone, is the spacecraft is using more fuel than our scientists originally calculated it would. Not by a wide margin, and we're absolutely certain it won't adversely affect the mission, but the fact is, the Ares Pilgrim's hypersonic nuclear thermal rocket propulsion system is not operating as efficiently as designed."

"Copy that, Pax." The timbre of Stone Godfrey's voice is matter-of-fact.

"There's one more thing. I need to remind you of something you already know, just so we're all on the same page here: After the Ares Pilgrim entered the Transfer Orbit Trajectory Vortex Anomaly, well, needless to say, there was no turning back."

"Copy that, Pax. We'll make it work."

"Ten-four, Stone. Our engineers are working day and night to find a solution. More to follow on that. Mission Control, out."

Maya reaches behind her head and bunches up her hair

with her left hand. And then she uses a pink elastic hairband to secure her hair into a tight ponytail. And that prompts me to make an entry in the Captain's Log:

> Captain's Log—Ares Pilgrim Mars Mission, Day 3
> The shape of Maya's ponytail as it floats above her head reminds me of something, but my brain can't place it because of all the other assignments it's tasked with right now.

"Possible fuel shortage. No turning back. Stone seems to be taking it all in stride."

There isn't a question in Maya's words, so I'm not obligated to respond, but I decide to honor my friendship with Maya, so I nod, which I conclude is the equivalent of saying *Copy*, but without saying the word, and then I decide to put Zeke's diary aside for now, even though I still have part of my daily allocation of pages left, and I hope the Ares Pilgrim's nuclear thermal fuel lasts as long as my supply of chili mac 'n' beef, because I don't want any of it to go to waste.

49

I Might Have Caved

We're exactly halfway to Mars, which I consider to be an Ares Pilgrim landmark event. Time has passed swiftly, as it often does when I spend most of my waking hours in solitude.

Conversely, the hours move at a snail's pace whenever Maya interrupts my math calculations to tell me more and more inconceivable details about her life, which is far more dramatic and colorful than mine, although some of the specifics she offers seem to be beyond belief.

As keeper of the Captain's Log, I've been tasked with maintaining a detailed record of watershed mission events, so I commemorate the milestone by making a log entry.

Captain's Log—Ares Pilgrim Mars Mission, Day 91

Chili mac 'n' beef remains a vitally important staple of the mission. I often wonder why more people back on Earth don't incorporate its consumption into their daily lives. After all, proper nutrition is a cornerstone of good health.

I've fallen into a routine with Stone Godfrey—he barks out a command for me to run fuel expenditure and exhaust velocity calculations, and I deliver the results so swiftly that he often questions the accuracy of my work.

Most of the time, I'm confident in my computations, but there's a microscopic sector of my brain that wonders whether I've processed the available data correctly.

Maya has been keeping to herself, except when delivering communiqués from Mission Control or attempting to coerce me into swapping one of her vegetarian meals for a packet of my chili mac 'n' beef. I always tell her no because I don't want to deviate from my established routine.

I notice the lower hatch opening, which means Maya is going to come in and talk endlessly, so I conclude my Captain's Log entry with a scientific observation.

Mars is now clearly visible through my hatch window. I can see its subtle geographical features and eerily exotic reddish-gray undertone in greater detail with the passing of each day.

Maya guides her way into my compartment. Her ultra-dark, wavy hair flows in weightless countermovement to the direction her body is traveling.

"Any interest in exchanging a packet of your macaroni beef chili thingy for this handsome container of kale and white bean casserole? Seems fair."

"It's called chili mac 'n' beef. And I thought you were mostly vegetarian."

"I am. Just looking to experience what it's like to fuel my body with the Sherman Tuckerman meal of choice."

I'm not opposed to trading foodstuff commodities with Maya, but I can't afford to throw my meal forecasting system out of alignment.

"No."

"Bummer."

Maya pulls a pink hairband from her jumpsuit pocket and uses it to cinch her hair into a ponytail. Again. What is it about that ponytail?

"Received a message from Mission Control. Need to do a software update on your computer system."

I'm all for it, especially if it means Maya will momentarily concentrate on something other than negotiating a meal exchange. I use the time to service my compartment's water purification filter.

Nothing can go to waste on an extended space mission, especially something as vital to human life as water.

My brain notes that the Ares Pilgrim is equipped with a state-of-the-art water recycling system that extracts particles and debris before passing the wastewater through a series of multi-filtration beds to remove impurities. In the final step, a catalytic oxidation reactor removes any volatile organic compounds and kills bacteria and viruses.

The system gathers humidity from the air, as well as water from when we brush our teeth and wash our hands. It also collects and processes urine, which might seem gross to non-astronauts, but the water produced by the system is cleaner than what most people drink back on Earth.

"All done here. Last chance to expand your palate with a savory array of kale and white beans and other stuff that tastes vaguely like food."

"Hard pass."

Maya returns to her quarters, and I make my final Captain's Log entry for the day.

> Captain's Log—Ares Pilgrim Mars Mission, Day 91 (continued)
>
> I'm beginning to feel ever so slightly homesick. I miss my bedroom, and my weekly chess match with Nathan, and Rigoberto asking me what the good word is.
>
> And three months is a long time to be away from Mike's pizza.
>
> If Maya had thrown in a warm slice of pepperoni during her failed meal-exchange negotiation, I might have caved.

50

The Pieces of the Puzzle Are Falling into Place

Captain's Log—Ares Pilgrim Mars Mission, Day 181

Six months have passed swiftly and without incident, not counting Maya's outlandish stories—which, I notice, never include anything about her personal life—and Stone Godfrey's erratic command of the spacecraft.

We are now one day away from sample container retrieval.

I set aside my Captain's Log responsibilities for a moment to reflect on the precise nature of the mission's framework.

The SFC's operational planning team established a regular routine for us, scheduling our days down to five-minute increments, which I love, because I need structure in my life, and I always operate best when I know what's supposed to happen next, and I wish the rest of the world operated this way.

We sleep in three separate non-overlapping eight-hour shifts, each of us in our own one-person sleeping bag that attaches to the wall of our cabin. That way, at least two of us are always awake to keep an eye on the Ares Pilgrim.

We continuously check our support systems, perform routine maintenance, clean the water purification filters, update software on the computer equipment, conduct science experiments and medical exams, prepare meals, and maintain personal hygiene, which is way trickier here than it is back on Earth. We also monitor communication from Mission Control, and we even take out the trash. Well, we expel the trash into space.

It's important that we get enough exercise to prevent the bone and muscle loss that can occur while living in microgravity. We use resistive stretch bands to do a series of exercises we learned back on Earth, and we walk on the flight deck treadmill every day.

My favorite activity is looking out the airlock chamber's hatch window, especially to compare the relative size and level of luminosity of Earth and Mars as we travel deeper and deeper into outer space. From here, my home planet seems like nothing more than a fragile ball of life hanging in the void. And the closer we get to Mars, the more my brain works to reconcile my nervousness and sense of responsibility.

There's even time for stargazing, and the Milky Way has plenty to offer in this regard, with astronomers estimating that our galaxy is home to as many as four hundred billion stars. And it's humbling to consider the infinitesimal place our own sun holds in this spiraling mass of distant, shimmering stars, which scientists believe has a visible diameter of about 100,000 light years.

My second favorite activity is my running debate with Maya on what the seven wonders of the solar system are. We agree on nearly all of them, which is unusual for us:

1. The oceans of Earth
2. The surface of the sun
3. The rings of Saturn
4. The asteroid belt between the orbits of Mars and Jupiter
5. The enormous swirling vortex in Jupiter's southern hemisphere known as the Great Red Spot
6. The Olympus Mons, which is the largest volcano on Mars—and the largest in the entire solar system

But we've argued for days on end about the seventh wonder of the solar system. Maya thinks it's the dark side of the moon. My choice is Enceladus, the sixth largest moon of Saturn, because it is thought to have a liquid water ocean beneath its frozen shell, and it sprays its watery substance into outer space. Scientists have determined that Enceladus has most of the chemical ingredients needed for life, which is why it makes my list.

Mars, with its brick-red and grayish surface, is now in plain view through my hatch window as I float weightlessly to the galley to rehydrate and heat my dinner in solitude. What was once a tiny, mysterious image through the eyepiece of my telescope is now this massive body of inhospitable land beneath me.

I use my time away from the other crew members to make an entry into the Captain's Log, reviewing certain basic facts about the planet so I'm better prepared to perform my mission-critical sample-container-retrieval duties tomorrow.

Captain's Log—Ares Pilgrim Mars Mission, Day 181 (continued)

1. Mars is known as the Red Planet because it's covered in rock, soil, and dust made from iron oxide, which gives the planet's surface its rusty color.

2. The two moons of Mars, Deimos and Phobos, are named after the horses that pull the Roman god of war's chariot.

3. Scientists believe that these moons originated as asteroids captured by the Martian gravity millions of years ago.

4. There's no hard evidence of life on Mars, either past or present.

5. Mars has the best conditions to support life of any planet in the solar system except, of course, Earth.

6. Mars has a candy bar named after it. The Mars bar was invented in England in 1932, a little over fourteen years before the invention of Bazooka Joe bubblegum.

7. The Mars bar is my favorite candy bar.

With this task complete, I stir my meal as I reflect back on all that has happened in the months leading to tomorrow's sample container retrieval, summarizing everything in my brain thusly as I prepare to read the final allotment of pages from Zeke's diary:

Radio communication with Earth now takes fourteen minutes, each way, which I note is an obvious simple multiple of seven. It means we're on our own should we need to react swiftly to a life-threatening event, because waiting twenty-eight minutes for instructions from Mission Control would be less than useful.

With each passing day, Stone Godfrey is more irritable with the crew and more abrupt with Mission Control. And he continues to question the accuracy of my work, to which I respond by sticking up for myself and saying *Copy!* a lot.

Maya spends an inordinate amount of time putting her hair into a ponytail, which I find to be oddly distracting.

And she keeps digging for information and trying to coerce me into telling her too much about my private life and my thoughts about Zeke's diary and my dad and the mission and Stone Godfrey and Dr. Murakami and Flint Garrison, and even Ryker and Brock Decker.

My brain concludes that there are parts of Maya's life she's careful not to reveal, which is okay because I already know more about her than I want to.

And Zeke's life in the time we've spent together, at least according to his diary, has been a whirlwind of pain and joy and self-discovery.

Zeke writes that basketball is the prism through which he views the world. My brain determines he isn't referring to a transparent triangular object that has refractive surfaces at an acute angle with one another and separates white light into a spectrum of seven colors.

Yes, seven.

Instead, Zeke is using the word *prism* figuratively, which means he is referencing the comparative clarification afforded by a particular viewpoint.

And this leads my brain to theorize that the abstract science of mathematics serves a similar purpose in my own life to the one basketball serves in Zeke's.

And then my brain concludes that Zeke and I are polar opposites and, at the same time, completely alike, which explains why we get along, and for the first time, my brain admits it has been protecting me by limiting the quantity of my friendships, and the quality of them as well.

And then I hear the sound of the lower hatch opening, and Maya slips in through the passageway.

"On your feet, soldier. Schedule says we're supposed to review tomorrow's sample container retrieval protocols."

I know that Maya's interpretation of the schedule is correct, but my brain wants to complete its summary analysis of Zeke's diary.

"I need more time."

"Giving you fifteen more minutes, and that's it."

And Maya retreats to her quarters, and then my brain continues with its data summary of Zeke's diary—this time, in numerical form—as I watch steam swirling from my chili mac 'n' beef:

1. Zeke convinces the 7th Dimension to allow basketball to remain on Earth.

2. Zeke graduates from McDerney, enrolls at Jefferson as

a freshman, earns a spot on the team, and airballs the potential game-winner in the regional title game.

3. While trying out for the team as a sophomore, Zeke runs a perfect fast break, which mysteriously transports him to an Afghan desert, where he witnesses his brother, Wade, being killed in action.

4. Zeke goes on to lead Jefferson back to the regional finals, where he runs another fast break to perfection, this time propelling him to Allen Fieldhouse, where he speaks with his dead brother about how free will allows people who've recently died to have one final chance to communicate with someone of their choosing before they cross over to the other side, and Wade chooses Zeke, and he tells Zeke that human consciousness survives death.

5. Zeke graduates from Jefferson and is invited by KU head coach Bob Worth to try out for the team as a walk-on.

6. Zeke rides his bike to Biffmann Self-Storage to retrieve his pickup truck to drive to KU, but discovers it has been dismantled.

7. Zeke learns that Brock Decker and I repurposed the truck parts to build a time machine, which Brock Decker uses to travel back in time to 1891 in Springfield, Massachusetts, where he alters the history of basketball and becomes the game's wealthy sole owner.

And I realize all of this is a lot for me to accept, but Zeke is my best friend, so I believe everything he says in his diary. And by this point, the pieces of the puzzle are falling into place, and I'm remembering more and more of our time together and the strange things that happened to us along the way.

And as I stare at the seven pencils that have been floating weightlessly in my cabin since shortly after we launched from Earth, I'm recalling bits and pieces of how I leveraged their power to help Zeke save basketball for all of humankind.

My chili mac 'n' beef has sufficiently cooled down for consumption, and the digital clock on my instrument panel says I've still got fourteen minutes left before Maya slides back through the hatch. I settle in for a warm meal as I prepare to speed-read my way through the final allotment of diary pages.

51

Maya's Lips Are Trembling

After basketball returned to its rightful place in history, Lawrence and I had one last encounter with James Naismith, basketball's original inventor but now the 7th Dimension's trusted envoy on all matters pertaining to the game. That's when Naismith granted me a lifetime basketball guardianship, and I have Lawrence to thank for helping me to achieve that honor.

It's what best friends do.

Naismith went on to say that in the seven days following his return to Entity headquarters, Lawrence and I were not permitted to say anything to anyone about all that had transpired with the 7th Dimension.

After that, Naismith said, all memory of our experiences with the Entity would be wiped away forever, and I would never be consciously aware of my selection for basketball guardianship. Instead, it would become an ethereal

part of me for the rest of my time on Earth. And Law-
rence's too, I suspect.

Zeke went on to write that under the terms of our verbal
agreement with James Naismith, I could never again intercept
7th Dimension communiqués.

The three of us shook on it because, as we all know,
a man's handshake is his word, and his word is his bond.

And now the light bulb in my brain switches to the on
position. That sentence from Zeke serves to completely restore my memory of the time we spent together attempting to
undo Brock Decker's unscrupulous deeds.

When I realized there was only one day left before the
7th Dimension would erase the memory of our journey
across the barriers of time, I decided to spend that last
night writing what is no doubt the world's most compre-
hensive diary, a complete recap of everything that hap-
pened since Lawrence and I first met inside the McDerney
cafeteria and became best friends.
    Last thing: Naismith told us we were forbidden to say
anything, but he didn't impose any restrictions that would
prevent me from writing it all down.
    I interpreted that to mean I had found a loophole in
the Entity's directive. It's a possible oversight on the part
of the 7th Dimension, but since Lawrence was no longer
permitted to communicate with the Entity, there was no
way to get an official ruling on it.

I take a deep breath before reading the final diary passage.

> *This diary enables me to express to Lawrence how important he is in my life, and how our friendship has grown over time to what it is today: bigger than basketball.*

Those words cause me to wipe my eyes with the sleeve of my jumpsuit, which isn't one-hundred-percent cotton like my dad's, so all it does is move the moisture around without blotting it up.

And then the hatch opens again, and Maya's head shoots through the passageway, and her forehead is wrinkled.

"Tried to reach Stone over the intercom to review the procedures for tonight's insertion trajectory maneuver and tomorrow's sample retrieval, but he's not answering, and I'm kind of concerned."

We crank open the hatch to the flight deck, and we shoot through the opening. And when we get inside, I see Stone Godfrey floating, apparently lifeless, in the middle of the cabin.

And Maya's lips are trembling.

And her hands are shaking.

"Stone!"

52

You Can't Talk to Me
That Way

"Stone, wake up!" Maya screams as she shakes his shoulders. There's no response, so she rears back and cracks him hard across the face.

Stone Godfrey moans and slowly regains consciousness. "What's happening? Where are we?"

He appears to be dazed. I'm not the chief medical officer, but I know it spells trouble.

"We're aboard the Ares Pilgrim," Maya says, "thirty minutes from exiting TOTVA. You're supposed to navigate the spacecraft through the insertion trajectory maneuver that'll enable us to recover the core samples that are circling Mars in a precarious elliptical orbit. Remember?"

Stone Godfrey shakes his head from side to side. I don't make direct eye contact with him, but I can tell he's groggy.

"Great, we're on our own in the middle of nowhere,"

Maya says under her breath, and her voice sounds different in that sentence than any of the other 23,275 sentences she has spoken since we blasted off from Vandenberg. My brain decides not to check divisibility by seven, because using my brainpower to stay alive takes priority.

"What should we do?" And now I'm asking a question again, which I would rather not be doing.

Maya doesn't flinch. "Can't afford the nearly half hour it'll take to get a message back from Mission Control on how to deal with this. Wait here and keep an eye on the man responsible for whether we live or die while I go grab my medical bag."

Maya takes off. Stone Godfrey moans again. I need a double wedge of Bazooka Joe, but all my bubblegum is in my cabin, and Maya said not to leave.

"Linderman, where's my sand wedge?" Stone Godfrey isn't making any sense. "Help me find it, caddie. That's an order."

I have no idea who Linderman is, but I deduce from the word *caddie* that he is talking about golf, and I've never carried a golf bag or calculated the yardage from a sand trap to the pin, and I don't want to touch Stone Godfrey, but I'm sensing we're in grave danger, so I grip onto his jumpsuit and guide him to his crew seat, and I strap him in.

Stone Godfrey stares at his instrument panel. He turns a knob, then another. "Can I get the Golf Channel on this thing?"

I try to ignore the question, but the predicament I'm in is worsening with each passing second, and Maya isn't back yet.

I buy some time by answering Stone Godfrey's question with one of my own.

"Did you know that the modern game of golf originated in Scotland in the fifteenth century?"

Stone Godfrey's eyes are glazed over. He doesn't respond, but Maya does as she shoots through the passageway. "How do you know so much about golf history?"

I ignore her question.

"Linderman, take the helm! We're sheering off to starboard! Jupiter, set the main sail! Trim the jib!" And now Stone Godfrey is suddenly barking out sailing commands. This whole mess is clearly headed in the wrong direction.

Maya pulls her sphygmomanometer and stethoscope from her medical bag. She slips the cuff around Stone Godfrey's upper arm, squeezes the bulb, and listens for his systolic and diastolic readings. Stone Godfrey offers no resistance.

"Your blood pressure is off the charts, Stone. What are you on, Commander?"

"I took a little something to help me get some sleep last night."

"What did you wash it down with?" And the volume of Maya's voice rises, and the expression on her face intensifies.

"You can't talk to me that way, Maya Jupiter—or whatever your real name is."

Real name? Stone Godfrey must be delirious.

"I can, because I'm the chief medical officer on this mission!"

"Chief medical officer? You're a high school dropout who flunked a biology course!"

And now the tone of their conversation is swiftly deteri-

orating, as is my confidence that we're ever going to complete the mission and return safely to Earth.

And I'm rocking from side to side, which is not easy to do
because I'm weightless, and my hands are clammy, and I'm
hyperventilating.

"STOP IT, STONE!"

Those words escape from my mouth with the same velocity as the sample container streaking around Mars.

53

Don't Let Me Down

Maya gives Stone Godfrey a container of water with a straw piercing its top and hovers over him while he drinks it.

The clock is ticking on exiting the vortex anomaly and performing the orbital insertion maneuver that will align the spacecraft with the sample container's elliptical orbit—also known as the reason why we're all aboard the Ares Pilgrim in the first place.

I scramble back to my quarters to run final trajectory calculations. My brain understands that if Stone Godfrey messes up, we'll either crash into Mars, or we'll carom off the planet's atmosphere and slingshot toward Maya's namesake planet.

Neither option allows for putting the truck back together, or playing chess with Nathan, or watching Zeke play basketball at KU.

I triple check my calculations before writing them down on a piece of paper from my dwindling supply. Then I return to the flight deck, only to find Stone Godfrey leaning back in his chair. His feet are up on the instrument panel's console. And Maya is packing up her medical gear.

"Did you feel that?" Stone Godfrey asks.

"Um, feel what?" Maya tilts her head to one side. I don't think she knows what Stone Godfrey is talking about. Neither do I.

"Exactly. Smooth as silk. We just exited TOTVA, and I'm pretty sure I did it with my eyes closed."

"Great." And now Maya is pressing her lips together so hard, I think they might fuse together permanently. But I'm wrong. "Maybe you can take a short break from being full of yourself to put us in orbit around the planet."

I glance out the flight deck window and notice the sharp contrast between the dimly lit, reddish Martian surface and the velvety blackness behind it. I feel the hairs on the back on my neck wiggle. I don't remember that ever happening to me before.

I work my way over to Stone Godfrey, and I hand him my orbital insertion data.

"About time you got here, Tuckerman." Stone Godfrey appears to be acting like his normal self again. "I'd hate to have traveled all this way, only to miss the insertion window because you were sleeping on the job."

My pulse speeds up. My body tenses.

"Don't be such a jerk, Stone." Maya is not letting it go.

"C'mon, I'm just horsing around here. You and Tuckerman seem to have lost your sense of humor."

I don't find anything funny in Stone Godfrey's words. I ignore him, and I point to the digital counter instead.

"I see it. We've got two minutes before I fire the rockets. Stick around, Tuckerman, you might learn something."

Maya and I grab hold of the tethers mounted onto the flight deck walls because we know it might get bumpy. Stone Godfrey's eyes are trained on the digital counter. I consider asking to do the countdown, but my brain intervenes by telling me it's best not to potentially distract the man who, minutes earlier, was unconscious.

Stone Godfrey stares at my slip of paper before punching the data into the computer on his console. And when the digital counter hits zero, he pushes a button, then six more in rapid succession, and then he guides a large silver lever into a downward position.

And I sense the spacecraft decelerating and changing course.

And then the instrument panel emits an audible burst of 3,000 Hz electronic tones. And Stone Godfrey flips three switches, and then he rotates a dial four clicks to the right, which causes the Ares Pilgrim to regain speed and level out.

And I glance over at Maya, who is fidgeting with her hair.

Stone Godfrey returns the silver lever to its original position and throws his feet back onto the console. "Jackpot," he says. "Anyone got a cigar?"

"You can't smoke in here. It's a rule." I can't believe Stone Godfrey wants to light up a cylinder of tobacco leaves inside the spacecraft.

"He's kidding, Lawrence. Lighting up a cigar is a culturally ingrained, time-honored way to celebrate a victory."

"Oh."

My brain analyzes the available evidence and concludes

that we've successfully entered Martian orbit, which means I'm twenty-four hours away from operating the Ares Pilgrim's robotic arm at a twenty-three-degree angle to retrieve the sample container.

"Gonna stay here with Stone awhile to make sure he's all right," Maya says as she straps her medical bag to a countertop. "You've got quite a bit of data to go over for tomorrow. Won't disturb you when I head back to my quarters."

I give Maya the Ryker two-finger wave and make my way through the passageway. Before I can secure the hatch, Stone Godfrey's voice catches my attention.

"We're only going to get one shot at this, Tuckerman. Truth is, I'm relying on you to be at your best tomorrow. Don't let me down."

It's not necessary for Stone Godfrey to say that, because tomorrow I will rely on the math. Truth is, unlike some humans I could name, *it* never lets *me* down.

54

My Brain Advises Me to Play It Safe

I self-settle my nerves by making another entry into the Captain's Log:

> Captain's Log—Ares Pilgrim Mars Mission, Day 181 (continued)
>
> I'm playing a game of chess against myself, using my miniature chessboard and magnetic chess pieces.
>
> The chess set was a birthday present from my dad, who purchased it from Chip's Sporting Goods when Nathan began working there as a part-time trainee sales clerk in charge of the store's chess and checkers section.
>
> At the time, my dad told me that the chess set was a dual-purpose purchase—he

thought it would encourage me to leave the house more often, and since Nathan was my best friend, my dad also wanted to help him build confidence in his new position at Chip's.

My dad is always doing stuff like that for people, and six months in outer space has afforded me the opportunity to see that more clearly.

And six months from now, after we splash down in the Pacific Ocean, I'll be in charge of that same chess and checkers section when I'm working for Nathan at Chip's.

And now I get back to my chess match, where I employ the Scotch Gambit strategy against myself, not only because it requires me to fearlessly place my bishop on its most active and aggressive diagonal when I'm locked in battle against a worthy opponent, but also because it calls indirect attention to golf's origins in Scotland, which means I am working tangentially in support of Stone Godfrey while I'm practicing being fearless.

I play myself to a draw, and then I run my sample-retrieval calculations, using my abacus to double-check my work.

Afterwards, I collect the seven pencils that've been floating around my cabin ever since we left Earth's atmosphere. I return them to my backpack for safekeeping, because I don't want them wandering out of the spacecraft tomorrow when I'm using the robotic retrieval arm to capture the sample container.

And now the flight deck hatch opens. And it's Maya.

"Just passing through now that I believe Stone is probably going to live."

I don't respond to her, as usual, because there's no question involved in the conversation, which I determine is a monologue because only one of us is participating in it.

"Gonna fire off a status update to Mission Control on Stone's condition. You're in the spotlight tomorrow, Sherman Tuckerman. Get some rest."

And Maya's ponytail bobs above her head as she disappears and closes the hatch.

I secure myself inside my wall-mounted sleeping bag, and I close my eyes and try to drift off to sleep, but instead, my brain conducts an analysis of the spatial characteristics of Maya's floating bundle of hair.

My brain tells me there's something about it that might be critical to the mission, but then my brain responds to itself by saying how ridiculous that sounds, and now I don't know what to think, so I fixate on her ponytail for several more minutes, but my concentration is broken by the sound of the lower hatch opening again.

"Got a response from Mission Control. Pax Booker told me not to let Captain Stoner out of my sight for the rest of the mission. Pax didn't actually call him that. I was *embellishing* the flight director's message for dramatic effect because this mission needs more theatrical arts to help muffle the boredom."

How am I ever going to get any rest with Maya's continual chattering?

And now she has me asking *myself* a question.

Maya keeps talking, but I ignore her while my brain

considers how accurate her use of the word *embellishing* is, because she is attempting to make Pax Booker's statement sound more interesting and possibly more entertaining by adding extra details, especially ones that are not true, although in Stone Godfrey's case, I'm not so sure.

"Are you even listening to me?"

And now Maya is asking me another question, and her face is tightening, and she is crossing her arms, and I just want her to leave my cabin so I can get back to unraveling the mystery of her ponytail, which is swaying from side to side as she admonishes me for ignoring her.

"Yes."

"Good, because there's one more thing. There was a communiqué from Flint Garrison that arrived a few hours ago. The general said to remind you, and I quote: 'Everyone knows there's no basketball on Mars.' I think he might have been making a joke. Hold on—didn't he say that to you after the flight activities specialist carded you for having copious amounts of unauthorized contraband in your backpack? And wouldn't that make you a *contrabandist*? And when you think about it, there's probably no such thing as *authorized* contraband because, well, you know, contraband is, by definition, unauthorized. Otherwise, they would call it something else, right? *Right?*"

Maya asks me four more questions in all those words, and I wish she would stop doing that, but if I ignore her again, odds are she'll ask three follow-up ones.

My brain advises me to play it safe.

"Right."

55

Wonder If I Struck a Nerve

Maya leaves my cabin again. And her ponytail is the last thing I see as she slips through the passageway.

And now I'm officially obsessed with it.

I close my eyes, and my brain speculates, without firm evidence, that Maya's ponytail might play a key role in the mission, and then my brain contradicts itself by saying I should let it go and mentally prepare for the robotic arm maneuver instead.

But rather than prepare, I take note of how jet black the insides of my eyelids are. And now I'm in a safe place, free to think about the variable elasticity of a wedge of Bazooka Joe, or the inexplicable number of consecutive identical consonants in Chett Biffmann's and dive training officer Pfeffermann's names, or how seven pencils organized in a heptagonal array can possibly . . .

"This is your Commander speaking. Rise and shine, Tuckerman. Look alive, Jupiter."

The sound of Stone Godfrey's voice blasting over the intercom jars me awake. I glance at the instrument panel. It is one hour prior to the scheduled intercept of the sample container. My knee bounces in sync with my heart pounding against the inside of my rib cage.

"All hands report to the flight deck."

The lower hatch opens, and Maya shoots through the passageway.

"Hope you got enough sleep, Sherman Tuckerman, because it's a big day in the neighborhood. And in case you were wondering, it's a proven scientific fact that otters hold hands when they sleep so they don't drift away from each other."

Why does Maya give me so much absurd information? And now she has my brain asking questions of itself.

"And dolphins and whales literally fall *half* asleep. Each side of their brain takes turns so they can come up for air."

Is she making these things up?

Maya and I float to the flight deck. Stone Godfrey is strapped in his crew seat. His eyes are bloodshot. His hair is more weightlessly disheveled than usual.

The Ares Pilgrim's operations manual is open on the console, and it looks like several pages have been torn out of it, because there are sheets of paper with diagrams on them floating about the cabin.

Maya's medical bag is strapped to the countertop where she left it. There's a digital clock on Stone Godfrey's instrument panel counting down the minutes and seconds until I'm supposed to intercept the sample container.

"Looks like you've been busy," Maya says.

"I spent the night analyzing Tuckerman's latest fuel expenditure and exhaust velocity calculations. Bottom line is we've only got enough gas in the tank for one pass at the prize. Then we'll need to fire the rockets to exit Mars orbit and re-enter TOTVA—and the window to do that will be fleeting."

Stone Godfrey's use of that acronym for the sixth time causes my brain to twitch. I don't know why exactly, but I just don't like that abbreviation. I respond with the minimum number of words possible. "Copy."

"Good, because if you and Jupiter drop the ball, we're going back to Earth empty-handed."

"Copy that." My eyes dart over to Maya, who's fidgeting with her ponytail again.

Stone Godfrey continues to put the squeeze on us. "I don't want to apply too much pressure, but the success of this mission will largely be in your hands."

Maya raises her eyebrows and gives Stone Godfrey a glassy stare. "Do your job, we'll do ours." And then she bolts out the hatch, leaving me alone in the flight deck with Stone Godfrey.

"Wonder if I struck a nerve," Stone Godfrey mutters under his breath.

But since he doesn't ask me a question, I don't respond, not even with a *Copy!*, and I follow Maya out through the passageway to prepare for the next phase of the mission.

56

Roger That, Flight Deck, Let's Do This

I'm strapped into my crew seat reviewing in my brain the seven attempts it took me to master the robotic arm maneuver and capture of the mock sample container.

And now my brain points out that my use of the phrase *master the robotic arm* is an exaggeration, because I only secured the mock container on my final try.

And the sound of the lower hatch handle rotating breaks my concentration.

Maya's brow is wrinkled. She clears her throat, but not the way Flint Garrison does. Her throat-clear is gentle.

"Just received a communiqué from Mission Control. They're saying the sample container's tracking device indicates the elliptical orbit is rapidly deteriorating. Pax Booker thinks there's a chance we might not reach it before it falls from the Martian sky and crashes back onto the planet."

"That's it?"

"Isn't that enough?"

"I'm confident we can do this." I try to sound as convincing as I can.

"Wait, there's more." And now Maya's eyebrows are so closely squished together, they're almost touching. "Mission Control says in order to make the capture, we'll need to fly closer to Mars than originally planned. That means we'll have to expend way more fuel than anticipated to break out of Mars orbit and reenter the vortex anomaly for the trip home."

I'm relieved that Maya doesn't use Stone Godfrey's acronym, but her additional news causes me to rock from side to side. "I'm not worried," I say. "I trust Stone."

"So do I, pretty much, but this involves a lot more than having faith in the guy." And now Maya is biting her lower lip, and she's playing with her ponytail again, and I'm careful not to stare at it, even though my brain is hypnotized by its shape.

"Twenty minutes to container intercept," Stone Godfrey says over the intercom. "Let's get ready down there."

I make another attempt to reassure Maya. "There's one more thing. The math. Once we reenter the vortex anomaly, I can induce the spacecraft's hypersonic nuclear thermal rocket propulsion system into operating more efficiently by continuously recalculating fuel expenditure and exhaust velocity to get us home safely."

"You can do that?"

"I got this. Go tell Stone. I need to suit up."

Maya disappears into the flight deck.

I unfasten the latch on my cabin closet door, and I pull out my bulky spacesuit, and my helmet and gloves. And I think about all the men and women before me who've worn a similar garment on the Space Shuttle, or the International Space Station, or even the seven moon missions.

Heroes, all of them.

My spacesuit, like the others, is white. It has a Strategic Federation Council logo patch glued onto the sleeve.

Without that spacesuit working as designed, I'll die a horrible death inside the airlock chamber long before I have a chance to operate the robotic arm. That's not a favorable option, so I'm careful not to damage the spacesuit as I climb into it.

Maya returns from the flight deck. I normally don't start a conversation with her, especially with a question, but this time it's different. "What did Stone say?"

"He said, 'That outer hatch is a lot bigger than you think, Jupiter. Don't let Tuckerman fall out of the spacecraft. I'd have a tough time explaining that one to General Garrison.'"

"Really?" Stone Godfrey sounds serious. I'd better be careful when I'm inside the airlock.

"Yeah, but I told him that if you tumbled out, I'd use situational mathematics to ration your Bazooka Joe so that the remaining crew members would have just enough to make it all the way home."

And now I know she's kidding and that I'll never know what to believe when she's talking.

And Stone Godfrey's voice bursts over the intercom again: "Ten minutes to container intercept. You should be in final preparation now."

Maya helps me to put on my gloves and secure my helmet

to my spacesuit. And she touches me while she does it, which I normally don't like, but I fight through my resistance because I don't want any oxygen to leak out when I'm operating the robotic arm in the vacuum of deep space.

"How's that?" she asks.

I respond with a Ryker two-finger gloved wave, and I make my way to the airlock's interior door.

It's Maya's job to operate the airlock controls. I watch as she pushes a button, and then the glass door slides open, and I step inside. I secure the airlock's nylon safety strap to the metal coupling on my spacesuit, and Maya closes the door behind me.

And I turn around and watch as Maya operates the controls to depressurize the airlock chamber. I can sense the air pressure in the chamber changing around me, but my spacesuit is operating as designed. The effect is minimal.

And then I review in my brain the seven robotic arm procedures I'll need to follow once Maya opens the hatch:

1. Release the robotic arm's protective harness.

2. Extend the robotic arm and adjust its angle to the requisite twenty-three degrees, just like dive training officer Pfeffermann told me.

3. Wait for the sample container to come into plain view.

4. Catch the container in the mesh netting at the end of the robotic arm.

5. Pull the container into the airlock chamber.

6. Secure the container inside the small compartment that's bolted to the airlock chamber floor. That compartment is insulated with lead to protect the crew from potential radiation exposure.

7. Signal Maya to close the exterior hatch window.

"Five minutes to container intercept. You good to go, Tuckerman?"

I would rather give Stone Godfrey the Ryker two-finger gloved wave, which doesn't involve having to speak, but it's not an option, because Stone Godfrey is in a different compartment piloting the spacecraft.

"Roger that, flight deck. Let's do this."

57

It's Now or Never, Tuckerman

I hear the sound of the rockets firing as the spacecraft decelerates and angles downward. My brain interprets it to mean that Stone Godfrey is at the controls, maneuvering the Ares Pilgrim into position for sample container intercept.

And I feel my heart rate increase. And I watch Maya as she pushes the button that operates the exterior hatch mechanism. And then I turn, and I see the hatch door move from left to right until it is fully deployed.

And I stagger backward as the planet comes into full view, and then I realize that my eyes are now physically closer to Mars than anyone else's in human history.

"Are you seeing what I'm seeing?" Stone Godfrey says from the flight deck. "It's absolutely breathtaking."

"Roger that, Stone," Maya says. "No words here to describe it."

They're right, and Maya being at a loss for words is a mission first.

The planet is dimly lit. The surface is a shade of red I've never seen before. And there are mountains and valleys and rock formations and canals. And I sense that my eyes are moist again, but there's no way to smear the moisture with the sleeve of my spacesuit, because I'm wearing a helmet.

Stone Godfrey and Maya were right about the hatch's opening. I feel like I could fit through there if I had to, which I'm hoping I don't.

Stone Godfrey's voice blasts through the speaker inside my helmet. "There it is, Tuckerman, the sample container! Do you see it?"

Using the Martian surface as a backdrop, I search for it.

Nothing.

"I don't see it."

And now my brain is beginning to panic. And my palms are sweaty. And then I feel the spacecraft adjust course. And I hear Stone Godfrey's voice blaring over the speaker again.

"See that mountain towering above the surrounding plains? That's the Olympus Mons! Put it dead center in your line of sight, then track your eyes diagonally downward and to the right at a forty-five-degree angle until the sample container comes into view. The container's yellow locator beacon is blinking. You can't miss it."

"Copy."

I follow Stone Godfrey's instructions to the letter, and to the number.

And I blink, and I focus my eyes.

And there it is.

Flint Garrison was right. That container is the size of a basketball. And I'm going to catch it in a net. I wonder what Zeke would say about that.

"Tuckerman, talk to me."

"I see it."

"Okay, I'm going to move us into position for intercept. Get ready in there."

During training back on Earth, I had mastered the glove work necessary to release the robotic arm's protective harness and extend the arm outside the spacecraft and adjust its angle to precisely twenty-three degrees.

But now I'm doing it for real in a zero-gravity environment and under tremendous, partly self-imposed pressure, with the weight of the entire mission on my shoulders, and I'm nervous, and I'm sweating, and I'm scared, and my space-suit feels bulkier than it did back on Earth, and my hands have all the dexterity of a pair of stiff new catcher's mitts from the baseball aisle at Chip's.

"Good luck, Lawrence." I hear Maya's voice, but I can't see her because she's standing behind me, probably fidgeting with her ponytail. And my brain elects not to give her a be-hind-the-back Ryker two-finger gloved wave because I don't have a free hand.

Stone Godfrey guides the Ares Pilgrim toward the sample container. And since we're traveling slightly faster than the container, my brain needs to anticipate where to deploy the robotic arm as the container comes within reach.

"It's now or never, Tuckerman."

I extend the robotic arm.

And I instantly realize that the angle is wrong.

I swipe the mesh netting at the sample container, but I miss badly, and the spacecraft barrels past it.

And I stare off at the planet's surface.

And now my fear of heights kicks in, and I'm hyperventilating.

"What happened? Do we have sample container capture?"

"Negative."

58

We Don't Have Enough Fuel, Food, or Oxygen to Make It

I've never felt so alone as I do in this moment.

"Tuckerman, say again."

Not all those times when I sat by myself in the back of the McDerney cafeteria eating my astronaut training meal in silence while the other kids were making fun of me, or even at Zeke's basketball games, when I calculated his shooting percentages and free-throw probabilities in solitude from the empty top row of the bleachers.

"Dammit, Tuckerman. Repeat!"

I stare out the open hatch at the vast Martian landscape below.

And now my eyes are playing tricks on me, because Mars dissolves into a gigantic basketball court, and my brain visualizes the Zeke Archer of two years ago in the closing moments of the Southern California regional title game, when he drove downcourt on a fast break, and he pulled up at the free-throw line, but Curtis and Stretch weren't open, so Zeke took the shot, a potential game-winning fifteen-foot jumper, and he airballed it, and what a crushing blow it was for him when he let down his teammates.

This must be what Zeke felt like.

And I blink my eyes, and I see Mars outside the hatch again.

And now my fear of heights disappears.

And I wonder about the dramatic outcrops of sedimentary rock that have recorded the planet's complex geological history, and the spectacular landscapes and canyons and volcanoes and dry lake beds and craters, and the famous red dust that covers most of the Martian surface.

"Jupiter, what's happening in there?"

I wonder what it might be like to be the first earthling to set foot on Mars, to be remembered by the world for something other than keen math skills, or acumen at chess, or slapping people.

"I don't know, Stone. He's just staring out into space."

I stick my head out the hatch opening for a closer look at the planet. It seems so close, I can almost touch it. And then I unclip the nylon safety strap from my spacesuit, and I push my arms through the opening.

And I can hear what sounds like Maya's fists banging on the airlock's thick glass door.

"Sherman Tuckerman!"

I ignore Maya as I force my shoulders outside the spacecraft. I'm surprised to find that even with my bulky spacesuit, I'm able to squeeze through. And I place my hands on the outer surface of the Ares Pilgrim, and I lift my feet off the airlock floor. And then I—

"LAWRENCE!"

Maya screams my name through the speaker in my helmet so loudly, I almost throw up. Her voice lifts the fog from my brain, and I focus on what I'm doing inside the airlock, and when I realize my body is halfway outside the hatch, I almost throw up a second time.

I grab hold of the sides of the opening, and I force myself back into the airlock chamber. And once I'm safely back inside, the hatch window closes. Maya must have hit the button.

"Tuckerman, I'm not going to ask you again. Repeat!"

"NEGATIVE!"

I sense a change of air pressure inside the chamber, so I know Maya is operating the controls to pressurize it. And then I turn around. And Maya is standing directly in front of the window staring at me. I try to avoid her eyes, but I can't. I'm drawn to them.

And then I hear Stone Godfrey's voice inside my helmet. "Jupiter, send a communiqué to Mission Control. Tell them we're coming home. Tell them we're empty-handed. Copy?"

Maya completes the pressurization process and opens the airlock door. I step inside my quarters and remove my helmet.

"Copy," she says, and she continues to stare at me, and then without saying a word, she floats toward the lower hatch leading to her quarters.

And I catch a glimpse of her ponytail bobbing weightlessly.

"Wait!"

Maya stops and turns to face me. "Now what? Want me to open the hatch for you again?"

I'm the one and only person in the world who the Strategic Federation Council chose to carry out this mission, out of 6,623,517,838 possible candidates. And I can't just walk away from the responsibility. This is on my shoulders.

I can do this.

I WILL do this.

"Follow me," I say as I float toward the flight deck hatch. It's a tight squeeze with my spacesuit still on, but I'm able to slide through the passageway. And I don't check to see if Maya is following me, because I know she is.

And now it hits me. It's time to take personal responsibility. That's something Zeke taught me. I got us into this jam. I'm the one who needs to get us out of it.

Stone Godfrey is there, waiting to confront us.

"What happened out there? You said you had this."

"I did. Almost. The angle was wrong."

"What are you talking about, Tuckerman?"

"We need to orbit the planet one more time and try again. I can do it."

"We can't. There's not enough fuel, and the window to reenter TOTVA is closing fast."

Stone Godfrey uses that acronym for the seventh time, and I want to tell him to knock it off, but there's the more pressing matter of completing the mission and returning safely to Earth.

And it's always time to take action when there's danger.

"Give me a piece of paper."

"What for?"

"I need to run some calculations."

Stone Godfrey's face reddens. "The only way I'm giving you a piece of paper is if you're going to use it to write me a letter of apology."

"C'mon, Stone, don't be a jerk." Maya steps in on my behalf. "Give Lawrence some paper."

Stone Godfrey complies, and I remove my gloves, and I clip them to the carabiner attached to my spacesuit, and now I'm floating in the flight deck running the most vitally important calculations of my life.

And when there's no room left to write on the front, I flip the sheet over and complete my findings on the back. And then I hand it back to Stone Godfrey.

"Here."

"What's this?"

"The calculations we'll need to capture the container and then get us back into the vortex anomaly," I say as I slip my gloves back on.

Stone Godfrey scrutinizes my math. And then he rubs his chin and grimaces. "What's all this about a ponytail?"

"I formulated a nonlinear shape differential equation that takes into account the stiffness of Maya's hair, and its overall curliness, and its estimated buoyancy in the weightlessness of my cabin."

"Tuckerman, have you gone insane?"

"Let him finish." Maya sticking up for me makes my hands less clammy.

I tell Stone Godfrey that I've been observing the ponytail's geyser-like springiness as it cascades from the back of Maya's head like root beer pouring from a twelve-ounce aluminum can.

Those words cause Maya to shove her hands into her jumpsuit pockets.

I tell Stone Godfrey that I calculated the ponytail's launch angle, where the outermost hairs emerge from Maya's pink elastic hairband, all the way to the ponytail's fan-like conclusion at the bottom.

"The angle of launch is precisely twenty-eight degrees, certainly a number divisible by seven, but more importantly, it mirrors the angle of Zeke's elbow when his arm recoils after shooting a free throw—knee, elbow, and wrist, all moving in perfect alignment and harmony."

"Who the hell is Zeke?"

"He's my best friend, and he's the best basketball player in the whole wide world, or at least in all of Lawrence, Kansas."

"I can't believe I'm asking this." Stone Godfrey cocks his head to one side and rubs his eyelids. "What does this Zeke fella's recoiled shooting arm have to do with capturing a sample container orbiting Mars?"

"That's easy. Two things. The sample container is the size of a basketball, and twenty-eight degrees is the perfect angle to capture it."

Stone Godfrey takes another look at my calculations. "Then there's the matter of fuel, or more specifically, our lack of it. How do I know I can trust these numbers?"

"It'll take us a hundred and nineteen minutes to orbit Mars for the second attempt. After capture, we'll secure the payload, pressurize the airlock chamber, and turn the space-craft toward TOTVA."

I thought that by using Stone Godfrey's acronym, I might persuade him to view my plan more favorably.

"But these calculations have us using thirty-five percent of our remaining fuel just to get us to the vortex anomaly entrance."

"It's all there in the math. If you can get us into TOTVA, I can formulate continuous energy-efficiency scenarios to max-imize our remaining hypersonic nuclear thermal fuel. It'll be close, but we should make it."

"*Should?*" I don't think Stone Godfrey is convinced.

"Sounds like a plan." Maya is on board, and now I can sense heat radiating from inside my chest.

Stone Godfrey presses his lips together. "What if we miss the vortex anomaly entrance? We'd have to take the long way home, and we don't have enough fuel, food, or oxygen to make it." Stone Godfrey runs his hands through his hair. "I can't risk both your lives hoping this wild fantasy of yours will actually come true."

59

And There It Is

I let Stone Godfrey's words sink in. He's saying he doesn't
want to put our lives in jeopardy to avoid failure. Simple
as that.

I grapple my way over to Maya on the other end of the
flight deck. Up to this point, she and I have been content to
let Stone Godfrey decide everyone's fate.

It's time to find out what she wants to do.

"You've heard both sides," I say. "What's your opinion?"

Maya sways her head in a tight figure eight, which causes
her ponytail to take flight. "I'm in. Let's do this."

I turn to Stone Godfrey, knowing that as flight engineer, he
makes the final call. And I also know we can't afford to wait
the twenty-eight minutes it would take to ask Mission Control for permission and then wait for Pax Booker's decision,
which would be no anyway.

We're on our own.

"This isn't a democracy," Stone Godfrey says. "I'm taking
us home."

"Guess *Astronaut Quarterly* had it all wrong." Maya jumps headlong into the conversation. "Ace test pilot? Wounded Iraqi war veteran idolized for his courage on the battlefield? Innovative and respected Space Shuttle astronaut? Guess you can't believe everything you read in the press."

Stone Godfrey's jaw loosens. "You're just a couple of kids. You've got your whole lives ahead of you. Why do you want to risk everything?"

"We're at risk no matter what we do," Maya says. "Lawrence thinks he has a way out of this mess. I trust him. I believe in him."

No one has ever said those words about me before.

I drift over to Stone Godfrey. "You do your job, we'll do ours." And then I extend my hand to him. "Let's shake on it, because a man's handshake is his word, and his word is his bond."

Stone Godfrey's bloodshot green eyes meet mine, and for the first time since I met him, I don't look away.

I meet his gaze head on.

And then Stone Godfrey grasps my hand. And even though there's a better-than-even chance we're all standing at death's doorstep on this mission, my brain steps away for a millisecond to recall the detailed handshake lesson Zeke taught me on our Kansas road trip.

I grip onto Stone Godfrey's hand, and with friendly sincerity, I look him directly in the eye, and I smile.

Three pumps.

Three seconds.

Release.

And then the Stone Godfrey I've read about so many times in *Astronaut Quarterly* takes over.

"We don't have much time. Jupiter, send Mission Control a communiqué. Tell them we're making a second pass, then we're coming home. Tuckerman, get yourself into that airlock and adjust the robotic arm angle. I'm going to swing this crate around the planet one last time and get us into position for intercept."

My brain operates best when it has an understanding of the game plan, as it does right now.

Maya makes a beeline for her cabin to send Stone Godfrey's message to Mission Control. And I hustle back to my quarters, where I reflect on basketball's influence in my life and the lessons Zeke has taught me.

My brain tries to think of a way I can express my appreciation to him, but my thought process is cut short when Maya shoots up through the lower hatch.

"Mind telling me what was going on in the airlock chamber before?"

I ignore Maya, hoping she'll concentrate on the upcoming deployment, not the previous one.

Stone Godfrey's voice rings throughout the entire spaceship. "Ten minutes to container intercept. Final preparations, crew."

Maya helps me secure my helmet and gloves. Then she stands in front of the airlock button, but she doesn't push it. "You're not going in there till you tell me what went down."

She's not letting it go. I respond with *the blocker*.

"I dropped a contact lens."

"Very funny," she says as she opens the airlock door. "Letting it slide for now, but you'll have six months to give me an explanation. Better make it a good one."

I float over to the ceiling and peel off the piece of duct tape that's connected to the two fuzzy basketballs. "It's for good luck," I say as I enter the airlock and stick the contraption onto the chamber's ceiling.

"You're gonna need it, friend. See you on the other side."

And Maya closes the airlock door, but I motion for her to open it again.

"I forgot something. Hand me the laptop."

"What for? You won't have time to make a Captain's Log entry in there."

"In case I need it for something else."

Maya stares at the floor for a second and offers a slight shake of her head, which causes her ponytail to sway again. "Whatever."

She hands me the laptop. The FOR THE CAPTAIN'S LOG label is still stuck to the lid. Using one of the nylon straps inside the airlock, I secure the laptop to the side of the chamber.

And Maya closes the door. And the depressurization process gets underway. And I sense the air pressure changing again.

"Five minutes to container intercept. It's all you, Lawrence."

It's the first time Stone Godfrey calls me by the same name my friends do. My brain determines he's got a lot on his mind right now. I decide not to say anything or read too much into it.

And then I hear the rockets firing like before. And the Ares

Pilgrim decelerates and eases downward. And my heart rate remains steady this time. And Maya opens the exterior hatch.

I release the protective harness and extend the robotic arm. And then I make the all-important angle adjustment to precisely twenty-eight degrees. And now I wait for the sample container to come to me.

And as I stare out the open hatch, Mars dissolves into a basketball court again. But instead of Zeke and Curtis and Stretch losing the championship game, the guys are on the sideline encouraging me to succeed. Even Brock Decker is there, although it looks like he's just standing around waiting to see what'll happen.

And then I hear Stone Godfrey's voice, and when I blink my eyes, the basketball court disappears, and the surface of Mars is once again in plain view.

"There it is again, Tuckerman. Can you see it?"

My brain notates that Stone Godfrey has gone back to calling me by my last name. I find comfort in that. I think it means he trusts me.

This time there's no need for him to give me geographical points of reference on the Martian surface below, because I can see the yellow locator beacon flashing like the turn signals on my 1965 Chevy pickup—at least when it was all in one piece.

Stone Godfrey guides the spacecraft toward the sample container, closer and closer, until it seems like I can practically reach out and touch it.

I know that the success of the mission is now entirely in my hands, which are encased inside a pair of thick gloves. And I'm nervous, but I'm confident too.

I extend the robotic arm, and I focus my eyes on the flying basketball's locator beacon.

Closer and closer.

And there it is.

And I reach for it.

Knee. Elbow. Wrist.

All moving in perfect alignment and harmony.

And I catch the sample container, dead center.

Nothing but netting.

Ballgame.

60

The Bird Is in the Nest

I retract the robotic arm back into the airlock chamber, being extra careful not to bang the frame of the mesh netting against the sides of the hatch.

If I were to accidentally drop the sample container overboard now, and Stretch were operating the airlock controls instead of Maya, he would size up my misfortune by saying: *Nice hands, buddy. You should have a pair of ping-pong paddles made out of those.*

I peek over my shoulder, and I catch a glimpse of Maya's ear-to-ear grin. And then I remove the sample container from the mesh netting, and I secure it inside the specially designed, lead-lined compartment that's bolted to the floor of the airlock chamber.

"Sample recovery crew, report status."

"We've got it, Stone! Lawrence came through!"

"Roger that, Jupiter. Button it up down there. We're going home."

Maya steps toward the airlock door. "Stand clear. I'm going to close the hatch window."

"Wait."

My brain replays verbatim every word Flint Garrison said to me when the flight activities specialist was rifling through my backpack as I prepared to board the spacecraft: *Basketballs, huh? Egad, Sherman, you can't take those with you. Everyone knows there's no basketball on Mars.*

And then I think about how Zeke always accepts me for who I am, and all the times he's helped me out of a jam, and how the sport of basketball is at the center of everything Zeke and I do whenever we hang out together.

And Zeke's two fuzzy basketballs are still duct-taped to the ceiling of the airlock chamber. Those basketballs have served their intended purpose. They brought us good fortune on the mission.

"I need to do something," I tell Maya as I peel the duct tape from the ceiling. "I need to honor Zeke. I need to honor basketball."

And when Maya smiles, her front teeth reflect the light coming from inside the airlock chamber. "Do what you gotta do."

I step to the open hatch, and I take one final unobstructed look at the planet below. I hope to return here someday and walk on the Martian surface, for the good of humanity.

But for now, I'm content with returning to Earth to tell Flint Garrison that there actually is basketball on Mars.

When my brain precalculated tossing those basketballs overboard, it concluded that they're so lightweight, they might remain in orbit forever and never fall to the planet's surface.

I free the laptop from the nylon straps, and I stick the duct tape and basketballs onto its metal lid, and then I fling the whole thing overboard. And I watch as evidence of my journey to Mars tumbles end over end until it disappears from view.

I'm glad that my dad didn't tell Flint Garrison I wouldn't need a laptop on the mission. Turns out it came in handy after all. I hope it wasn't too expensive.

I turn toward the airlock door. Maya's nose is pressed up against the glass. And her face is wrinkling in slow motion.

"Why'd you do that? Weren't you using the laptop for the Captain's Log?"

"No."

"What if we need it later?"

"We won't. It served its purpose."

Maya still has a look of concern on her face. "You said Zeke gave you those orange thingies for good luck, but you tossed them overboard when we're only halfway through the mission."

I hadn't thought of that, but it's too late now.

"We'll be fine. Get me out of here."

Maya closes the hatch window and pressurizes the chamber. And then she opens the airlock door, and she helps me out of my spacesuit.

And then we float to the flight deck to check in with Stone Godfrey.

"Good work, Tuckerman. You too, Jupiter."

"Thanks, boss." Maya is quick to respond.

But I don't, because Stone Godfrey doesn't ask me a question. Instead, I take note of how my lungs are expanding to their fullest as I draw in a deep breath, and then I hook my thumbs onto the pockets of my jumpsuit, and I stick out my chest.

"What was all that chatter before?"

"Nothing. Just Lawrence putting his stamp on Mars."

"I've had enough of this planet to last me a lifetime," Stone Godfrey says as he punches our new coordinates into the flight deck computer. "Tuckerman, run the fuel expenditure and exhaust velocity calculations for vortex anomaly approach. Jupiter, radio Mission Control. Tell them the bird is in the nest. Tell them we're coming home."

61

Hold On!

The Ares Pilgrim's nose is tilting upward like before. And my brain senses that the spacecraft is altering course.

"You two had better get to your crew seats and buckle up. If it's anything like last time, the ride is going to get choppy."

"Copy." Saying that word is second nature to me now. I like how it conveys an important message while using the minimum number of words possible.

I know that the spacecraft's computers are tasked with guiding us into the vortex anomaly's entrance, but protocol calls for Stone Godfrey to override the system if he thinks we're in trouble.

"We are T-minus thirty seconds from insertion. Tucker-man, after that stellar performance with the robotic arm, I'm going to give you the honor of doing the countdown."

And now I'm feeling so confident, I add an extra word to my response.

"Copy that."

"We are at T-minus fifteen seconds and counting. We're go for insertion. Astronaut Tuckerman, you take it from here."

"Sherman Tuckerman, in the spotlight," Maya says, but I don't let her break my concentration.

Just as I did when we launched from Vandenberg, I count down the next five seconds in my brain before pressing the intercom button.

"Ten. Nine. Eight. Seven. Six. Five. Four. Three. Two. One—"

There's the whooshing sound, and my cabin goes dead quiet, and then my brain senses that the spacecraft is pulsating and gaining speed.

"Hold on!" Stone Godfrey issues a directive from the flight deck, but I'm already white-knuckling in my crew seat long before he says it.

And the interior of my quarters goes dark again, just like before, and my hands are clammy and trembling.

But this time, the sensation of being an accomplished space pioneer forces something unfamiliar to happen.

It makes me grin.

And no matter how hard I try to make it stop, I can't.

62

I Make a Rare Attempt at Humor

Captain's Log—Ares Pilgrim Mars Mission, Day 273

We're exactly halfway home. Similar to when we arrived at the midpoint of the outbound journey to Mars, and in the interest of symmetry, I'm making this Captain's Log entry to record my observations.

Stone Godfrey's behavior has become progressively more unpredictable ever since we captured the sample container. On some days, he's overly friendly. On others, he says mean things to Maya and me.

And then there are the times when he blurts out words that don't make any sense. This concerns me the most, because I was around kids in my special needs school who did that, and sometimes it didn't end well.

Maya has been keeping to herself more and more on the return trip home. She's not as cheerful as she was when we began the mission, and she has stopped telling me bizarre and colorful stories about her past.

I fight boredom on the journey back to Earth by performing a continuous comparative analysis of the relative size of Earth and Mars as I view them through my hatch window.

And I spend the rest of my free time doing theoretical topological studies of the effect that the rocket propulsion system might have on the space capsule's structure. I do this by running differentiable equations of the deformations in geometrical shapes that might occur under conditions of stretching, crumpling, bending, and twisting.

During my JPL internship, Professor Bellwether suggested that this type of detailed examination would allow for greater insight into what a Mars-bound spacecraft might endure over the course of a lengthy spaceflight. And as the mission's mathematics flight specialist, I need to be ready for anything.

And now I'm running out of things to write, which is okay, because I hear the

lower hatch opening, which means Maya
wants to talk, which is annoying because
she talks too much, but is occasionally
favorable, because I've been in near-total
isolation for most of the past 273 days,
and I'm finding that it isn't as much fun
as it was when we first launched from
Vandenberg.

Maya is carrying her medical bag. And her hair is no longer in a ponytail. And she's not smiling like she used to.

"You busy?"

"Yes."

"Captain's Log?"

"Yes. Important entry."

"Was wondering if you'd like to swap a meal packet today. Little variation in the routine."

"No."

"I'm long on corn pudding with asparagus. Whaddaya say?"

"No."

"Green bean and garlic cashew stir-fry? Zesty noodles in avocado sauce? Spicy quinoa bowl with lentils?"

I wonder whether it would be a mission infraction to say the word *no* three times in a row. Instead, I channel my inner Dr. Tidewater by choosing diplomacy.

"I'm kind of busy."

"While I'm here, might as well take your vitals." And Maya uses her medical devices to measure my heart rate, blood pressure, body temperature, and oxygen saturation level.

"Cool as a cucumber, Sherman Tuckerman."

My brain notes that cucumbers are mostly comprised of water and are therefore cool to the touch, so I surmise that Maya's use of the word *cool* refers to my imperturbable nature rather than my body temperature being low.

And then I make a rare attempt at humor, opting for a double entendre, which my brain recalls is a word or phrase open to two interpretations.

"Cool."

There's no reaction from Maya. She packs her medical equipment and heads back to her quarters, but before she disappears, she turns and asks me a question, which by this point in the mission, is no longer a big deal because I'm used to it, so I let it go.

"Stone hasn't allowed me to take his vitals for a couple of weeks now, and he's been acting more crotchety than usual. You think he's okay?"

I've also witnessed Stone Godfrey's changing behavior, and I don't know what's causing it, and I don't want to upset Maya, so my brain searches for a strategically innocuous grouping of words to address her concern without causing undo alarm.

"Interesting question."

"Yes, isn't it," she says as she retreats to her compartment. But before she closes the hatch, she pops her head back through the passageway. "Hey, how about I offer you a couple packages of chicken noodle casserole with potatoes? Two-for-one swap."

"No."

63

No One Will Miss Us, No One Will Care

Captain's Log—Ares Pilgrim Mars Mission, Day 364

This will be my final log entry before splashdown in the Pacific Ocean two hours from now. I'm starting to get the hang of this Captain's Log assignment. I hope the SFC scientists back at Mission Control find it useful and appreciate my attention to detail.

I've been running ongoing calculations to maximize our fuel expenditure and exhaust velocity, and I can report that the Ares Pilgrim is responding as intended.

And in my spare time, I've reread Zeke's diary six more times. I've also attempted to reestablish contact with the 7th

Dimension on several occasions using seven interlocked No. 2 pencils, but no luck so far.

I will conclude this final log entry with a message to young people like me who struggle to find their place in the world: Never ever stop trying. You might make it to Mars someday, or wherever your hopes and dreams take you.

It's time for my final meal of the mission. I think I'll have the chili mac 'n' beef.

Tuckerman, out.

The sound of the lower hatch opening interrupts my food preparation. Maya drifts into my cabin.

"Kind of busy in here. Chili mac 'n' beef waits for no man."

"Not here to interrupt your breakfast," Maya says. "Here to talk to you."

I don't think we can separate the two activities, but Maya is my friend. I listen while I squish around the food inside the package.

"Want some?"

"No, thanks. Not hungry. Anyway, there's some stuff I need to tell you. All those things I said about—"

THUMP! BANG!

Maya stops talking, and I think the Ares Pilgrim just bounced off the side of a mountain.

The spacecraft is wobbling like an out-of-balance gyroscope, and it's making me dizzy.

And the lights are flickering.

And the smell of burning insulation is wafting through the air.

"Medic!"

It's Stone Godfrey, shouting the last word you ever want to hear over the intercom from the person piloting the spacecraft. Maya rushes to the flight deck. I follow behind her.

Stone Godfrey is strapped to his crew seat, leaning back and clutching his heart.

"What happened?" There's panic in Maya's voice.

"It came out of nowhere. We hit some space debris. I think I'm having a heart attack."

"Wait here and keep an eye on him. I need my medical bag." And Maya disappears through the hatch.

And Stone Godfrey is gasping for air. And his face is chalkier than Flint Garrison's.

"I knew we weren't going to make it, Tuckerman."

"Don't try to talk. Wait for Maya."

Where's Maya? Why isn't she here yet? If Stone Godfrey dies, we're sunk.

The wobbling and flickering stop, but the burning smell is still in the air.

"This whole mission has been a lie." And now Stone Godfrey isn't making any sense again, and he's struggling to breathe, and I don't know how to help him.

Just then, Maya darts through the passageway, medical bag in hand.

"How is he?"

"He can't breathe, and he's talking gibberish, something about the mission being a lie."

Maya removes an oxygen mask from a compartment on

the instrument panel, and she straps it to Stone Godfrey's face. He takes a deep breath, and then another, and then he rips off the mask.

"You don't get it, do you?" Stone Godfrey's breathing is labored and shallow. "We're expendable, all of us. I'm a has-been loser. You're just a couple of snot-nosed kids. One of you can change the station on a radio dial, the other has memorized his multiplication tables. If we don't make it back to Earth, no one will miss us, no one will care, and no one will ever know what happened."

64

And Then I Hear a Familiar Voice

"That's not true," I say as I move closer to Stone Godfrey and cross my arms. I feel my blood pressure rising. "We're not expendable. We're highly skilled astronauts on a mission to recover Martian stromatolites that can possibly lead to sweeping new advances in medical science."

And Maya straps the oxygen mask back onto Stone Godfrey's face. And tears are flowing from her eyes as she takes his blood pressure, and then she pulls a syringe from her medical bag.

"I need to give him something to calm him down," she whispers to me. And she injects the contents of the tube into Stone Godfrey's neck.

Stone Godfrey grabs my jumpsuit and pulls me in close as he whispers to me through his mask.

"I've read the research," he says. "The SFC thinks the Martian stromatolites might contain trace amounts of a previously unknown fifteenth isotope of Lawrencium, one with a half-life that extends well beyond the known origins of the universe. If that's true, then the chemical compound we're bringing home has the potential to be used as a building block for an advanced new type of biological weapon."

I break away from Stone Godfrey's grip to process what he says.

"Mission Control to Ares Pilgrim, come in." It's Pax Booker's voice blaring over the intercom.

Maya keys the microphone on the instrument panel. "Ares Pilgrim. Go."

"We're getting some unusual readings down here, Maya. Our instruments have detected some sort of collision, followed by a fuel leak. And you're veering off course too. What's the sitrep?"

My brain remembers from my week of training that *sitrep* is a military abbreviation for *situation report*, which is a type of status update that provides decision-makers like Pax Booker with an immediate understanding of the current situation.

"We hit space debris. Then Stone had a heart attack."

There's a lengthy pause before Pax Booker responds. "What is the flight engineer's status?"

"Vitals aren't good and he's super agitated. I gave him a mild sedative."

Those details are met with another protracted delay before Pax Booker responds. "Maya, stay with Stone and do everything you can to get him stable. Sherman, I'm afraid I might have to ask you to do more than you signed on for. Can you do that, son?"

"Copy that." Without knowing exactly what the flight director might ask me to do, it's the only way I can respond.

"Ten-four. Give us a few minutes to figure this thing out. Stand by, flight crew."

And now Stone Godfrey appears to have lost consciousness.

"Stone, stay with me!" Maya says, and then she smacks him across the face, not as forcibly as before, but hard enough to get his attention. There's no response.

"I need to go," I say to Maya.

"Go? Go where?"

"To my cabin. I need to think."

"Better hurry. Don't have much time."

I work my way back to my compartment, open my backpack, and pop seven wedges of Bazooka Joe into my mouth from my dwindling supply. No sense waiting for a rainy day.

The sweet goodness calms me down. I can think more clearly now. I close my eyes and concentrate. And when I open them, there are pencils drifting about the cabin. Seven of them. They must have floated out of my backpack again.

I have an idea. I grab the pencils and interconnect them using the notches I carved into them when they were brand new. I'm attempting to use neusis construction to create a heptagonal antenna to communicate with the Entity, just as Zeke describes in his diary. I need to ask the 7th Dimension for help.

I release the seven-sided device to float about the cabin while I close my eyes and concentrate on making contact.

Nothing.

And then I remember the time when the 7th Dimension altered its spectral broadcast subcarrier, which rendered me unable to tap into the correct nonneutral linear half-frequency until I invented a workaround by using bubblegum fortified with my own DNA, which is the self-replicating chemical building block present in all living organisms and the main component of chromosomes.

In doing so before, I self-sequenced my own genetic code to activate the heptagonal antenna so that the Entity would know it was me trying to make contact.

I pull the giant wad of already-been-chewed gum from my mouth, and I wrap chunks of it around the notches where the pencils are interconnected.

And then I release the device to float about the cabin again, and I close my eyes, and I concentrate harder than I ever have in my entire life.

Again, nothing.

And then I hear a familiar voice.

"Hello, Lawrence."

65

The Universe Is a Pretty Big Place

I open my eyes and turn around, and James Naismith, the inventor of basketball, is floating with me in my cabin.

"It is good to see you again, old friend," James Naismith says. "I heard your distress call."

"Copy."

I'm too stunned to say anything else. And my hands are clammy. And I'm hyperventilating. James Naismith reaches into his satchel and hands me a brown paper bag.

"Breathe into this. It will put some of the lost carbon dioxide back into your lungs to assist in balancing the flow of oxygen in your body."

It works. I'm no longer panicking, and my brain is thinking clearly again.

Reading Zeke's diary during the mission helped to jar loose my memory of the time Zeke and I spent in the presence of James Naismith, which only happened when the sport of basketball was in grave peril.

But the catastrophic situation brewing aboard the Ares Pilgrim has nothing to do with basketball.

"I am here to tell you that the 7th Dimension representative who is the most well-versed in matters of space travel just went all-in on the final hand of a poker tournament with Neil Armstrong, Christa McAuliffe, John Glenn, and also Gus Grissom, Ed White, and Roger Chaffee, the three crew members of Apollo One."

There's an Entity-sponsored poker tournament, and the players are seven deceased space program legends?

"Copy."

And now I'm wondering whether I've breathed in too much of what was burning inside the space capsule after we glanced off that space debris, because what I'm witnessing in front of me can't be happening.

"Emotions can run close to the surface when you are at the edge of the human experience," James Naismith says. "You may wish to consider keeping your composure in this crisis. Your crewmates are relying on you to remain mentally healthy and make sound decisions."

James Naismith's reality check sends a shudder through my body.

"Copy."

"With that settled, Lawrence, I must be going. Take good care, my friend."

"Lawrence!" I turn toward the hatch, and Maya's head is poking through the opening. When I swing back around, James Naismith is gone. "Are you talking to yourself?"

"No."

"I need you up here. Whatever it is you're doing, hurry up."

And Maya disappears back through the hatch, and when I turn around, there's another person floating in my cabin.

He's familiar to me, but I've never met him.

Until now.

"Hello, Lawrence," the man says.

"Hello." I would have written that word on a note if I had a pencil handy that wasn't stuck to six other pencils with bubblegum.

The man points toward the hatch window inside the air-lock chamber. Planet Earth, spinning on its axis against a sea of darkness, is visible through the glass. It reminds me that I'm a long way from home.

"I understand you're trying to make it back safely to that pale blue dot over there, that small stage in the vast cosmic arena. That's home?"

"Yes."

And now my brain realizes he's the same person who's on the poster hanging on my bedroom wall. And he's even wear-ing the same dark green suit, light blue shirt, and gold knit tie.

It's Carl Sagan.

"Sorry to have suddenly appeared as quietly as an amoe-ba's footstep. I hope I didn't startle you."

"No."

"Good. Sometimes these appearances can catch people a little off guard."

"Yes."

"It seems that Zeke's diary—that assemblage of flat, flexible parts imprinted with dark graphite squiggles, perhaps the greatest of human inventions, your best friend's voice speaking clearly and silently inside your head, directly to you—has brought us together in this moment of crisis."

"Yes."

I wonder how long before Maya shoots through the hatch again, and what she'll say when she sees me talking to the man who spent a lifetime on Earth researching extraterrestrial life.

"Lawrence, you've been given the lead in this cosmic drama. As you might imagine, the answers you seek are resident within you. It's important that you have purpose beyond instinct, that you move toward what you want, rather than away from what you don't. Let your imagination carry you to new worlds. Your options, like the stars visible in the divine darkness through that hatch window, are infinite."

My brain is still processing what Stone Godfrey whispered to me, that the contents of the sample container might be used to build an advanced new type of weapon.

"What about the—"

"Yes, the Martian sample container. You're concerned, and rightly so, about what might happen with its contents back on Earth. What I will tell you is that the 7th Dimension strongly endorses the time-honored belief that life looks for life, not death."

Carl Sagan's words provide much-needed relief.

"Mission Control to Ares Pilgrim. What's the sitrep?" It's Pax Booker over the intercom. I know Maya will soon be looking for me.

"One last thought to leave you with, my young colleague. The universe is a pretty big place. If it's just us, it seems like an awful waste of space, wouldn't you agree?"

"Lawrence!" Maya's head is poking through the hatch again.

I turn back to Carl Sagan, but he's gone.

66

My Real Name Isn't Maya Jupiter

"Who are you talking to?"

I know I can't tell Maya the truth. If I say I abandoned her to have an ethereal conversation with two 7th Dimension emissaries while the Ares Pilgrim was rudderless and barreling toward Earth in a doom spiral because the only person who can pilot the spacecraft is on death's doorstep, she might think my brain has lost its mind, and there's no mathematical upside to that.

And I've never told a lie.

And I'm not going to start now.

So I ignore her.

"Wait. Your answer to this crisis is to talk to yourself down here while I'm trying to keep the flight engineer alive?"

Maya seems like she's about to lose it. I know, because I've been there so many times in my own life.

"Mission Control to Ares Pilgrim. We need to know the sitrep. Talk to us, Maya."

"And why is there a brown paper bag floating around your cabin? Is there something going on down here I need to know about?"

"No." That is the truth.

I follow Maya back to the flight deck, and she grapples her way to the instrument panel and presses the mic button. "Stone is unconscious. I'm trying to keep him alive, but I don't know how much longer I can do that."

"Copy that, Maya. Sherman, it looks like it's just you and me and that space-age hunk of metal you're riding in. You ever fly any type of aircraft before?"

I move to the instrument panel and key the mic. "No, but I sat behind Stone Godfrey when he was flying the T-38 Talon jet trainer, and I once drove Zeke Archer's 1965 Chevy pickup truck all the way from Utah to Kansas nonstop."

"Good. That will help."

"Pax Booker sounds like he's trying hard to be optimistic," Maya says, but I ignore her because her words are less than helpful.

"Sherman, let's start by getting Stone out of the pilot's seat and you in it. Can Maya safely secure him to another part of the flight deck?"

"Affirmative." I say that word for the first time in my life. I know it conveys hope, support, and encouragement, things I suspect we'll all need.

Maya unlatches the harness and guides Stone Godfrey to the other side of the flight deck, and then she secures him to the floor. I slip into the pilot's seat, and I strap myself in, and then I key the mic again.

"Mission Control, this is Tuckerman, in the catbird seat, awaiting instructions."

I know from watching TV crime dramas that *catbird seat* is a phrase used when a person is in an enviable position and has the upper hand, and that's clearly not the case now, but I say it as part of my master plan to keep Maya calm.

"Ten-four, Ares Pilgrim. After you exit the vortex anomaly, the spacecraft's autopilot will perform a course-correction maneuver and adjust your trajectory. This will scale down your fuel consumption, minimize deceleration forces on the spacecraft, and reduce the risk of a misaligned reentry. After that, the guidance system will automatically set a course for splashdown."

"Copy that."

Looks like I'll only need to say *Copy* a lot and babysit the spacecraft while the autopilot does all the work.

"There's one more thing I need to tell you. According to our data, we believe that the heat shield was damaged when the spacecraft nicked that space debris, and there's no way to know the extent of the damage. The guidance system is going to fine-tune your angle of reentry into the atmosphere, and we think it'll minimize the possibility of anything going wrong. Copy?"

"Minimize the possibility of anything going wrong? Is he serious?" Maya sounds worried. "We're all going to die, I just know it."

"Copy that, Mission Control."

And now, in addition to landing a crippled spacecraft, I need to ask Maya a bunch of questions about her life to distract her from coming apart at the seams.

"You said there was stuff you wanted to tell me before Stone Godfrey tried to land the Ares Pilgrim on an asteroid. What was it?"

"Nothing."

"It's my spacecraft now. I get to make the rules. As your commanding officer, I'm ordering you to tell me."

"Wow, put a guy in charge and watch it go to his head."

"Mission Control to Ares Pilgrim. We've sent you the coordinates for deceleration, orbital insertion, and Earth atmosphere reentry, in case you need to input the data manually. Maya can access everything over the datalink on the flight deck's instrument panel."

Maya drifts over and downloads the data.

"Everything I told you about myself was a lie," she says, and now I notice that her hands are shaking.

"Copy that, Mission Control, download successful." And now I turn to Maya. "A lie?"

"For starters, I never played point guard in middle school."

Totally harmless. Maya joins the long list of teenagers who've inflated their sports accomplishments prior to entering high school.

"That's it?"

"Mission Control to Ares Pilgrim. Sherman, check your fuel readings. Copy?"

"Copy that."

"No, there's more," Maya says.

My plan to keep Maya calm by distracting her appears to be working. "Like what?"

"Never had a butler. Never went to Sorbonne University."

Okay, that's not so bad. "Is that it?" I ask as I scribble my fuel calculations onto a scrap of paper from atop Stone Godfrey's console.

"Never hitchhiked across Europe, never built a pirate radio station, never was arrested by police in Luxembourg."

"What about the Planetary Society's Tuckerman Clause?"

"No such thing."

"The runaway combine harvester incident in the Iowa cornfield?"

"Nope."

"Was any of it true?"

"Yeah. I did build a transistor radio when I was two. And my father did ask General Garrison to secure my release from custody, but it wasn't in Luxembourg, it was county lockup in East L.A. My dad isn't Flint Garrison's Air Force buddy. He's an auto mechanic at the garage where the general takes his car for servicing. Dad pleaded with Flint to bail me out after I was arrested for driving on a suspended license for the third time, and then other things happened after that, and now here I am, moments away from being vaporized."

I choose not to lecture Maya on the characteristics of the vaporization process or ask her why her driver's license was suspended multiple times. "Anything else?"

"Yeah, my real name isn't Maya Jupiter. It's Mary Jones."

67

Godspeed, Commander Tuckerman

I am surrounded by total chaos, and things are happening all around me that I cannot control, and my life might end instantly at any second.

All of which makes this an odd time for my brain to remind me that I never lie.

And now I think about how people have judged me all my life because I'm different, and because of the choices I make.

Maya has made choices in her life I wouldn't make in mine, but not everyone has to be like me. If they were, then that pale blue dot we're streaking toward would be a pretty boring place.

I'm glad Maya is my friend. My brain concludes that the lies she told are not harmful to anyone but her. And I still respect her, and I won't judge her for her decisions, or her lies, and I don't need to know why she did it.

"Wanna know why?"

"No."

"Till I met you, never had a friendship that lasted longer than six weeks, seven tops."

"I said no."

"You're different from anyone I've ever met. You're honest and direct. I made up everything because I wanted you to like me, to accept me."

I don't need an explanation from Maya because I liked her from the moment I met her. And it's her life. She gets to make her own decisions, just like I make mine, except when my dad makes them for me.

And now my brain returns its focus to the crisis we're in, and I radio the data on the spacecraft's remaining nuclear thermal fuel to Mission Control.

"Roger that, Ares Pilgrim." Pax Booker confirms that our calculations are in sync.

"Changed my name after the general posted my bail. Wanted to leave Mary Jones in the rearview mirror. And that's everything."

I'm most relieved about the Tuckerman Clause not being real, because I wouldn't want nepotism to play a role in my possible future selection for space missions.

"Mission Control to Ares Pilgrim, come in."

"Tuckerman. Go."

"I've got some news, and I'm not going to sugarcoat it, Sherman. Our computers are telling us the spacecraft's auto-pilot function has failed. It's completely offline. The collision must've taken it out. But don't worry, we'll walk you through everything on the fly. Piece of cake."

"Is it just me, or does Pax Booker sound excessively positive about the outcome of this looming disaster?"

I don't answer Maya because her question is rhetorical, meaning she said it to create a dramatic effect rather than to elicit an answer. Instead, I change the subject. "How's Stone Godfrey?"

"Out cold. Breathing is shallow. Blood pressure's dropping. There's only so much I can do for him with the limited resources I have here."

"Before he fell ill, he said you failed a biology course, but I can tell you learned some important medical stuff."

"It was Biology 101 in high school, and I didn't flunk. I got a D because I cut class on the day of the final."

"How come?"

"Mission Control to Ares Pilgrim. Two minutes to vortex anomaly exit. Sherman, would you like to do the countdown?"

"Raincheck me on that, Mission Control. We've got our hands full up here."

"Ditched class to go to the downtown federal building to take the test for my FCC Global Maritime Distress and Safety System Radio Operator's License."

"But you must've learned some important stuff in biology."

"Best experience I got was when I posed as a nurse's assistant in the ER of a local hospital for a couple of days. That's where I learned how to treat trauma victims. Turns out it was enough to earn a spot on this mission of death—but maybe not enough, because Stone just stopped breathing!"

And now there's a whooshing sound, the same as when we

entered the vortex anomaly when the mission began, and my body feels the spacecraft vibrating and gaining speed.

I hear a hollow thumping sound behind me. I glance over my shoulder, and I watch as Maya administers CPR to Stone Godfrey. She's applying repeated compressions to his chest in an attempt to restart his heart. Mine feels like it's ready to explode.

"Mission Control to Ares Pilgrim. We're showing successful vortex anomaly exit. Nice work up there, Sherman."

"Copy."

And now I hear Maya performing mouth-to-mouth resuscitation, forcing air into Stone Godfrey's lungs in an effort to restore his circulation and breathing.

She removes a medical reference manual from her bag, and she flips through it until she lands on the page she needs.

Then she pulls another piece of medical equipment from her bag, but it's a lot smaller than the one she used to check Stone Godfrey's blood pressure. It's the device she uses to measure oxygen saturation level. She clips it to his finger, and she reads the display monitor, and then she shakes her head.

"Sherman, you've got the wheel now, so I'm going to give it to you straight." Pax Booker sounds calm but serious. "You'll need to thread the needle, otherwise the Ares Pilgrim will either burn up on reentry, or it'll skip out of the atmosphere and strand you in interplanetary space. I'm going to be honest with you, son—if we don't get this just right, we're going to have a problem."

"By *problem*, I think he means we're all going to die."

"Shut up, Maya."

"Once you've input the data into the guidance system,

you'll be bringing the spacecraft in manually. I know you've had a chance to look over Stone's shoulder on this mission. I need you to draw from that experience. You've got good instincts, Sherman. I need you to follow them."

"Copy."

"You'll begin to hit Earth's atmosphere in two minutes. When that happens, you'll lose all radio contact with Mission Control, and it's going to get bumpy and real warm inside the flight deck. After that, splashdown is the only detail left on the docket. Copy?"

My brain concludes that I've developed enough of a relationship with the flight director to call him by his first name.

"Roger that, Pax."

"Got a pulse. Got him breathing again."

"Good. Now get down below and strap yourself in."

"No way. I'm not leaving him. If Stone can hang on, so can I."

"Keep an eye on your descent angle, Sherman. It needs to be precise so that you minimize the adverse effects of the damaged heat shield tiles."

I find comfort in Pax Booker's voice. I hope I'll be able to write him a note to thank him in person. Or better yet, I might even give him the ungloved version of the Ryker two-finger wave.

"Copy that, Mission Control." I cinch my crew seat harness as tight as I can.

"Godspeed, Commander Tuckerman."

68

Mayday! Mayday! Mayday!

My body feels like it's riding a rollercoaster inside a cement mixer encased in the pizza oven at Mike's.

"Hold on, Maya!"

My brain remembers the seven-button sequence Stone Godfrey punched into his computer when he guided the spacecraft into Martian orbit. I follow the same pattern, but I change the order to account for the difference in Earth's atmosphere versus that of Mars before I guide the large silver lever into the downward position.

My feet feel like they're on fire. I glance at the on-board thermometer. It's 112 degrees Fahrenheit in the flight deck. My brain calculates the conversion to Celsius at 44.44444 degrees, which doesn't help me to control the spacecraft any better, but the unexpected number of consecutive fours temporarily distracts me from the realization that if the Ares Pilgrim crew perishes instantly in a massive nuclear fireball, it'll be all my fault, because I'm the one at the controls.

The speaker on the instrument panel snaps me back to

reality when it blasts out a series of 3,000 Hz electronic tones. And my brain recalls that when it happened before, Stone Godfrey flipped three switches and rotated a dial four clicks to the right. I repeat the process, but my instincts tell me to do it in reverse order.

And now alarms are going off everywhere, and it sounds like someone is blowing a basketball referee's whistle inside my head, and I don't know how to make it stop.

And then I key the mic.

"Mayday! Mayday! Mayday!"

And now sparks are flying past the flight deck window so fast that they're a bright yellow blur, and smoke is pouring in from the instrument panel, and it smells like burning insulation, and all I can do is use my instincts to punch buttons, and slide the large silver lever up and down, and hope.

And then all the lights go out.

And then it gets eerily quiet.

And then I wonder if this is what it's like to be dead.

To be free of fear.

And pain.

And bullies, and people who don't understand me, and endless calculations coursing through my brain.

And then I hear a muted *whoosh-flap-bang!* sound from outside the spacecraft.

And I feel the Ares Pilgrim rapidly decelerating.

And then my brain concludes that the parachute has deployed.

"Mission Control to Ares Pilgrim, come in."

I try to key the mic, but my brain can't move my hands. It doesn't matter, though, because I'm unable to speak.

"Mission Control to Ares Pilgrim, do you read me? Come in."

And I hear the sound of Stone Godfrey moaning, and then I sense something drifting toward me, but I'm unable to turn my head to see what it is.

"Mission Control to Ares Pilgrim, do you read me? Come in."

Smack!

Maya cracks me hard across the face.

"What'd you do that for?"

"It's an old chief medical officer's trick. We use it to bring a catatonic hero back to reality. You going to answer that?"

My brain notes that the word *catatonic* is used to describe someone who is immobile or in an unresponsive stupor. I've been called a lot of names in my lifetime, but nobody has ever called me that one before.

And come to think of it, no one has ever called me a hero. Until now.

"Mission Control, this is the Ares Pilgrim Commander speaking. Parachute deployed. Flight engineer stable. We're headed for splashdown."

"Roger that, Ares Pilgrim. You roast any marshmallows in the flight deck on the way down?"

"Negative, Pax. But we sure could've if we had some aboard."

69

Life Might Well Exist Beyond Earth

The space capsule bobs up and down in the Pacific Ocean a few miles off the Central California coast. We're scooped up by an AgustaWestland AW139 Air Force helicopter.

A second chopper arrives soon after to secure a supplemental flotation device around the ailing but valiant Ares Pilgrim and recover the sample container.

It's my first-ever helicopter ride, which would've ordinarily been a thrilling experience, but after cheating death in a confined space for 364 days, the copter is simply the means to an end, and I'm looking forward to walking on terra firma again.

A medical crew treats Stone Godfrey at one end of the helo's fuselage, while Maya and I hang out together at the other.

"If I get to cast a vote for this year's Nobel Prize in Physics, I'll vote for you, Sherman Tuckerman. What do you think of that?"

I think that even though Maya is asking me a question, I don't mind it one bit.

"Copy."

"What are your plans now?" Even back on Earth, Maya cannot keep from grilling me.

My brain already has a firm plan in place.

I'm going to ask Ryker to drive me home, and then I'll get takeout from Mike's Pizza with my dad, and then I'll get my work permit, and then I'll take the bus to Chip's Sporting Goods to start my new job working for Nathan, and then I'll go to Biffmann Self-Storage to put my truck back together, and then I'll get my driver's license, and then I'll take a road trip in my truck to KU to see Zeke play, and then I'll wrap up high school, and then I'll go to a prestigious research university like Caltech to get my degree in applied mathematics.

"Dunno. Stuff, I guess. What about you?"

"Got fences to mend back home, then I'm going to start college. Need to decide between majoring in electronic radio technology or medicine."

For someone who excelled equally at both on the mission, the choice seems clear.

"Why not both?"

"Hadn't thought of that."

My legs feel like jelly as I walk unsteadily into SFC Central Command. I'm accompanied by Dr. Murakami. Flint Garrison is already seated in his usual black leather chair. And there's no sign of Maya.

Even though I am wobbling on my feet, which is normal after being weightless for so many months, I've passed the flight surgeon's comprehensive medical exam, so this meeting is my last one before I get to go home.

Pax Booker is at the table's co-vertex again. "Why don't you take a seat, Sherman, and we'll begin our final debriefing."

An attendant closes the door. I set down my backpack. I'm careful to leave a chair unoccupied between Flint Garrison and myself when Dr. Murakami and I sit down. That way, if Maya ever shows up, she can serve as *the blocker*.

I hear the faint sound of footsteps approaching Central Command from the hallway. And the door swings open, and Maya bursts in and steadies herself against the door frame.

"Sorry I'm late. Was at the base diner grabbing some breakfast sushi to go. Mind if I eat it in here?"

And Flint Garrison grunts. And Dr. Murakami flips open her journal. And Maya stumbles to her seat. And I unwrap my last remaining wedge of Bazooka Joe.

And then I look around the room. The entire mission team is here.

Pax Booker begins the meeting. "I'd like to start with an update on Stone Godfrey's condition. Maya was right. Stone had a heart attack. Surgery was touch and go, but he's as tough as they come, and he survived it. The doctors say his prognosis for a full recovery is excellent."

That leads to a polite round of applause in Central Command, and then the flight surgeon rises to her feet. "I also want to add that Maya Jupiter is the reason why Stone is still with us," she says. "Maya did the near impossible to keep him alive, with only the bare minimum of medical resources, and in a heavily damaged spacecraft."

Maya leans in and whispers into my ear: "Maybe I can get Stone to cover my breakfast."

And then Pax Booker turns his attention to me.

"I also want to recognize our intrepid hero, Sherman Tuckerman. He was nails up there, exhibiting a kind of intestinal fortitude and grace under pressure I've never witnessed before. Sherman saved the lives of the entire crew, and he preserved the Martian sample container while doing it. Our scientists have it now, and we're optimistic that our preliminary scientific assessment of its contents was accurate."

I stand and offer Pax Booker my best rendition of the Ryker two-finger wave. And then I walk around the conference table to where he's sitting.

"The bumping of fists can only occur once the mission is accomplished," I say. And I extend my clenched fist, and Pax Booker bumps his fist against mine, and immediately after contact, I spring open the palm of my hand in a symbolic galactic supernova finger explosion.

After the laughter in Central Command subsides, I clear my throat in a gesture of solidarity with Flint Garrison, and then I summon the courage to address him.

"May I have my plaque from the preflight staging center, the one with my name on it? I'd like to mount it on my bedroom wall, next to my poster of Carl Sagan."

"Of course, Sherman," Flint Garrison says. "And while we're on the subject of SFC property, the inventory list I received from the flight activities specialist indicates that your laptop computer is MIA. Know anything about that?"

I sit back down. The palms of my hands are instantly sweaty, and my right knee is bouncing up and down.

"We tossed it out the airlock hatch as excess ballast," Maya says, coming to my rescue.

Flint Garrison silences the chuckles in the room with a monstrous throat clear, and I take comfort in that being his twenty-first, and thereby divisible by seven.

"Is that so," the general says.

And that's where the meeting ends.

Maya walks with me to the parking lot, where Ryker is standing next to his black four-door Dodge Stratus sedan. And he's wearing dark sunglasses, which makes sense, because it is shortly after daybreak, and the sun is hanging low and bright in the early-morning sky.

And I hand Ryker a note.

Okay to ride shotgun?

"Sure thing, kid. Get in."

And Ryker opens the passenger-side door for me, and I plop onto the bench seat, and then I set my backpack on the floor, and Maya walks up to my window and motions for me to roll it down.

I push the button that operates the power window.

"Maybe we should get together sometime and, you know, hang out," Maya says as she blows a strand of hair away from her mouth.

I pull a sheet of paper and a No. 2 pencil from my backpack, and I write her a note.

(323) 746-9241

I wonder if I will ever hear from her.

The ride home gives my brain time to reconcile everything I've experienced in the past year.

I start with the conversation I had with Carl Sagan, who has been dead for nearly ten years, so my brain confirms I was successful in reestablishing contact with the 7th Dimension's communications network.

The philosophical words of advice Carl Sagan offered me as the crippled spacecraft was plummeting toward Earth saved my life. I'll always remember that.

And then I think about what's actually inside the sample container, and I'm hoping my mission was for the good of humankind, and not to its detriment.

And then I think about how my autism has provided me with challenges and opportunities in equal measure, and how proud I am to have led by example.

And then I think about how my life is no longer defined strictly by mathematics, or by my limitations, or by what others think about me.

And for the first time, I see the world as a living, breathing superorganism, one small, tangible, interconnected place, where everything fits together as if by some grand design, where the only border that matters is the thin blue line of Earth's atmosphere, and I am a step closer to understanding the shared desires of people, and the commonality of the human experience, and how wildly perfect the planet is in all its sublime imperfection.

Planet Earth.

What a thing.

And now my brain wants to expand its understanding of perfect order in the universe by exploring the possibility that life might well exist beyond Earth.

And then Ryker pulls up in front of my house, and he puts the sedan's transmission into park.

And my dad is standing on the front lawn waiting for me.

70

I'm Here About the Job

Ryker reaches into the glove compartment and hands me a small box that has the SFC insignia printed on the outside of it. I open the box. There are dark sunglasses inside, just like Ryker's.

"Any astronaut who rides with me after returning from a mission gets a pair of those."

And then Ryker gets out of the car and opens the door for me, and I sling my backpack over my shoulder, and I walk toward my dad.

My dad gives me a hug, and for the first time ever, I hug him back, and I don't let go for a long time. And it's a good thing my dad is wearing a long-sleeved cotton shirt.

"Come with me," my dad says, "I want to show you something."

And then my dad walks past our 1987 Ford LTD Crown Victoria station wagon, all the way to the garage, and he unlocks the padlock, and he lifts the garage door.

And my mom's forty-nine boxes are gone, and the garage is empty.

"It was time," my dad says. "I hauled the boxes to the community rec center, the one where Zeke and Curtis and Stretch play basketball, and you and Nathan play chess. Mr. Shields was grateful for the donation, and now you have a place to park your truck. You don't have to leave it at Biffmann Self-Storage anymore."

Sure, if I can get it running again.

And my dad and I circle back to the front yard, and we head for the door, but the sound of a car horn stops us.

I turn toward the street. It's Ryker, and his window is rolled down.

"C'mon, *Mister* Tuckerman, let's see it!"

My brain recognizes that Ryker hasn't addressed me as *Master* Tuckerman, the way Wolf did when we first arrived at the guard shack at SFC headquarters. It means Ryker is addressing me as a colleague rather than expressing authority over me.

I flash Ryker the two-finger wave, and he nods in approval, and then he disappears down the street as a mail truck pulls up to our mailbox, and out steps Bernadette.

"My goodness, Lawrence," Bernadette says, "I haven't seen you around in a long time. Where've you been?"

"Not walking on Mars."

Bernadette smiles and drives off to deliver the mail to the rest of the houses on Laszlo Lane.

And now everything in my neighborhood is back to normal.

My room looks exactly the same. All of my stuff is where

I left it when I took off for the mission. I pick up my bus pass from my desktop, and I wave goodbye to my dad as I head out the front door, and then I race-walk my usual 868 steps to the bus stop.

And when the bus arrives, Rigoberto opens the door.

"Wow, a face from the past! What's the good word, Lawrence?"

I hand Rigoberto a folded-up note as I walk past him to my usual spot, an unoccupied window seat in the seventh row.

"Mars!" Rigoberto shouts to me over his shoulder. "That's a real good word, Lawrence. *Real* good. I have a real good feeling that someone might walk on Mars someday."

And then the bus rolls to a stop in front of Chip's Sporting Goods.

And I walk through the store's double doors, and I find Nathan at the cash register hassling a customer. My chess master best friend is opinionated and consistent.

And I hand Nathan my employment application and a note.

I'm here about the job.

71

I'm Going to Walk on Mars One Day

"You mean the one I promised you more than a year ago?"

"Yeah, that one. My dad said you got my letter."

Nathan confirms that he received my letter, and he placed it inside my employee file for safekeeping. I interpret that to mean he has already put the wheels into motion to hire me.

And then he explains that he kept my job open because he's a man of his word, and he worked tons of overtime to keep the chess and checkers section in good order until I arrived, which cut into his chess-playing time, but that the reduction was minimized to the extent that I wasn't around to play against him.

And Nathan reaches under the counter, and he pulls out a Chip's polo shirt, size medium. And there's a shiny gold nameplate attached to the shirt with LAWRENCE stamped onto it.

"Wear it with pride, rookie."

"There's one more thing. I need to take a couple of weeks off, starting today. Road trip to Kansas."

Nathan reacts by pulling the store's employee handbook from a shelf behind the counter and flipping to the Vacation section. "Looks like an egregious violation of company policy to me."

Just then, Chip Spears, the store's owner, appears out of nowhere.

"Welcome aboard," Chip says. "I couldn't help but over-hear your request to take time off before you've even started working here."

Nathan glares at me. "As assistant store manager, I don't think—"

"It's all right, Nathan. I like that kind of bold, independent thinking from my employees. Lawrence's vacation request is approved. And as soon as he leaves, have a look at the chess and checkers aisle. It needs attention."

I exit the store before Nathan can unload his rage on me, and I race-walk the 1.4 miles to Biffmann Self-Storage. When I arrive at the main office, Chett Biffmann is behind the counter to greet me.

"I was wondering when you were coming back to put that ol' jalopy back together," Chett Biffmann says as he sends a stream of chewing tobacco juice in the general direction of the brass spittoon on the carpet next to him.

"It's not a jalopy. It's a 1965 Chevrolet Fleetside shortbed pickup truck."

"Whatever it is, there are a couple of juvenile delinquents hanging around space 1046 waiting to lend you a hand."

I race-walk the rest of the way to my storage unit. When I

arrive, Curtis and Stretch are standing in front of the roll-up door.

Curtis's dented 1968 Plymouth Belvedere surfmobile is sitting in visitor parking, and there's a surfboard strapped to the roof rack.

"Dude, about time you got here," Curtis says. "Your pops told Ezekiel you were back in town. The Zekester called us on the hotline and asked us to give you a hand with the cruiser."

Stretch is holding a large box of pizza from Mike's. "Speak for yourself, amigo. I'm not interested in getting my hands dirty, but at least I brought lunch."

"Let's get 'er done," Curtis says. "Those heavy sets at Zuma aren't going to wait. Outside break, LT. Need to get Woodrow back onto PCH, pronto."

And I flip on the light to reveal all the parts that will add up to one vintage Chevy pickup.

And the three of us get to work putting the Chevy back together. And forty-nine minutes into the process, there's a knock on the storage unit's corrugated steel wall.

It's Brock Decker.

Curtis moves swiftly to the entrance and gets in Brock Decker's face. "What are you doing here, cement-head?"

"Cool your jets, surfer boy. Nathan let it slip that the brainiac surfaced, and Mr. Tuckerman told me where I could find him. I helped Lawrence take apart the truck. Who better to assist with putting it back together?"

"He's got a point." Stretch must sense that the math supports everyone doing less work if Brock Decker gets involved. Very basic arithmetic.

And from there, it only takes us another four hours and

fifty-four minutes to resurrect the pickup truck. And the engine turns over on the first try. And Curtis and Stretch and Brock Decker exchange tough-guy words with each other, and they all take off.

And I close the roll-up door, and even though I only have my learner's permit, I grant myself an exception before maneuvering the Chevy to the front parking lot just prior to the close of business, and I walk inside the office for the last time.

"Here's the padlock key."

"You sure you don't want to leave your truck in space 1046 for another year? I can make you one heckuva deal, Larry."

"Not interested. That space number isn't divisible by seven. And my name isn't Larry. It's Lawrence. Lawrence Tuckerman. And I'm going to walk on Mars one day."

And for the first time ever, Chett Biffmann is speechless.

72

I Think I Can Get Us
an Interview

My dad accompanies me to the Department of Motor Vehicles the next day so I can apply for my driver's license.

I ace the written exam, scoring one hundred percent on all forty-two questions. And after safely landing a heavily damaged spacecraft in the Pacific Ocean, the driving test isn't much of a challenge.

I leave the DMV with my temporary license, which is exactly what I need to put the truck on the road to Kansas.

And we pick up a pizza from Mike's on the way home, and then I park my truck in the garage, and for the first time in a long while, dinner is something other than chili mac 'n' beef.

After dinner, I take my SFC name plaque out of my backpack, and my dad helps me mount it on my bedroom wall, next to my poster of Carl Sagan.

"I don't imagine there are a lot of young folks with a

plaque on their wall that says they were the mathematics flight specialist on a mission to Mars."

"I think it's a limited edition, Dad."

"I'm so proud of you, son. Your mom would be too."

And I turn in early, because I've got a long drive ahead of me in the morning. Before I crawl into bed, I part the curtains of my bedroom window, and I gaze out toward the southwestern sky.

And there it is.

Mars.

The Red Planet.

It seems different now.

Less mysterious. And more familiar.

And there's basketball on it. Two basketballs, actually.

I'm up with the sun, which has been my celestial alarm clock since I was four years old.

And I take a shower, and then I organize my backpack for a week on the road. I'm careful to pack enough paper and pencils, clean underwear, and Bazooka Joe.

And I also pack a map of the United States. Not because I need one. I have all the highways memorized. I pack the map because I think it will make my dad not worry so much.

And I don't pack a cell phone, because I don't own one. The one time I used one, it made my brain feel like it was on fire. I carry around a bag of quarters in my backpack instead. I know I can dial home from any pay phone in the country for $1.75.

And I've decided to take time off from my chili mac 'n' beef astronaut training regimen. I'll be eating greasy cheeseburgers at truck stops all along the interstate highway system instead.

I make sure everything in my room is exactly as it needs to be while I'm gone, and then I sling my backpack over my shoulder, and I walk to the kitchen. My dad is there sipping a cup of black coffee and reading the newspaper.

"Can I make you something for breakfast, son?"

"No. I'll grab a cheeseburger on the road."

And I pick up the handset from the green telephone that's mounted on the kitchen wall, and I dial Zeke's number. It's time to express my appreciation.

"Hello."

"It's me, Lawrence."

"Whoa, a voice from the past."

"Yes."

"Curtis and Stretch said you got the truck running again. I think that's great."

"I need you to leave me a ticket at the will call window for Tuesday's Dartmouth game."

"Lawrence is driving to Lawrence. Talk about symmetry."

"Road trip. One thousand, six hundred and three miles. See you soon. Bye."

I hang up the phone. And then I hug my dad again, not for as long as I did when I returned from the mission, but long enough to let him know I'll miss him while I'm gone, and I head for the garage, and I back the Chevy out onto the street.

And I'm about to drop the three-on-the-tree gearshift into first gear when my dad comes running out the front door.

"You've got a phone call, son. She says her name is Mary Jones."

I cut the engine, and I race-walk to the kitchen.

"Hello."

"Hey, Linderman."

"Shut up."

"Just called to tell you that I brought you back a surprise souvenir from the mission."

My brain concludes that no one has ever brought me back a souvenir from anywhere, and especially not from a mission to Mars.

"What is it?"

"If I told you, it wouldn't be a surprise, would it?"

Maya is asking me a question, but I don't mind, because all throughout the mission, she withstood my mathematical friend-making qualification process, which means I can now afford her some leeway to be pesky and irritating.

"No."

"What's going on in your world, Sherman Tuckerman?"

"Nothing. Going on a road trip."

"Where to?"

"The University of Kansas to watch Zeke play basketball."

"Kansas! The Sunflower State, admitted to the Union on January 29, 1861 as a free state, where slavery was abolished. Capital is Topeka, and it's bordered by Nebraska to the north, Missouri to the east, Oklahoma to the south, and Colorado to the west. Home to two-point-eight million Kansans. State bird is the Western Meadowlark."

"You seem to know a lot about Kansas. You been there before?"

"No."

"Oh."

"When are you leaving?"

"Now."

"Need anyone to ride shotgun?"

"No."

There's a long pause.

"Okay if I ride shotgun?"

"Yes."

And my brain conducts a rapid comparative analysis, and it concludes that Maya is pushier than Nathan.

"Great! Pick me up. Lots to talk about. Been hearing some stuff through the grapevine. Thought you might be interested. Get a pencil. Here's my address. I'll be waiting out front."

And Maya gives me the address to her apartment, and I hang up, and then my brain calculates that she lives 147 blocks to the northeast.

And I pick up the green landline phone, and I call Zeke again.

"Hello."

"It's me, Lawrence."

"Wow, twice in one day. What's up, podner?"

"Make that two tickets to the Dartmouth game."

"Wow, Lawrence Tuckerman, mysteriously changing plans on the fly. Two ducats to Big Green versus the Jayhawks. Check."

"Thanks. See you soon. Bye."

And I hang up.

And then I race-walk back to my truck, and I pick up Maya.

"Nice wheels. A real classic." When Maya says that, I sense heat radiating from inside my chest for the second time since I met her.

"Thanks."

"Here we are again, yin and yang."

Inseparable and contradictory opposites, interconnected and interdependent. "Uh-huh."

"Need me to drive?"

"No."

"Is it okay if I drive?"

Maya is as pesky as ever. "No."

With that settled, I notice that her long wavy hair that verges on black is no longer bunched up in a ponytail with a pink elastic hairband. And then I notice she smells like a lemon that's been cut into seven wedges and dipped into a beaker of rose-scented root beer.

"Here. This is for you."

Maya hands me a brown paper bag. I open it, and inside, there's a smaller brown paper bag, and this one is crinkled up, and I immediately recognize it as the one James Naismith handed me as I was hyperventilating when we were about to die a fiery death as we reentered Earth's atmosphere.

And there's a note inside the crinkled bag, and it's folded in half, like the one Maya passed me in Central Command when we first met. I open the note, and I see that it's written in pencil, using a simple substitution cipher.

My brain quickly decodes the message.

You left this inside the Ares Pilgrim. Thought you might want it back.

"Thanks."

"In case you were wondering, the machine that makes square-bottom paper bags with pleated sides was invented by Charles Stilwell."

Maya seems to know a lot about the history of paper bags.

"Interesting."

"Isn't it? And the invention enabled paper bags to stand upright and have a larger capacity than their predecessors. Stilwell patented his machine in 1883, but the first bag didn't roll off the assembly line until 1884."

And my brain notates that square-bottom paper bag manufacturing began exactly seven years prior to James Naismith's invention of basketball.

"Interesting."

"You ever going to tell me why it was floating around your cabin?"

"Maybe." That's the truth. Someday, I might.

And I steer the Chevy onto eastbound Interstate 10, and the road trip is underway.

"You know how your superpower is mathematics? Well, mine is sushi, and I was having the loveliest conversation with the sushi chef at the base diner at Vandenberg, and he was insisting that fresh fish is the most important ingredient of good sushi, but I told him that the rice was the key component, because using fresh fish was a given, but preparing the rice properly is what makes sushi so amazing, and I told him about my secret recipe for homemade rice vinegar, and how sushi rice, for optimal taste and texture, should be served just below body temperature so it's not gummy and it melts in with the fish."

"Oh."

Maya makes friends easily, and she seems to know quite a bit about sushi.

"Anyway, the sushi chef said he overheard some SFC scientists saying that the preliminary analysis of Sojourner's for-ty-two core samples confirmed the presence of Martian stromatolites that contain a trace amount of a previously un-known fifteenth isotope of Lawrencium—at least I *think* that's what he said."

And then Maya tells me that those same SFC scientists are saying there's nothing like it on Earth, and they believe that the discovery will lead to a medical breakthrough in the treat-ment of antibiotic-resistant bacterial infections.

"Stone Godfrey's theory that the discovery would be used to build an advanced new type of weapon was bunk," she says.

And I think back to what Carl Sagan said to me in the moments before I was handed the responsibility of bringing us home safely.

He said that the 7th Dimension strongly endorses the time-honored belief that life looks for life, not death.

It leads me to believe that the Entity might have influenced the outcome of what was eventually found inside the sample container.

"The sushi chef said he also overheard the SFC scientists complimenting you on the amount of detail you put into your Captain's Log."

"Thanks. I tried to paint an accurate portrait of what life was like up there."

"Last thing is I heard that the SFC is planning to go public with news of our mission and the discovery. That means we're almost famous! And Flint Garrison is rumored to be meeting with JPL engineers, as we speak, to hammer out the frame-work for a state-of-the-art mining operation on Mars. And that means there'll be another mission to the Red Planet in a couple of years."

"Another mission? Copy that."

"I think I can get us an interview for it. You interested?"

A chance to walk on Mars?

A chance to hang out with Maya Jupiter again?

"Affirmative."

ACKNOWLEDGMENTS

Marco Pavia, who directed the creative process for my Zeke Archer Basketball Trilogy, returned as book producer for this one as well, handling the book's design, production, distribution, and marketing. I could not ask for a more generous and knowledgeable mentor.

My editor, Christopher Caines, has also been with me since the beginning, keeping me on the path with his expertise in the English language, his sharp basketball acumen, and his deft sense of humor. If NASA ever needs an editor on Mars, they should definitely ask him first.

My developmental editor, Jenna Winterberg, walked into our initial meeting wearing a U.S. Space & Rocket Center Space Camp jumpsuit. Her superpower is combining a passion for the subject matter with a deep understanding of the dynamics of human relationships.

Tabitha Lahr (cover designer), Brent Wilcox (interior page designer), and Kammy Wood and Cecile Garcia (proofreaders) returned to throw down again. I'm grateful to all of them.

I read four books that helped me to concoct what Lawrence Tuckerman's dream mission to the Red Planet might look like. They are: *The Case for Mars: The Plan to Settle the*

Red Planet and Why We Must, by Robert Zubrin with Richard Wagner (Free Press, 2021); *Mars: A Cosmic Stepping Stone*, by Kevin Nolan (Praxis Publishing, 2008); *Pale Blue Dot: A Vision of the Human Future in Space*, by Carl Sagan (Ballantine Books, 1994); and *The Big Book of Mars*, by Marc Hartzman (Quirk Books, 2020).

I attended a course at the Osher Lifelong Learning Institute called Mars! Fictional and Factual Explorations of the Red Planet, taught by Dr. John Doveton, a senior scientist at the Kansas Geological Survey, a research and service division of the University of Kansas. The session offered abundant details on the rich cultural history of humankind's long fascination with Mars.

Bob Conroy, an engineering faculty member emeritus at California Polytechnic State University, San Luis Obispo, once again served as my math and science arbiter, which gave him ample opportunity to enhance his own suspension-of-disbelief skills.

Kevin Whipp, a mechanical engineer at NASA's Jet Propulsion Laboratory in Pasadena, California, provided keen insight into what might take place behind the scenes during a Mars mission.

Science journalist Natalie Wolchover assisted me with her lucid explanation of how a physicist might attempt to describe the topologically curious contours of a ponytail.

Father Zacchaeus of the New Camaldoli Hermitage in Big Sur, California, offered insight into what human beings might encounter in the divine darkness of outer space.

I remain forever grateful for the support of numerous book clubs around the globe, in particular, Susan Whitebook's Blakely Peeps Book Club.

Samuel Adam "Shmuli" Weber remains my first choice to play the role of Sherman "Lawrence" Tuckerman when the trilogy and this follow-up effort are made into a feature film or TV miniseries. Shmu is *the Man*.

My distinguished young-adult beta-reader squad included Hailey Star Dowthwaite, Bryson Montgomery, Stiles Montgomery, and Santos Rodriguez. Warm thanks to all of them.

I have a shortlist of supporters who regularly looked in on me as I was pounding out the book's first draft, even as COVID-19 threatened to turn the world on its ear. They are Rob Anker, Steve "Junior" Aronson, Michael Benner, Stephen Bookbinder, Chris Coppel, Ted Dayton, Jim Gentilcore, Theo Gluck, Joey Held, Stephen Hertzog, Mike Hulyk, Jasmine Ilkhan, Greg Klein, Bernie Larsen, Neal Laybhen, Mason Nesbitt, Cary Osborne, Gregg Sandheinrich, Shirley Strickland, John Walker, Angela Weber, and Steve Williams.

My son, Zachary, and my daughter-in-law, Erika, have a unique way of challenging me to go deeper into the well than I ever have.

My wife, Andrea, provided the love and support that fueled the creative process and inspired me to keep going, even when the only thing visible on my computer screen was my own reflection staring back at me. I definitely married out of my league.

ABOUT THE AUTHOR

Despite being relatively earthbound most of the time, Craig Leener has long maintained a keen interest in space travel. He's also a big fan of basketball, having immersed himself in the game since his youth as a player, coach, referee, fan and, later in life, as a sportswriter.

Craig has an above-average ability to go to his left and maintains a solid perimeter jumper. His free-throw percentage on his backyard home court is an implausible 87 percent—and to this day, that number remains 100-percent officially unverified. And what the author lacks in foot speed, leaping ability, and defense, he makes up for in court smarts and post-game snacks.

Craig is a lifelong opponent of the instant replay in sports. He maintains this contrarian point of view because of the intrinsic value he places on the human element's potential to influence the outcome of athletic competition, inadvertently or otherwise.

Craig holds degrees from Los Angeles Valley College and California State University, Northridge. He sits on the board of directors of CSUN's Journalism Alumni Association and serves as the organization's director of scholarships. Although

Craig possesses an innate curiosity about what might reside beyond the heavens, he lives in the suburbs of Los Angeles with his truly otherworldly wife, Andrea.

There's No Basketball on Mars is his fourth young-adult novel, following the publication of the Zeke Archer Basketball Trilogy.

The author and his publishing company, Green Buffalo Press, will donate a portion of proceeds from the sale of this book to Exceptional Minds, an academy and studio that prepares young adults on the autism spectrum for careers in animation, visual effects, 3D gaming, and other related fields in the entertainment industry. The organization is headquartered in Los Angeles.

Made in USA - Kendallville, IN
18247_9780990548980
01.10.2023 1458